In the
Small Hours
of the Night

In the
Small Hours
of the Night

An Anthology of Sundanese Short Stories

Including works by

Aan Merdéka Permana, Absurditas Malka,
Dadan Wahyudin, Déni A. Fajar, Déni A. Héndarsyah,
Érwin Wahyudi, Fitria Puji Lestari, Héna Sumarni,
Lugiena Dé, Mamat Sasmita, Mulyana Surya Atmaja,
Nina Rahayu Nadéa, Usép Romli H.M.,
and Yus R. Ismail

Translated and with an Introduction by
C.W. Watson

Jakarta, Indonesia

In the Small Hours of the Night:
An Anthology of Sundanese Short Stories

Publication of this volume was made possible by
the generous assistance of The Ford Foundation.

Additional thanks must also be given to
Rachmat Taufiq Hidayat, former director of Kiblat publishing house;
Purwanto, current director of Kiblat; and the publishers of
Tribun Jabar and its former editor, Cecep Burdansyah.

Design and layout by Cyprianus Jaya Napiun

Printed in Indonesia by PT SuburmitraGrafistama

ISBN No. 978-602-6978-90-5

Contents

Introduction

The Sundanese Language Spoken in West Java: Some Context

Sundanese is spoken by approximately 35 million people in west Java as their mother tongue. This point needs to be understood in context. Java itself is the most highly populated island of Indonesia. It has a population of around 110 million, almost half of the total population of the country, which now contains 250 million and in terms of population is the fourth largest country in the world after China, India and the USA. Indonesia, as might be expected of a country which consists of a huge archipelago comprising thousands of islands, is composed of many different ethnic groups, each with its own traditions and language. On Java itself there are two principal languages—Javanese, spoken in central and eastern Java, and Sundanese spoken in west Java. There are strong resemblances between the two languages, but they are different and are not mutually comprehensible, any more than are, say, Dutch and German.

This reference to the plethora of vernacular languages in Indonesia is not, however, the end of the story. After all, one finds the same phenomenon in India. The difference between the two countries with respect to language is that in Indonesia, unlike in India, there exists only one national language, Indonesian (Bahasa Indonesia), which is spoken the length and breadth of the country from the most extreme western tip of the archipelago in north

Sumatra to the most eastern border on the island of Papua. It is true that not everyone speaks the language with the same fluency, but all Indonesians recognize the significance of the language and its importance in the economy and governance of the country. Furthermore, again unlike in India, the language of the former colonial power—in the case of Indonesia, the Dutch—plays no part in contemporary cross-ethnic communication at any level of society.

The historical circumstances which led to the development of the national language—which in its evolution from the Malay language spoken on either side of the Straits of Malacca became a lingua franca of commerce and later of island-wide colonial administration—are too complex to recount here; but some salient issues are worth mentioning. First, because the nation of Indonesia was born out of a long violent struggle against the Dutch in the period 1945–1950, which had been preceded by a period of Japanese occupation in which the Dutch language had been outlawed, the use of Dutch, which had never been widespread and had indeed been discouraged by the Dutch except in relation to a very small elite minority, gradually disappeared—somewhat like Spanish in the Philippines. In direct proportion to the decline of Dutch, Indonesian was rapidly developed through formal and informal education.

Second, the Indonesian language was not only an important symbol of national unity, it was also a defining constituent element of national culture from 1928 onwards. An unfortunate corollary of this promotion of the national language was, however, the relegation of regional and vernacular languages to minor status. The process was accelerated after 1950, when the vital importance of consolidating the new national unity through the dissemination of a national language was immediately recognized, and it continues today.

And third, following the depreciation of local languages at an official level, the transmission of these languages was largely confined to the immediate local and family environment and domestic, private occasions. All public ceremonies were and are performed in Indonesian. As a concession, however, to the recognition of the importance of vernacular languages as a medium of instruction in the early years, the first three years of primary education in rural areas is delivered in the vernacular; but this practice seems to have waned over the last four decades. With the advent of local radio channels and one or two local language programs on television, there has been some innovation in the use of vernaculars as a medium for social communication; but their scope is limited. The central government in Jakarta, for its part, does not concern itself with matters of local literatures and languages, except when they can be harnessed in terms of artistic performance, dance and drama, to demonstrate the vibrancy of national culture.

The decline in the use and development of regional traditions has been a source of anxiety to many at a local level who regret the increasing ignorance of the younger generation of the language of their parents and grandparents. And it is these concerned activists and scholars who have been at the forefront of cultural movements to revive and develop the use of local languages and, alongside that, to instill a pride in local historical and artistic traditions. Nowhere is that more the case than in west Java, where various initiatives by individuals and lobby groups are now vigorously pursued to restore a sense of local pride, including pride in Sundanese literature and historical traditions.

The Origins of Modern Sundanese Literature

Thanks to scholarly research over the last forty years, much is now known about the origins of a specifically modern literature in Indonesia. Most research has been about Indonesian-language publications. But the paradigm explaining the emergence of the literature can be profitably extended to understanding what has happened with the modernization of local languages, especially those which have been used in printed works.

The account runs like this. In the nineteenth century as trade and commerce began rapidly to develop in the archipelago, especially in Java after the invention of the steamship and the telegraph, and after the opening of the Suez canal, it became necessary to increase the speed and volume of communications to facilitate the growth of trade. In addition to the efforts of Dutch entrepreneurs and government civil servants to this effect, an important role was played by the Chinese population, which had been encouraged to come to the Dutch East Indies ever since the seventeenth century and whose numbers had increased dramatically in the nineteenth century as a consequence of push and pull factors leading to substantial immigration from Fujian in south-east China. It was these Chinese who began to make use of local languages as a means of facilitating communication and to embed themselves into local society. Many of these early immigrants were single males, and they subsequently married native Javanese and Sundanese women. After a generation or two, these Chinese families lost their facility in the Chinese language and spoke Javanese or Sundanese as their mother tongue while still retaining a sense of their Chinese distinctiveness. (As far as I can see, this phenomenon still exists in west Java. Several families of Chinese origin speak Sundanese among themselves, though whether this is a Sundanese Creole or orthodox Sundanese will have to be determined by research.) These new Chinese commercial communities required a quick and easy written medium to communicate among themselves and with the native population. This lay to hand in the form of a creolized Malay spoken through the archipelago, and this they subsequently used in the commercial news sheets which they began to print in Roman script. These news sheets later evolved into fully-fledged newspapers carrying political as well as commercial news and also reporting on local events. The Chinese example was followed by entrepreneurs from other ethnic groups in large towns on the major islands. By the end of the nineteenth century, printed newspapers in Romanized Malay were widely available throughout the archipelago. At the same time, publishers were also beginning to bring out fictional stories, often translations of popular European literature, via Dutch versions—Conan Doyle, Jules Verne, Alexandre Dumas—as light reading matter for the growing urban populations of Java and the port cities of the outer islands.

In the second decade of the twentieth century, the colonial government, alarmed by the nature of the publications that were now being widely disseminated—some of which were salacious and a few of which had become the vehicles of strong anti-colonial sentiment—decided to intervene in the publishing market. This they did through the establishment of a government publishing house, Commissie voor de Volkslectuur, later named Balai Pustaka (Hall of Reading), designed to provide "wholesome" literature. The latter was defined as the modern printing of classical stories from the archipelago as well as text-books for use in schools and translations of popular children's literature, such as *Robinson Crusoe*, *The Broad Highway* (J. Farnol), *King Solomon's Mines*. These translations were soon followed by original indigenous stories set in contemporary times.

Thus from the second decade of the twentieth century we see throughout Indonesia, but especially in Java, a proliferation of modern reading materials, including fiction. The publications put out by Balai Pustaka, mainly in "standard" Malay (the Malay of the Straits of Malacca), rather than the pidgin or creolized Malay of commercial publishers, but also in vernacular languages—for some languages, including Javanese, using indigenous scripts—competed alongside the publications of Malay–Chinese publishers and some independent Dutch publishers. The fictional content of these novels, short stories, and popular magazines, had as their setting the everyday experiences of people in contemporary society, and often drew heavily on real, sensational events which had been reported in the newspapers. Many of the stories had romantic themes and melodramatic plots, and described the problems faced by young men and women struggling to get to grips with modern lifestyles, which were at odds with their traditional upbringing. Much of the content of the narrative was devoted to descriptions of the sights, sounds, personalities, and experiences of modern urban life.

Balai Pustaka also published pioneering modern prose fiction in Sundanese, hoping by doing so to inculcate an ethic of modernization, in which the key values were a scientific education, a rejection of superstition, and an awareness of the possibility of self-advancement through conscientious hard work. It is remarkable that the Sundanese publications of Balai Pustaka covered a broader span of social classes than most of the publications in Malay, and, to my mind at least, more clearly and realistically reflected the social changes that were occurring at the time than the Malay–Indonesian novels of the period. There is more political satire, more detailed description of social situations, professional occupations, class and ethnic difference, than is to be found in Malay–Indonesian novels, only a few of which discuss the political issues of the day.

This close attention to domestic and economic problems arising from rapid social change is even more evident in the Sundanese novels published by small independent publishing houses throughout west Java, where writers and publishers did not feel constrained to follow the moralistic and political guidelines tacitly imposed by Balai Pustaka. Thus one finds several novels that deal with conditions in the plantations and agricultural estates owned by the Dutch, or novels criticizing the *mores* of the feudal aristocracy and its hangers-on.

In the second half of the twentieth century, this modern literature continued to be written and published despite competition from Indonesian-language publications and the government promotion of Indonesian as the national language described above. Sundanese writers founded new magazines and journals and established publishing houses in Bandung, Bogor, and elsewhere in the region. Many of these journals were short-lived, but others emerged to take their place and publishers reinvented themselves, reprinting the very popular stories of the pre-war period as well as encouraging younger writers.

Today in terms of the promotion of writing in the vernacular, west Java is far ahead of other regions, including, counter-intuitively for those who are aware of the significance of Javanese in oral communication, Javanese. There are monthly and weekly journals in Sundanese, one of which, *Manglé*, has been appearing regularly since 1957. Moreover, there are several publishers, of which the most visible today is Kiblat, which bring out new novels and reprints almost every month. This growing emphasis on Sundanese in the last decade or so has been strengthened both by local government initiatives in particular, but, more importantly, through the work of local scholars and writers, who use every opportunity to advance Sundanese. In addition to the traditional avenues for publication, flourishing virtual communities have sprung in social media, such as one devoted to what is known as *mini-fiksi*—short stories of usually less than 300 words, which circulate widely on the net. There are also annual drama festivals and regular performances of traditional singing styles. Every two years in Bandung, there is a drama competition for schools that takes place over a period of three weeks in which schools throughout west Java are invited to put on one of six selected plays in competition with one another.

Sundanese is also the beneficiary of a Sundanese patron of the arts, Ajip Rosidi, a writer who has done more than anyone else to encourage the development of Sundanese by offering a literary prize, the Rancagé prize, for the best work in Sundanese published the previous year. In addition, he has established publishing houses and given his support to younger Sundanese figures in publishing and in higher education. He has also been responsible for bringing out in Indonesian an authoritative and beautifully produced large encyclopedia of Sundanese history and culture, and has played a major role in the organization of two decennial international conferences on Sunda in the last twenty-five years. In his own writing, both in Sundanese and Indonesian, he has been responsible for the comprehensive critical documentation of modern Sundanese literature. His work in these different spheres has deservedly brought him national and international recognition through the award of several honors.

Sundanese is, then, undergoing what I see as a golden period in its literary development. However, the competition from Indonesian and, more recently English, is strong. There is a trend among elite urban Sundanese families to avoid Sundanese; and the children of such families, although they may be familiar with a limited Sundanese vocabulary, have neither the ability nor the inclination to read Sundanese journals or fiction. Furthermore, if they do read fiction at all, it is likely—with the exception of one or two recent best-sellers of indigenous romantic, especially Muslim, stories—to be translations of popular English-language novels. But it has ever been the case that there have been pressures of this kind, leading doom-mongers to prophesy the end of regional literatures. The current proliferation of Sundanese publications, as well as the use being made of the new virtual networks, however, give grounds for optimism, at least as far as Sundanese is concerned.

Sundanese Short Stories Today

Every week there are three publications which carry Sundanese short stories. *Manglé*, mentioned above, is a glossy weekly carrying stories of personalities and feature articles about developments in west Javanese society, as well as dedicated opinion columns written by house journalists and a separate section of humorous features. Fiction constitutes the major part of the weekly material, and besides translations from other literatures—the Arabian Nights has been running for the last few years—there is usually a serialized short novel or sometimes a reprinting of an older novel. In addition, there are at least three new short stories every week, one of which is a supernatural story. The print run of the magazine is now about five thousand.

Galura is a Sundanese language tabloid, with a circulation of around seven thousand, published by the west Javanese press group of *Pikiran Rakyat*, the name of an Indonesian daily newspaper produced from Bandung. Besides items of news and descriptions of cultural performances, *Galura* contains one serial and one short story in the paper, as well as a semi-fictional full-page column entitled *Satukangeun Lalangsé* (Behind the Curtain), giving an account of an individual's personal experience within a family setting. Finally, in the Indonesian-language popular daily newspaper, *Tribun Jabar*, a Sundanese short story is carried over three days, Tuesday, Wednesday and Thursday, the total length of each story varying between 2,300 and 3,300 words.

For anyone wanting to read Sundanese fiction there is, then, plentiful weekly provision. The contents of the stories, even when they deal with the supernatural, anchor the plot within the context of everyday circumstances familiar to readers, always making reference to common situations and experiences. There is an almost equal distribution of rural and urban settings for the stories, ranging from well-known locations in Bandung to isolated villages in the southern areas of west Java. These two features, the accessibility of the stories through the familiarity of the experiences described, and the variety of rural and urban settings, make them recognizably different from the contemporary Indonesian short stories that also flourish in the national press.

The trend of the latter, in my reading of them over the past few years, is to focus largely on unusual or highly particular situations featuring eccentric characters or absurdist scenarios. Fantasy is carried to extremes, and the point of the story seems to be to create as bizarre a world of the imagination as one can: Ionesco, Beckett, Borges, are tame by comparison. When writers do set their stories in a recognizable everyday milieu, the characters are almost exclusively drawn from a wealthy cosmopolitan elite whose lifestyles bear no resemblance to that of the majority of Indonesians.

Indonesian short stories found in the weekly press are consequently very narrow in scope compared to their Sundanese counterparts, and do not have the same broad appeal. One can imagine very few readers of *Manglé* stories deriving the same satisfaction of instant recognition from reading the stories in, for example, *Kompas* or *Republika*, two of the national newspapers with the largest circulations.

There are differences not only in the readerships to which the two appeal but also in the way in which writers in Indonesian position themselves compared to their Sundanese counterparts. (That is not to say that those who write in Sundanese never write in Indonesian. Many of them do, but their voices tend to be muted in the context of their fellow-Indonesian writers.) In part this is because Indonesian writers, even those who come from regional backgrounds and are familiar with a vernacular, as would be the case for many Javanese writers, do not, it seems to me, have the variety of experience of the Sundanese writers. They live in much more compartmentalized urban environments, and no longer have that intimacy with the experience of rural society or the non-educated elements in society that are still closely observed by Sundanese writers. Furthermore, Sundanese who write in Indonesian—influenced by foreign literature, either in English or in Indonesian translation—tend to emulate the models with which they are acquainted. The type of anecdotal story of everyday experience favored by Sundanese readers and writers does not appear to have the same cachet with them. With the increasing incorporation of an educated elite into an intellectual world with global points of reference—including, it should be said, a greater awareness of non-Indonesian forms of Muslim lifestyles—Indonesian fiction has moved away from the regional and local contexts that used to define it fifty years ago.

Sundanese writers frequently belong to strong support networks and writers' communities, not only around Bandung but in cities throughout the region, and often meet and share experiences and ideas or cross swords in ideological debates. Although many of them are equally at home in Sundanese and Indonesian, they still have strong roots in rural communities and with relatives and friends who reside there. This is not to suggest that they are obsessively parochial, but more to emphasize that they cherish those connections and value them more highly than the alternative lifestyles to which they have access but prefer not to embrace to the exclusion of other possibilities. This is partly a function of having opportunities of which their fellow-writers in Jakarta are deprived. It is simply not easy to move in and out of Jakarta at will for half a day to visit family and friends or to receive the latter at home. Nothing could be simpler in Bandung. It is, therefore, only to be expected that the stories Sundanese writers hear, and the observations of everyday experiences they note, after they have been transformed into fiction and addressed back to the community from which the original sources of inspiration derive, have a very different character and tone from Jakarta-oriented writers in Indonesian.

The Translated Stories and their Themes

All the stories translated here, with the exception of one, whose inclusion is explained below, are taken from the weekly *Tribun Jabar* stories. I have been reading these with great pleasure for a number of years and have tried to cut out and keep many of them as clippings. Not all of them are equally good or appeal equally to me, but I almost always enjoy reading them, if not for their immediate literary value, at least because I constantly learn from them in various ways. Of the hundred or so I have preserved, I have selected twenty-three which have appeared since 2011, when *Tribun Jabar* first started publishing them in a three-episode serialized form.

All but three of the writers are relatively young, born since 1970, and the stories they tell all reflect issues which are the common currency of everyday conversations and experiences. The only difference between the young writers and the three older ones is that the latter often refer to historical events and experiences of the period before 1970, and as result often carry references which the younger generation would know only vicariously through the accounts of their parents' generation or their place in the national historical imaginary.

In this respect, three historical episodes stand out in modern west Javanese history: the period of *perjuangan,* the struggle for independence against the Dutch involving physical armed conflict in Bandung and surrounding areas in west Java; the time of the *gerombolan* (groups of armed terrorists), whose actions led to a long period of anxiety in west Javanese villages around Garut and the Priangan region outside Bandung in the years between 1952 and 1962; and the period of civil unrest just prior to the coup d'état of September/October 1965 and its aftermath, leading to the extermination of the Indonesian Communist Party and the mass killings of the time. In Sundanese short stories and novels written by the elder generation, accounts of these three periods figure very strongly, but for younger writers they do not have the same resonance.

I have chosen one story to represent each period; *The Tek! Dung! Widows* by Mulyana Surya Atmaja recounts an episode in the revolutionary struggle. It is a well-known story, and has become a symbolic instance of what the Revolution meant to those who lived through it and how it is conceived by the people of west Java today. I have read other versions of the same story, but this one, through the device of presenting the events through the prism of the experience of a young widow then newly married, captures for me not just the historical significance of the event but the poignancy of individual experience. It conveys the emotion as well as a description of the experience, surely something we all look for in our reading of fiction.

The period of the *gerombolan* also features strongly in both written and oral traditions of the recent Sundanese past, but it is not well understood by the present generation, some of whom, very mistakenly in my opinion, have recently tried to make of the leader of the movement Kartosuwiryo, a Muslim martyr. I have not come across any *Tribun Jabar* story recounting the experience of those times—though see the story *The Star Spring* for a brief mention—but I did read such a story in an issue of *Galura* by Aan Merdéka Permana, a regular contributor to *Tribun Jabar*. As far as I can make out the story, *All Quiet in the Small Hours of the Night in Cijeléreun,* told in the first person by a man recalling an experience of his boyhood, is written out of direct personal experience. There is very little in terms of action and plot in the story—it is simply an account of going back to the village for a visit—but there is an immediate vividness of fear and anxiety which captures for me the numerous stories I have heard from Sundanese friends about the difficulties of that time.

The third story with a historical background is Usép H. Romli's *The '66 Album*, which also corresponds closely to stories told to me by friends who were students in 1966. The story is related through the reminiscences of someone who was strongly anti-Communist, but the point of the story is not to attack the PKI and what it was doing, so as much as to document the hopes of the reformists of that period and how those hopes were frustrated by the opportunism of those who subsequently came to power. (It may be worth noting that although there are now many Indonesian stories which are told from the point of view of the victims of the time, members of the PKI and their families, I have not found any Sundanese short stories of that kind.)

The remaining stories translated here, although each is highly individual, can be roughly assigned to six recognizable thematic clusters, with some stories open to classification under more than one category. The six are:

1) Stories contrasting urban and rural lifestyles
2) Political satire/criticism
3) Fantasy and stories of the supernatural
4) Humorous stories
5) Romantic stories
6) Stories of everyday happenings

The lost rural idyll is of course a common trope in many national literatures, including those in English, but each version has its own particularity. In the three stories by Mamat Sasmita in this collection, he tells the stories of individuals from the rural area south of Bandung. Describing the experience of these individuals—the old basket-maker, the religious teacher, the young bachelor—the account Mamat Sasmita offers the reader depicts rural inhabitants as not always finding it easy to come to terms with modern times and ever prey to the city slickers coming in to the village and trying to put one past them. But as with stories of this genre from other literatures, the city slickers often come off worse.

Usép Romli's story, "Somewhere to get Away from it All" and the story with which it has strong affinities, Yus R. Ismail's "The Neighbor" also contrast rural simplicity with urban luxury which outsiders try to introduce into a village environment. Both implicitly make the argument that the two are incompatible, since the life of luxury is inevitably compromised through owing its existence to fundamental dishonesty.

Dishonesty, corruption, double-dealing, the subjects of the second category of stories, are very much the stuff of daily gossip in west Java. Everyone has had some experience of being forced to pay a bribe or at least a "sweetener" in order to expedite an entitlement or obtain a privilege, and the circumstances for such occasions abound. The stories here reflect examples that one daily hears or reads about in the newspapers. "Corrupt" shows how easy it is for those who are honest to be deluded and tricked by politicians who claim to have their best interests at heart. The same theme emerges from "The Election Promise," where the writer describes in highly credible detail (with which scores of schoolteacher readers must sympathize) the experiences of a large group within Indonesian society today, the honorary unofficial teachers, who throughout the country work for a pittance in the hope that they will one day soon be appointed to permanent positions.

A third cluster of stories center upon the supernatural, though this takes many forms in the world of the Sundanese imagination, as these stories indicate. And the title given to this present collection of stories was deliberately chosen because it reflects the preponderance of stories with this element. Yus R. Ismail, who is represented here by more stories than any other writer, specializes in stories of this kind, all of which have a twist in the tail and one or two of which employ humor to convey social criticism. The translation of one of these stories, "The Rented House" has been published elsewhere with an extensive introduction and footnotes intended to convey some idea of the social context. One of the stories which I would include in this category is a particular favorite, "The Whirlwind." I don't want to go into detail about it here for fear of spoiling the story for the reader, but let me say that when I first read it I was very moved by the poignancy of its depiction of the bond between a son and his mother.

Other ethnic groups in Indonesia often associate the Sundanese with humor. The Sundanese are known for their, sometimes excessive, sense of fun and for their love of jokes and word play. In *Manglé* every week, in addition to a long one-page humorous story, there are two pages of short jokes sent in by readers. One stock repository of humorous stories in Sundanese is the tradition of oral literature centered upon a wise fool character, sometimes a trickster figure, known as Si Kabayan, whose exploits are familiar to all Sundanese and are very much part of well-known Sundanese folklore. There are modern avatars of Si Kabayan, and readers can perhaps see a little of what the character signifies for Sundanese in the two Ramal stories of Déni A. Fajar and Lugiena Dé's "Orange."

Stories of thwarted love or unsuccessful liaisons also fall into a separate, easily recognizable, category. Personally I am not so taken by such stories, but they do have a remarkable resonance in Sundanese society, and there are innumerable twists and permutations on the themes of mismatches, adultery, polygamy, arranged marriage, divorce, and misplaced sexual attraction, which have a ready following of readers, and explain the popularity of the *Satukangeun Lalangsé* page in *Galura* mentioned above. Here in this collection they are represented by "Birthday Tomorrow" and "Decided by a Stroke of Fate," both of which are written from the viewpoint of young unmarried women.

The final category is that of stories of social criticism and observation which describe the experiences of people pursuing common occupations within Sundanese society. The author of "The Boy in My Class," in a first-person narrative where he adopts the persona of a female teacher, shows how a child's behavior in class can be dramatically changed by the loss of a parent. "Traffic Jam" focuses on the life of minibus driver, but at the same time describes how worsening conditions in Bandung over the last decade have led to frequent traffic holdups with consequent frustration for all. Finally, "My Wife" illustrates the dire consequences of the increasing escalation of competition in conspicuous consumption which is so evidently a part of contemporary middle-class lifestyles in the towns of west Java.

Some Points about the Translation

In translating these stories, my intention has been above all to create versions which are as faithful as possible to the original in terms of reproducing not only the meaning of the sentences but also their tone. By tone I mean the weight that the original Sundanese reader is being asked by the writer to ascribe to the sentences in relation to the emotion felt by the narrator or the characters of the story. This has been very difficult, since the exact translation of the meaning into English using the descriptive metaphors, analogies, and even the simple empirical details of the Sundanese writer and observer convey very different sensory, emotional, and psychological impressions for English readers. It is difficult to overemphasize the problems that arise, but one can perhaps understand them better if one thinks of how the literature of other languages fares in English translation.

Comparing original works in French or German, for example, one is often aware of the lack of fit between the original and the translation into English. This is not because the translation is inaccurate in any literal sense, but because the rhythm of the sentences or the choice of words in English does not seem to match the fluency of the original, or, when one does not know the original, how one imagines how the original must read. This lack of fit, however, is occurring between languages which often employ very similar metaphors and descriptive terms drawn from the common experiences of people living in Europe who share the same or very similar habitats and natural environments, as well as being heirs to a common literary and mythic heritage stretching back over almost three millennia. Furthermore, European languages have the same linguistic origins and have developed similar inflections of verbal forms to denote tense and mood.

This common linguistic heritage is absent when one tries to translate non-Indo-European languages into English, and is especially noticeable when translating languages which are not inflected for tense and mood but convey these aspects by different means, through additional lexical items or an extensive use of particles, for example.

It is therefore inevitable that good translations into English of, say, Chinese literature often read oddly in English: do people really speak like that to one another, one finds oneself asking, or what a strange way of describing a strong emotion, or what is the significance of that cultural reference? That the reader of the translation should feel this is not only a proper response, but the right one. Conversely, one should be wary of a response such as: the characters sound just like us; I'd say the same thing; that's how all women feel; or, that's exactly the way we experience a sensation of disgust or physical pleasure—because the translator has worked too hard to assimilate the writing to an English equivalent and thus has sacrificed the particularity of the original which it should have been her duty to convey. One does not want a story by Lu Xun to sound as though it had been set in a small town in the north of England. A sympathetic and intelligent reader reading a story set, for example, in a village in Bengal, or a rural homestead in Africa, or a small town in Japan, both expects oddity and strives imaginatively and intellectually to comprehend it, and thus absorbs the literary experience into herself.

This is the frame of mind that I trust I can count on from the reader of these translations. Of course this may sound like special pleading, preemptively trying to deflect the criticism of the reader who finds the English wooden and unappealing. It is not intended to be. If the English is consistently awkward throughout, then the translation is bad. And even if it is not awkward throughout, but there are sentences and passages which jar, not because of the strangeness of the expression or the unusual metaphor but because the English in some places is not of a tone with the English used elsewhere in the same story—a sudden inexplicable colloquial rendering in what is otherwise conveyed in a formal register—then something is wrong. I am sure that the reader will find several instances of this occurring in places where I have made an inept choice of word or phrase, despite my best efforts. However, I would ask the same reader to distinguish between those weaknesses in the translation and those deliberately preferred instances of strangeness as mentioned above. By retaining the latter I have hoped, paradoxically, to make the reader more in possession of the original by extending her imagination.

Of the many examples that I could give to demonstrate more precisely what I mean by strangeness, in this case by reference to the particularities of Sundanese experience, let me confine myself to two: the different lexicons of speech which obtain between speakers of different social statuses addressing each other, and the heavy use of onomatopoeia in Sundanese.

The use of a specific vocabulary in Sundanese speech, like Javanese, is heavily dependent on who the parties to the conversation are. Different words carrying the same semantic weight are used if one addresses a social inferior and if one is addressing a social superior. This phenomenon of different language levels has been well described for Javanese and there is no need to dwell on it here. The very weak analogy in English might be the different registers which a teenager uses when speaking to their friends and speaking to their parents. The nuances in Javanese and Sundanese are, however, much more pronounced and one risks giving serious offence if one uses the wrong word in context. I remember, for example, when I was first learning Sundanese, picking up two words for "much." These were *seueur* and *loba*. After learning their meaning I forgot which of the pair was the polite word and which the impolite word. (There are third and fourth words refining the social nuances even more, but at that stage I had not been introduced to them.) Consequently, when in a friendly greeting I once asked a street-seller of vegetables whom I had got to know whether she had sold a lot that day, I said in my broken Sundanese, "Have you sold *loba*?" and I was swiftly put in my place and told that it was improper to use *loba* and that I should have said *seueur*, no quarter given even though I was a foreigner clearly taking my first steps learning the language. The choice of words and expressions is thus crucial to social intercourse, and that is reflected in the stories. Differential social status and the positioning of speakers vis à vis one another constitute a major element in the tone of the story. This is almost impossible to convey in English without sounding archaic or Victorian. The use of expressions such as "your honor," "your ladyship," "my good man," "your humble servant," "woman" simply will not do, yet somehow one has to try to convey the social distance deliberately being created between speakers. I have tried to do this without making a speaker sound too obsequious or too arrogant by using different terms of address or mixing registers, but I am aware that I have not always been successful. I would ask the reader to try to pick up the hints when it seems as though the dialogue between two speakers of different status, say a villager speaking to a wealthy city man or a farmer speaking to his son's teacher, seems a little strained.

The onomatopoeic character of Sundanese soon becomes apparent to the learner when he learns the vocabulary of sensory impressions: the different sounds a voice makes conveying different emotions, from anger and rage at one end of a highly differentiated scale to affection and tenderness at the other, are all indicated by clearly onomatopoeic words for which there is no easy English equivalent—although when I search for them it is surprising how many English words are also onomatopoeic: one talks of growling and snarling with rage, and sighing with love, something which would be immediately recognizable to a Sundanese. But the onomatopoeia in Sundanese has a much wider range of reference and covers not only empirically observable phenomena, but feelings and thoughts in subtle metaphorical ways that require considerable periphrasis in English. Again I have done my best to convey this, but at times when the effort was too great and I felt that the reader would stumble over the contortions of the English, I have opted for a simple direct translation. Bar the exceptions I have referred to above in relation to the necessity of occasionally having to force the reader to recognize strangeness, I have always tried to make the translation fluent and readable, and I hope that comes across.[1]

---

[1] I want to enter a small caveat for the benefit of English friends and readers. The original version of the translations, as might have been expected of me, used words which conform to British usage, for example, "torch" rather than "flashlight." Because the house-style of Lontar follows American usage, I was required to use American replacements for some words, and I did not have the energy to resist. My apologies for this *petite trahison*.

The sympathetic English reader, if she avoids the temptation to make comparisons, will find that these stories are not only entertaining in themselves but, and perhaps as someone trained as a social anthropologist I find this more significant, they also allow an entrée into a very different social world from what the reader has been exposed to through her own immediate experience in the milieu of her own society. By this I am not referring to what is immediately observable, the sights and sounds of west Java and the accompanying "social facts" as they used to be referred to by British anthropologists describing a society's peculiar institutions. There is that aspect of things, of course, but more important than that should be a reader's attempt to reach beyond this empirically observable local universe into the minds of the people of west Java, extending one's sympathies, learning, in however tentative a fashion, to comprehend the aspirations and values of others, their understandings of their own society and the motivations underlying their everyday behavior—in short, the variety of ways through which Sundanese live out what it means to be human. The critical appreciation of the literature that communities use to convey their thoughts and emotions to their intimates is one of the best ways I know of moving in that direction of sympathetic understanding, and I hope that, even in translation, these Sundanese short stories convey to the reader some of the excitement of entering imaginatively into the universe of a society that will inevitably retain some of its strangeness but has now become at least partly accessible.

Aan Merdéka Permana

All Quiet in the Small Hours of the Night in Cijeléreun

In the 1950s the region round Garut was not safe, because it was the center of operations of the rebel groups of the Darul Islam movement, which was waging war against the government. At that time I was still a small boy. In 1956 I had just started at primary school or "People's School" as it was called then.

"Take care, Aman, if you're setting off back to Cijeléreun. Don't leave it too late lest you're waylaid by the rebels," my grandmother used to say if my uncle Aman happened to be visiting Bandung from Cijeléreun.

There were means of getting from Bandung to Garut, only it wasn't so easy as it is now. That was because of threats to safety, and that was even more the case if one was going to Cijeléreun. If you wanted to go there from Bandung, you had to set out in the very early morning after the *subuh* prayer. First you travelled to Garut in a big shared minibus called a *suburban*, then from Garut you took the train to Cikajang. That's what Grandmother used to say about it not being safe in Garut, and she said it every year at Lebaran, at the end of Ramadan, when everyone was going back to their villages, in our case Cijéléreun. They call it "*mudik*," going back to the hills, today.

"If we go back to the village at Lebaran, Ma, won't we be stopped by the rebels?" I said. I called my grandmother "Ma."

"Yes, well, who knows?" It was my grandfather who replied.

As far as I remembered, this was the first time that I was going to spend Lebaran in the village. Before this, every Lebaran had been spent in Cicadas, just at the outer limit of Bandung to the east. But Mother said that once in the past I had been taken back to the village at Lebaran, only then I was very small, only a few months old. "You didn't know anything at all, let alone remember going to a faraway place on a visit," she said laughing.

At the time I didn't understand why, just after saying "if God allows it," her gaze suddenly clouded over and she seemed to be looking in the distance. She said that once there had been a lot of rebels in the vicinity of the village, and Uncle Jumsi, Mother's elder brother, had fallen victim to their cruelty. In the middle of the night when it was very quiet, the rebels had descended on the village. Many of the villagers were killed, including Uncle Jumsi. What had been his fault that he should be on the black list of these gangsters?

"It's probably because when he was asked for a rice contribution by the army unit there, Uncle gave them a sackful. And after that he was classed as an army collaborator," Mother said.

At that time the people in the villages lived in constant fear, tense from one moment to the next. Whatever they did was wrong. It came from being in an area which was caught right in the middle between the army and the rebels. At times the village was preyed upon by the rebels who forced the villagers to give them food that they could take back to consume in the jungle. If people gave them food and the army found out, then they would be arrested and interrogated and accused of being in league with the rebels. On the other hand, if those they gave rations to were the army who were on patrol there, then it was the rebels' turn and they murdered them.

After Uncle Jumsi had been killed by the rebels, Grandfather and Grandmother decided to take refuge in the town. They wanted to take all their family with them, but Aki Padma, Grandfather's younger brother, insisted on staying in the village. "And even Aman wants to stay to keep an eye on our small-holding. The age one reaches is up to God," Aki Padma said.

Grandfather brought Father and Mother to Bandung. Mang Aman, mother's younger brother, stayed behind in Cijéléreun to look after the small orchards.

So now if Mother said "Perhaps God will allow it," it was though she had taken to heart what Aki Padma had said.

And now coming up to Lebaran, Grandfather and Grandmother were taking me back at the age of six. Mother and Father had chosen to go to Cicadas.

"It's expected of me," said Father, "since I am a member of the Lebaran committee there for the collection of *zakat* and *fitrah* alms to be distributed. I can't shirk my responsibility. Mind you behave yourself in the village, lad."

"Take care of him, Father, and don't let him splash about in the fish pond," said Mother. "Town boys are not used to washing in the pond. He would probably get a rash."

To get to Cijeléreun, Grandmother had decided to take the train from Bandung to Cibatu and then from Cibatu to take another train going to Cikajang.

I remember well that the engine which pulled the carriages on that route from Bandung to Garut was called Si Gombar, but in front of Si Gombar there was a special steel carriage on which several soldiers were sitting armed with Bren guns.

"They are there to guard us," said Grandfather." I didn't know what the intention behind this was, but I had heard some news that in Trowék (which now lies in the district of Malangbong in Garut) a train was attacked by rebels and went off the tracks into a ravine, causing the deaths of hundreds of passengers.

During the train journey I sat on a suitcase, because the carriages were full with passengers since everyone was going back for Lebaran. On the stretch between Cibatu and Cikajang, I was constantly rubbing my eyes, because I couldn't avoid the smuts that were entering the carriage from the smoke coming from the coal-burning engine. The whole carriage was made of wood, like a carriage in cowboy films. The windows were not shuttered and there was no glass in them. So if it rained the rain came in and the wind rushed past carrying particles of soot. Throughout the journey the passengers said nothing; many of them were sleeping or pretending to sleep. It was very clear that there was a reluctance among them to engage in conversation and make each other's acquaintance. There seemed to be a fear that people might want to talk to them. They said only what they had to.

We had left Bandung at *subuh* and we got to Cijeléreun at *ashar*. When we got off at the station halt, there was Mang Aman waiting for us. And not just him; there were in fact four people there to escort us, all with machetes in their belts. It could have been simply that at that time people in the village were always working in their gardens and so it was usual for them to carry their machetes around. But it's also likely that they had them because there were always things happening which endangered public safety.

From the small station we had to climb up to the village. Sometimes we were following the paths along the dykes of the rice fields going upwards on the terraced plots, sometimes we skirted the bottom of the hills and pushed a way through the bamboo clumps, which never saw the sun from one day to the next. Because of that, even in the dry season, the climb was slippery since everything was wet with dripping water.

I was led by the hand by Grandmother, and I kept imagining all sorts of things. Soon we would be going through an especially thick bamboo forest and from the edge of the forest out would jump black men wearing only loin cloths, their bodies covered in chalk, carrying axes and spears. Perhaps I had been seeing too many Tarzan films in the Cahaya Cinema. Wasn't Tarzan constantly being waylaid by people like Dayaks? Were the rebels going to appear like that in the same way?

But thankfully our small party didn't encounter any danger. We arrived at the house, and I flopped down to sleep, tired out as well as very hungry because I was fasting. Grandmother told me that I should break the fast and eat, but I didn't want to. Not because I didn't want to, but because I was embarrassed in front of Aki Padma. If I had been in Cicadas, I would have been hoping all the time in the middle of the day that Grandmother would invite me to eat. Grandmother really did spoil me.

"Quickly go down to the spring by the river and have a wash before it gets dark," said Aki Padma. Grandmother and I went off hastily to the place where a stream had been diverted into a bamboo pipe which gushed water. Aki Padma and Grandfather soon fell into talk and became engrossed in the stories they were telling each other.

Mang Aman, who had accompanied us to the spring, said that people in the village always went there before *ashar* or before *subuh*. It was rather far to the bamboo pipe; in the time it took us to reach there you could have chewed a betel quid. The young men of the village, carrying machetes, watched over the people who went there to wash.

As far as I remembered, that was the first time that I had eaten the *saur* pre-dawn meal in such a cold place. In Cicadas by contrast, the boys used to walk along together setting off fireworks. Before eating we would keep a watch on the road, and then after *saur* we would walk along it. But now in this remote village called Cijéléreun there was just silence. Before *maghrib* the only noise was the murmurings of Aki Padma, who was muttering prayers. And it was the same after we had broken the fast while we were waiting for the additional *taraweh* prayers: Aki Padma would mutter a few verses from the Quran.

I chose to perform the *taraweh* prayers in the small neighborhood prayer-house, which could hold only thirteen or fourteen people. And indeed there were then thirteen or fourteen inside the prayer-house; outside in the yard were the young men with their machetes. It was even quieter in the night. One could of course indistinctly hear the voices of those doing the ritual *tadarus* reading from the Quran after *taraweh*. I felt sleepy, but it was difficult getting to sleep. The others were not going to sleep. The situation in the village made everyone anxious and on edge. I don't know, perhaps it was because Aki Padma had told us the story of how Uncle Jumsi had met his death in the room in which I was now sleeping. In those days one just slept on a mat laid out on the stamped bamboo floor. According to Aki Padma, Uncle Jumsi's luck had run out because he had been sleeping inside the room where he was hiding away, when through a crack in the floor he had been stabbed with a knife, and his guts spilled out everywhere.

The story made me fearful and it was impossible to sleep.

And then in the small hours of the morning before *saur*, from far away we heard several times the echoing sound of rifle shots. Everyone was alarmed.

"It sounds as though it's far away. Our army patrol is probably flushing the edge of the forest," said Aki Padma.

After we had finished *saur*, it was time for the *subuh* prayer, and everyone went off quickly to the bamboo pipe to get washed and do the ritual ablutions. The young men, with their knives in the belts, carried flashlights because it was still pitch black.

While we were there, we heard the sound of a footstep.

"Who's there?"

One of the young men responded with, "Who's there?" also.

"It's the army," came the reply from a footpath round the corner of the hill.

"I'm a member of the village watch," said the young man in a whisper.

Hearing that, everyone felt relieved.

"Be careful, the enemy is on the bank of that bamboo grove," said one of the soldiers.

And then of course our hearts started beating fast again.

"But don't be alarmed. The army is here to guard you," said the same soldier.

When the day came for the special Idul Fitri end-of-Ramadan prayers, the army was still there, keeping watch over all the villagers praying in the open, until the prayers were over and nothing had happened.

But I hope that my children and grandchildren will never have to go through times like that. I find it incomprehensible that there should be fighting among us, one people, one nation, each side claiming that it is in the right.

Mulyana Surya Atmaja

The "Tek! Dung!" Widows from Rawagedé

T he rainy season had really set in. For a week it had been
raining without stop. The rivers were overflowing, the rice
fields were becoming water-logged, and pools of water lay
in the yards of houses. The roads were muddy and slippery. It made
people reluctant to go out. Especially someone like Warman who,
it needs to be said, had just become a husband. He had tied the
knot just two days ago. Now he had shut himself up in his room
and covered himself with a blanket and was curled up in bed. He
didn't know what to do with himself; he was stiff and sore between
his legs after having watered the new pot which he had begun to
make use of. The sun had slowly crept up the sky and it had now
reached its zenith. Warman gradually eased himself out of bed.
A quick shower and after that his stomach began to rumble. He
looked at the food that had been prepared for him by Nyi Imi,
who was now officially his wife. He enjoyed the food, eating his
fill to the point where he found himself belching several times in
succession. Then he rinsed his hands and sat down on the veranda
in front of the house to have a cigarette. He inhaled deeply and
then blew out the smoke and felt the chill in the air.

"Reporting, commandant," came an unexpected voice from the
side of the house. Someone had approached very quietly. He was
taken inside quickly, lest he should be observed by one of those
"white lizards," the Dutch-paid spies.

"What's the news?" he whispered.

"Our forces, made up of forty to sixty rifles with one automatic machine gun, have been detected by the commander of the Dutch company from the Karawang sector, Major Alphons Wijman."

"Where did you get the news from?"

"From a cockroach, a Dutch spy: Dayat. He is the son of a policeman currently working as an assistant *wedana*, as appointed by the Dutch in the village. Dayat is from the village of Bubulak. He was caught red-handed when he was spying the layout of the hamlet here."

"If that's the case, you'd better warn everyone, so they are ready to deal with possible consequences. What's happened to Dayat?"

"According to a report, he escaped when he was in custody in the village hall."

"Is there any other news?'

"Yes, there is, sir. An undercover contingent drawn from different groups of fighters assigned to ambush the steam train from Karawang to Réngasdéngklok was successful. The train was seized, with all the weapons it was carrying. The incident was reported to Dutch headquarters, to that same Wijman who is now yelling that he will avenge all the deaths."

For the moment, the freedom fighters were lying low, disguising themselves as ordinary people of the village community. They were mingling in the safety of the crowds of people in the vicinity of the train station of Rawagedé. Wijman was thinking out tactics. His "roaches" were moving about observing every action that looked suspicious. The Dutch barracks were full of soldiers. Dutch support troops were coming from the Third Infantry Battalion and the Ninth Infantry Regiment (stationed at Cikampék), the Second Infantry Brigade from Purwakarta, and the Seventh Division whose headquarters were in Bandung. They would all come together on Tuesday, December 9, 1947. The hour for the operation they were going to undertake was set at half past five in the morning. Meanwhile Dayat, the roach who had escaped, was reporting to his father and describing his ordeal to Kalim. Kalim was a fellow roach, a close colleague of Tanu, who was employed in the detective department of the Dutch police. Kalim and Tanu passed on the news to the Dutch headquarters in Karawang.

Rawagedé was the center of things, not because it lay strategically twenty-five kilometers from the town square of Karawang and was on the train route from Karawang to Cikampék to Réngasdéngklok, nor because it was the former arms depot of the Japanese army, but more importantly because Rawagedé was the principal base of the combined Force of Freedom Fighters, the former headquarters of the PETA, the home army established by the Japanese, and furthermore it was to that place that the "Gangster from Karawang" was coming, that elusive charmed enemy of the Dutch, Captain Lukas Sutaryo, the commander of the combined force of fighters who had just attacked the Dutch headquarters at Cililitan. The Dutch had promised a reward of ten thousand guilders to whomever could bring them Captain Lukas Sutaryo's head, dead or alive.

"We'll assemble everyone." That was Wijman's thinking while he looked through all the intelligence reports and considered the appropriate tactics for a surprise attack on the area round Rawagedé. Everything was prepared with great attention to detail, carefully, precisely, everything calculated to the last jot. There was to be no further embarrassment. Wijman had felt uneasy from the time that the Dutch had seized Karawang, and he had not once ventured as far as Rawagedé. Every time one moved out, there was immediately a ferocious attack. The Dutch were in no position to make polite requests for considerate treatment and so avoid being caught up in a fire-fight or comprehensively destroyed in battle.

It was Monday, December 8, 1947, 7:00 in the morning. Captain Lukas Sutaryo, after having attacked the Dutch headquarters at Cililitan, had sought refuge with his troops in Rawagedé. They were resting at the same time as regrouping their forces. There was hardly time to smoke a cigarette and then they were off again to carry out follow-up guerilla attacks on Dutch outposts in Pabuaran, Pamanukan, Subang and Cikampék. It was only an hour since Captain Lukas Sutaryo had moved out of Rawagedé. At the Dutch barracks in Karawang, the combined Dutch troops were beginning to move in the direction of Rawagedé, which they intended to burn down in a scorched earth action at the same time as finishing off once and for all the "Gangster from Karawang" and all his men. "Fanatics always cause trouble," Wijman said as he took command of the scorched earth operation that day.

The morrow, Tuesday, December 9, 1947. Nature was at its best, calm and peaceful, not a cloud in the sky. The birds were chirruping, accompanying the dawn just breaking and gladdening the hearts of the people of the village, who were on the way to their rice fields or were setting off to the market to sell their produce or who were engaged in other small jobs. Getting on with their tasks, doing their chores, each was grateful for God's bounty.

Warman had spent the whole night gathering his men together to complete the task of blocking the roads. They had just finished as the pitch black of night receded and the shapes of the pillars of houses could be made out. All the roads leading into Rawagedé from all directions were cut off. The Garungung road to the north was blocked off completely. The Cilempuk road to the west was impassable, covered with all sorts of obstacles. And the Palawad road to the east had been cut off for some time. To the south, the Tegal Sawah road had been made unusable by digging huge potholes which were covered over so that anyone walking there would fall into a snare-trap. The Dutch columns were stuck on the road, held up. Their attack had to be put off beyond the planned time.

Warman was still drowsy after being shaken awake by Imi. Very agitated, she told him the news: the Dutch had arrived. This wasn't the usual kind of visit, intended to scare people. They had come this time to attack. They were rounding up all the men in the village, making them stand in a line the length of the village road; and it was the same for all the men who were at the station. Everyone was being herded together in the same manner. Everyone was being pushed along, no one was let by.

"Akang, quick, hide," Imi urged him. She was frantic, clutching at her sarong. Her face was white and she was trembling. There was no place to hide. It was too late to jump out the window. Her head was spinning. She grasped at the pile of clothes in the laundry basket. She grabbed a long *kebaya* blouse and wrap-around skirt and the long white headscarf she had worn two days ago when they were married. Quickly she dressed Warman in them and told him to go back and lie in the bed with his face covered with the veil so that no one would suspect he was a man. *Bang! Bang! Bang!* The door was being hammered. *Crack!* It was kicked in from outside. It flew open; the door hung on its hinges. The Dutch rushed in, looking around inside the house. Imi trembled by the side of the bed where Warman was pretending to be asleep. A Dutchman yelled at her and glared, shouting, "Who's that there sleeping?"

"It's my mother, Tuan. She's ill. Please be kind to her. Please, Tuan. Please," she said cowering. A hard shove. The Dutchman tried to strip away the blanket covering the person there. Imi tried to obstruct him and was kicked out of the way. Imi held on tight to her husband. Another Dutchman drew back the blanket of the sleeper with the end of his rifle. To his surprise, the person there was wearing a *kebaya*. Imi was crying even more loudly. Eventually the Dutchman relented, believing her. They turned everything upside down, and then went out again. Everything in the house lay scattered. The Dutch continued looking for adult men in each house.

Then the neighbor's house just to the side of Imi's was set on fire. The flames spread and reached Imi's house, and soon the whole house was ablaze. The man in disguise lying there could feel the flames scorching him. With a jump he crashed through the window. But the veil covering his face was lifted by a gust of wind which was blowing the gathering clouds. Seeing a man running, the Dutch gave chase, and fired. The bullets whizzed. Warman jumped and swerved as hard as he could. When he came to the river he plunged in, then hid by a clump of water hyacinth. For the moment he was safe. The Dutch had lost track of him. They were at a loss and, not knowing what to do, with a sense of urgency they reported back to their commander.

"Dogs. Use the tracker dogs to hunt these dogs of fanatics." Wijman gnashed his teeth as he went in pursuit. His face was red, red as a red-hot iron brand. The Alsatians were set free. Sniffing here and there and panting hard, they followed the tracks of those who were hiding.

They barked at a place by a clump of *talas* plants. Out came of a group of Warman's friends. Five of them were caught and bound. More barking at a stand of bamboo, then a clump of banana trees, a clump of shrubs, another stand of bamboo alongside the Rawagedé river. Tens, indeed hundreds, of people were found by the Dutch, including Warman. They were taken to the village road and lined up. Then they were interrogated one by one. They were prodded by rifle barrels, hit repeatedly, trodden on, stamped on, trampled, and violently beaten. And boots slammed into them, kick after kick making them shake and tremble even more.

"You know Lukas Sutaryo? If you all want to tell me where he is, then you will be safe and I shall give you a reward." Speaking

13

Indonesian, Wijman tried to win them round. Those addressed remained silent. Three times he asked, but no one replied. They maintained their silence. *Thud, thud,* one by one they were hit on the head with rifle butts. They flinched, trying to bear the pain, while within themselves they chanted, "Freedom or death." Wijman was black with rage. His patience was at an end and he vented his anger on them. He lashed out right and left, losing control of himself as he realized that his mission had failed. The "Gangster from Karawang" together with his men had got away. Those lined up in front of him were told to turn around, their backs facing the Dutch soldiers. "*Tek,*" the triggers of the Bren guns were cocked. "*Dung!*" the triggers were pressed. "*Tek! Dung! Tek! Dung! Tek! Dung!*" again and again. Those who were lined up fell, their bodies jerking. Hundreds of fighters dropped. Martyrs in the field of battle. Rawagedé was awash with blood.

The sun at the tops of the mountains seemed unwilling to witness the blood streaming into the valley of Rawagedé. The blood was now mingling with the falling rain, which from being a drizzle now came down in torrents; tears were flowing in profusion. No adult male survived. It was only Imi and the women of her generation and the children who were left moving unsteadily on their feet as they went to tend the corpses. The bodies were buried simply, some by the side of the houses, covered by boards made from what had been window frames or palings of a fence. They were buried only a few centimeters under the ground. And all the time the rain was becoming heavier and causing floods. A lot of bodies were washed away into the Rawagedé river, whose waters churned as the stream became a flood. The water of the river changed color. It was red; and the stench of the fresh blood was carried into the air by the breeze, which accompanied the martyrs to more beautiful streams in heaven.

"*Tek! Dung! Tek! Dung! Tek! Dung!*" The sound still filled their ears if they chanced to remember the scene. Lots of people continue to this day to refer to Imi and her fellow heroines as the "*tek, dung* widows.*"

This did not grieve them, poor as they were. But what did cause them pain was when those Dutch again offended them. They had now come again, sixty years after they had destroyed them body and soul. The Dutch had been declared in an international tribunal to have done wrong, but they still did not have the moral courage to ask for forgiveness. On the contrary, they behaved as if they were giving, not because they recognized their fault, but providing a sort of compensation for the war, which they described as charitable donations. And they had no hesitation in pitting people against one another by exploiting the situation. The money that was given out was silence money, distributed in a manner that was far from even and fair. Quarrels broke out. Imi and the widows like her could only pass their hands repeatedly over their chests in a gesture of astonishment when they saw the descendants of the fighters letting themselves be caught up by events and arguing about the insignificant silence money. The reason for the revolutionary struggle all those years ago had not been for any other cause than the sacrificial pursuit of freedom, had it not?

Now when that freedom was being given shape, the tragedy of Rawagedé was being recalled in a ceremony by crowds led by the VIPs of the nation who had come for the occasion, and it was being attended by many people from other countries. Imi and those of her generation who were left could only look on at the upright gravestones standing there in the specially constructed cemetery. "Even though it is only a handful of bones brought here from the yards of the houses, this is the evidence. That they once fought and gave their lives for the sake of their land," Imi said softly to herself.

She still heard those stirring words of Warman's when he was rousing the fighting spirit of the members of his company before they went out to fight. "Today our hopes depend entirely on you. If we return only in name or if you hear that we are now only bones lying on the field of battle, it is you who must bring to fulfillment the values and hopes of this struggle of ours for freedom. Or will only the bones remain and will we have died in vain? If anyone should ask who we were, I and the others, then reply that we were the soul of Rawagedé."

"*Tek! Dung! Tek! Dung! Tek! Dung!*" The sound of the firing still echoed without respite in their ears. The cinematic projector of their imagination still turned the reel of that scene of sixty years ago. Imi and the other heroines who were left stood looking at the cemetery. Their eyes were heavy with tears as they looked hard at the row of the many gravestones laid out in the special heroes cemetery, Taman Makam Pahlawan. The sight suddenly seemed transformed to that time when they had all stood side by side together. A sense of peace and calm overcame Imi as tears now coursed down her cheeks, no longer firm and taut as they had once been. "*Tek! Dung! Tek! Dung! Tek! Dung!*" That is the name by which the heroines of that time are still known today.

Usép Romli H.M.

The '66 Album

His mobile phone rang. Kasan was startled. He had been nodding off in the doctor's waiting room. He was there as usual; every week he had to come to have a checkup. He had heart problems. He found it difficult to cope with sudden shocks and noises. His wife had advised him to turn down the volume of his mobile so that it did not ring so loudly. In fact it would have been best if he put it on silent and just left it on vibration mode. But he hadn't listened to her.

He groped around for his thick spectacles. Even so the letters on the screen of his mobile were rather blurred, but he made them out finally. It was from a number he did not recognize. But the contents of the message were written in Sundanese in a friendly by-the-way manner. In fact you could say too by-the-way, a bit abrupt.

"Is that the number of Kasan Kosala? If it is, do you remember your old mate, Soron Siregar?"

Soron Siregar? Kasan frowned. He tried to recall. One by one he went through all the names of his Batak friends who could speak Sundanese. No, nothing came. He replied quickly. In the same friendly manner.

"Yup, I'm Kasan Kosala. And you, mate, Soron Siregar, I'm afraid I've forgotten who you are."

A reply soon followed.

"You really are over the hill. And you're not yet seventy are you? I seem to remember you are the same age as me; you've just turned sixty-eight.… December 1966, you and I went together to Tamblong Street to collect payment for our newspaper articles and then we went to that small restaurant in Kebon Kelapa…."

Kasan frowned again. Tamblong Street, 1966. That meant the era of the newspaper, *Mahasiswa Indonesia*, which was at the peak of its fame then. That was when the student demonstrations were at their height, calling for the overthrow of the Old Order, calling for the overthrow of Sukarno from his position as President.

"Blow me!" Kasan smacked his forehead. He remembered now. Old Soron was from Kisaran, a student who had only managed to complete his preliminary qualifying degree, his *sarjana muda*. He'd entered the university in 1962. And then there had been the strikes. And in 1966 classes stopped altogether. The universities were closed by the Minister of Education, because they had become the basis of KAMI, Kesatuan Aksi Mahasiswa Indonesia, the United Action Front of the Students of Indonesia, who were leading the demonstrations. It was they who had given rise to the term, "Angkatan 66"—The Generation of '66. It was a movement against the Old Order. The students from Bandung were known to be more active and more outspoken than those from Jakarta or other towns. And this became even more apparent with the publication of *Mahasiswa Indonesia*, a better paper than *Harian KAMI* which came out of Jakarta. Then came *Mimbar Demokrasi*, which was also anti-Old Order.

As soon as he remembered, he didn't bother sending another sms. He telephoned straightaway, going out of the waiting room to use his phone.

He got through. They spoke for a long time, both asking about each other. How many children, how many grandchildren? What had each been up to in the forty-five years since they had last met?

It seemed that Soron had been a civil servant in the tax department in Jakarta. Only he hadn't liked it there. He'd left and changed his job and tried to become a businessman. But there was too much competition from all the big conglomerate companies that had sprung up. Finally he had become a flower farmer on the slopes of Mount Semeru.

"I also grew apples. They were good, too, and there was a flourishing market for them. But recently they haven't been able to compete with apples imported from China.... I don't know where our country is heading. We fought all those years ago to free our people and our country from the shackles of the Old Order regime which tyrannized us. But now the government is even more repressive. But what about you...?"

"Oh, me, I've just been a teacher. Up to my retirement. But let's wait until we meet, we'll continue then...." Kasan switched off his mobile, since he had been called by the doctor.

When he returned home, he undressed and put on casual house clothes. He took his medicine and then lay on his bed. He thought about this and that and his mind began to wander. He thought of Soron "Samosir." He'd said that he had got his telephone number from a magazine in which one of Kasan's short stories had been published. And Soron had been complimentary about the story, observing that although Kasan was getting on in years he was still productive.

"When I was a student during that time of the demonstrations I could write, too. But now that's all stopped. Even finding time for reading is difficult," he said.

But in the past Soron had been very productive. Almost every week in *Mahasiswa Indonesia* there appeared an article of his sharply criticizing the Old Order, not to mention other articles which appeared in Bandung. Kasan, on the other hand, had written only one or two such articles, though he had written a lot of fiction, short stories or poetry. Sometimes he had done translations. Not political analysis or opinion like Soron.

A sound from his mobile indicated another sms. He opened it. It was again from Soron.

"I've just read on the internet of the *bupati*, the district head in your home district, by the name of Jampana. He wants the new swimming pool to be named after him. Is that true? But the money for that swimming pool came from the central and regional government budgets, not from his own pocket. If it's true, it seems that we failed in our fight to wipe out the cult of the individual."

He didn't reply immediately. Kasan wanted to give a full description of the situation to Soron. At the same time he wanted to recall those memories of the times when the idealism of the student struggle of '66 was at its height. The slogans "Defend our Rights," "Destroy the Wrong" were uttered by those who not only took positions but matched them with actions. It wasn't just empty words. One wrong that had to be destroyed then was the cult of the individual. The worship of institutions and individuals. The Old Order and those who led it.

At that time the center of the cult was Bung Karno—Sukarno, the first president of the new Republic from the time of its declaration in 1945. However, after twenty-one years in office, he had floated slogans such as "Guided Democracy," "The Revolution is not yet Over," and all sorts of crises had broken out in different arenas. There was a political crisis, an economic crisis, a cultural crisis. And there followed a moral crisis. One particular activist from KAMI, a student at ITB, MT Zen had written an article in the paper *Mingguan Indonesia* entitled, "Nine Sufferings for the People of Indonesia." He criticized the speech of Bung Karno to the national assembly (MPRS) in July 1966 which had had as its title, "Nine Readings for the People."

According to MT Zen, that speech described exactly the opposite of what the Indonesian people were facing at that time.

From the beginning of the 1960s, the Old Order had behaved stupidly and had tried to take the people along with them in their stupidity. It was cruel. Harsh. Totalitarian. They had only wanted to establish a superficial prestige and standing, while not caring in the slightest for the needs of the people. The suffering was hidden behind the ideology of power. The price of rice and basic needs had risen astronomically. The import of all sorts of items had also risen, but that did not affect the majority of people. It was only a matter that exercised the elite. As for exports, they had collapsed, because nothing was working. Agricultural harvests were being destroyed by pests, industry was being destroyed by corruption and bad management. Bribery and graft were rife everywhere. Personal and collective connections dominated everything. The situation was made worse by political parties and the bureaucracy, which arbitrarily used the people's money for the personal use of individuals and their cronies. The money from taxation was dishonestly manipulated. There was horizontal conflict between different sections in society, which could erupt at any time and in any place. The climax was reached in the rebellion called the "Movement of September 30, 1965" which involved the Indonesian Communist Party (PKI).

MT Zen's article was distributed widely and became the subject of discussions everywhere. It fueled the anti-Old Order sentiment, and the opposition to the cult of the individual. And indeed Soron Siregar and several other writers participated in the discussion and commented on MT Zen's article.

> All the chaos which has taken place over the last two years has derived from the cult of the individual. President Sukarno has been elevated to ridiculous heights. He has been loaded with all sorts of titles. Titles such as, "Mouthpiece of the People," "Great Leader of the Revolution," which were

deliberately popularized by Sukarno himself. And then other titles were added which of course Sukarno was not averse to. And when it came to the point that he was elevated to "President for Life" by the MPRS assembly of 1964, the cult of Sukarno as an individual became even more pronounced. At that time there emerged KOTRAR (Komando Tertinggi Retoling Apperatur Revolusi, The Highest Authority for the Retooling of the Revolutionary Structure), headed by the deputy prime minster Subandrio, who also held the position of head of Central Intelligence. Its function, in addition to spreading the "Teachings of the Great Leader of the Revolution," was to carry out spying activities in case there were individuals or groups who dared to obstruct or misapply the teachings of the Great Leader. It was from that time that the prisons and the places of detention of the police, the army, and the public prosecutor were full of people who were accused of being anti-revolutionary, who had dared to criticize Sukarno. Those who reported them and arrested them were sycophants who only wanted to win praise from the regime in power.

That was the kind of thing that Soron wrote that raised the political temperature.

And Kasan for his part had written several short stories and poems. They were published in literary magazines which appeared in Jakarta. They appeared alongside poems by Taufiq Ismail, Mansyur Samin, Abdul Wahid Situméang, all of which condemned the wrongs of the Old Order and looked forward to the establishment of the New Order. Those poems were read out aloud in front of student demonstrators at the traffic circle by the Hotel Indonesia, in front of the presidential palace, and elsewhere. They were read out in broadcasts put out by KAMI on the radio.

The Old Order—which had been so strong, supported by political parties and by the military, especially by the special presidential guard, the Cakrabiwara—finally fell. On March 11, 1966 President Sukarno issued the "Surat Perintah Sebelas Maret," the Governing Decree of March 11th, which later became known as "Supersemar." It gave authority to General Soeharto to maintain national law and order. In the month of February 1967, President Sukarno returned his mandate to the MPRS. And then the MPRS appointed General Soeharto to the position of President of the Republic of Indonesia and this was confirmed in the special assembly of the MPRS of March 1968.

The students yelled with joy. Their struggle had been successful. And one of the leaders of the student movement in ITB, Aldy Anwar, wrote an article over five issues of *Mahasiswa Indonesia* in February to March 1967 with the title, "De-Sukarnoization has Ended the Cult of the Individual."

But triumph turned to failure. The New Order, which it was said would correct all the mistakes of the Old Order, was no different. Especially in terms of the cult of the individual. Soeharto was in power longer than Sukarno: more than thirty years, from 1966 to 1998. The cult of the individual in relation to Soeharto was even worse; it applied shamelessly to his family and to his cronies. Sayings such as, "as the chief has instructed" and "it depends on the one above" became indications of the new cult. If, before, Sukarno had set up KOTRAR so that his teachings could be the instrument for the making of the cult, so Soeharto set up the BP7, P4, and Pancasila for the same purpose.

Kasan tried to tap out a reply to Soron:

"Yes, our fight ended in failure, Ron. You could see this after so many of our fellow fighters of those times went and entered the circles of power, both in the legislature and in the executive. They forgot about the hard times of the demonstrations when we were all in it together. They forgot about the aspirations of the people for which we were fighting…"

He sent it off quickly. The reply was soon in coming:

"The Reformation post-1998 should have completely transformed that failure of ours. But look: it's now fourteen years later and it's as though we had turned back to the past. To the cult of the individual again. Look at the uncritical acquiescent talk of those executive and legislative star performers if they start spouting on television. There is not one of them who dares to criticize the individual figures or the parties in power. Just the opposite, they praise each other, conceal each other's crimes. What else is this if it is not the cult of the individual?"

Kasan sighed. Soron was right. It was especially noticeable if you saw everything in the context of events that seemed to have no end: the cases of corruption among the elite, the millions spent on the expenses of members of parliament who went on study tours to foreign countries, the President's private plane, the cost of special tents erected for the President costing about fifteen billion rupiah when he went to inspect the scene of a natural disaster. That was the cult of the individual gone mad.

"And imitation of this behavior goes right down to the provinces. The new regional autonomy has created petty princes who hold absolute power. They are free to order expenditures for whatever they feel like. The provincial parliamentary assemblies, which should exercise control, can be bought off to collude in these goings-on. They all conspire together in their corrupt dealings. They are all in it, the subordinates and the boot-lickers; they all participate in the schemes. They misappropriate social welfare funds, and money from religious charitable foundations and other bodies. Or they propose their names for roads, for bridges, for stadiums, and all kinds of other constructions, since this could possibly bring long-term advantages for them. No matter that these projects have been paid for by the people's money, as you said just now with respect to the swimming pool to be named "Jampana." The name was given because it was built when Jampana was district head and wanted to make his name known, and he wanted to put himself forward for a second term." Kasan typed out this lengthy reply to Soron.

There was a breeze. The breeze of the dry season. Kasan felt it blowing through the cracks of the window frames. It had been a long dry season and water sources had dried up. In some places people had been forced to drink waste water. The rice fields were parched and cracked. Crops had died. The leaves on the trees were withering. And all this time there was a profusion of banners and posters in the names of parliamentary candidates who were putting themselves forward for election. The writing on them was full of self-praise. Narcissistic. They said that they were honest, could be relied on, were clever and dedicated, and other things of that sort, which all encouraged their own cult of the individual. This had not even been known during the times of the cult of the individual in the Old Order or New Order periods.

"History tends to come round again, as the French say," Kasan wrote. And he wrote it in French, "*l'histoire se répète*." He knew the phrase because he had once written an essay that looked at the cult of the individual as it was surreptitiously being practiced in a new way by the incumbents of the New Order. The essay was sharp but within bounds. If it had been frank and outspoken, the writer would certainly have been arrested by the security or intelligence forces. He would have been locked up just like that. Just like WS Rendra and other leading critical figures. Like Mochtar Lubis. Like Adnan Buyung Nasution. Or his civil rights would have been suspended because he had shown opposition to the president and

25

his views. Like General Nasution, Ali Sadikin, Mohammad Natsir and many others.

Kasan's mobile went off again. A text message from Soron: "And Jampana is a young man at that. When people were risking everything in the demonstrations, he was not even of school age. He was just five years old. And now he's got to the top. To the point where he is in a position to make a cult of himself. His reason is, he says, because a proposal was put forward by one or two community organizations that the swimming pool should be named after him. Can you believe it? You know better what the case really is."

Kasan smiled grimly. Although they had been together for several years on the campus and in the demonstration posts, Soron still didn't realize that Kasan was not heavily involved in political matters. He listened to the debates, but that was all. If it was a question of literature or culture, then he participated fully. But nonetheless he did think that he knew about political events that were occurring these days. Including the dispute over the name for the swimming pool between those who were for it and those against. But he had only read about it in passing.

He hesitated before replying. Besides, he was having difficulty with his breathing. The gusts from the dry season wind were building up. They brought unpleasant smells. The smell of garbage piled up on every street corner filled the air. There was no rubbish collection. There was no one cleaning the streets. The workers and the people in charge of them seemed to be busying themselves with matters that were more important or more lucrative for them; for example, putting up as many banners as possible, even though they were becoming real eye-sores.

"Yes, it's exactly like that. When we were doing our bit during the student campaigns, Jampana was still in short trousers," Kasan forced himself to reply to Soron's sms.

The reply from Soron again came quickly.

"Yes, we failed. Our efforts failed. Students were just ammunition, something used to protect others. And so idealism was used up, eaten away by the greed for power."

How could he agree with this, and how could he disagree? Kasan took a deep breath. His feelings stirred as though he were opening an album of the student movement of 1966. Full of heroic pictures. Of the stream of blood of the students who were victims of the cruel bullets of the authorities. Arief Rahman Hakim, Zaenal Zakse, who died during the "Tirta" demonstration in Lapangan Banteng in Jakarta. They had been demanding that the ministers in the Old Order cabinet be replaced, that prices be lowered, that the PKI, the Communist Party of Indonesia, be disbanded.

In Bandung, Julius Usman was shot and died on August 19, 1966 in Jalan Lembong, when demonstrators rejected the national address of President Sukarno to the legislative assembly in Jakarta, the speech entitled "Jas Merah" which was an abbreviation of "Jangan Sekali-Sekali Melupakan Sejarah"—"Don't Ever Forget History." In that speech Sukarno had described the service of the PKI in the struggle for Indonesian Independence. He had mentioned the many members of the party who had been arrested by the Dutch and exiled to Boven Digul.

This was the album of the student struggle, which according to Soron had failed. Because what they had wanted to clean up then, namely the cult of the individual, narcissism, self-praise had now grown again in profusion. The open license to do what one wanted had as its consequence a decline in public morals, and it had become increasingly extensive. This was occurring not only in elite circles and among the older generation but even at the lower rungs of society and among youngsters who were still wet behind the ears.

Garbage carried the smell of rotting carcasses of dead animals. It seemed as if it was evoking the stench of the cult of the individual that was beginning once more to pollute the contemporary social system. The album of '66 that Kasan was imagining became suddenly clearer. Even brighter was the flow of the tears and blood raging purple with pain, because nothing had any effect. The old idealism had gone; the past had been swallowed up by the present, and all were trapped in a period in which everything was rushing headlong into a deep, bottomless ravine.

Mamat Sasmita

Grandfather Oleh

It was a small village by the name of Cangkudu. To the south you could see the steep slopes of Mount Sawal. To the west of it was the river Cikidang. To the east, rice fields spread far and wide. And to the north was the line of the road to Sukamahi. It was there that Grandfather Oleh lived. His daily work was making kitchen utensils of woven bamboo—storage baskets, baskets for steaming rice, sieves, and larger baskets with flaps. These four kinds of utensils were what he made most often.

The *boboko* baskets were normally used to bring back the rice from harvesting the extensive paddy fields. The rice-steaming *aseupan* baskets had tall sides like Mt. Sawal, rising high. And the small hand-size sieve-baskets were used as scoops for catching fish in the Cikidang. As for the larger baskets, *tingkem*, they were for carrying whatever one had if one was going to take the road to the north. The things he made never disappointed. They were all carefully finished; they were strong, the weaving was tight, and the plaiting was smooth. The weave was interspersed with strips of the fine outer bamboo bark. And of course you could use these things for a long time. All the kitchen utensils used by people in Cangkudu and Sukamahi were Grandfather Oleh's work. Sometimes he wove other things, such as winnowing trays or deep baskets for carrying fruit and vegetables, but that depended on orders. As for the four main objects, he made those whether there were orders or not.

When it came to obtaining the raw material of the bamboo, it could not be cut down at just any time; there was a season for it. He used to do this at that time of the year when the crickets and cicadas were tuning up especially loud, the period of transition between the wet and dry seasons. Grandfather Oleh used to say that that was the time when the bamboo was especially fine, not too dry, not too wet; and the bamboo which he harvested had to be stands of at least three years' growth.

One late afternoon after the *asar* prayer, when Grandfather Oleh, was relaxing in his sarong, stretched out on the small front veranda, some visitors unexpectedly came to call. There were three of them, and they seemed to be townspeople; you could tell from their clothes. They had been brought there by a young lad, one of the villagers.

"Grandfather, some visitors; they said they wanted to meet you, Grandfather," said the boy.

Grandfather Oleh at first said nothing; he was a bit anxious; he felt uneasy about visitors from town. Usually the only people who came to see him were small traders selling baskets from the market at Ciawi. And now here were visitors from town, three of them. It was natural that seeing these visitors he should feel his heart beat a little faster. He spread out a mat; he had to shake it out first, since it was a bit dusty because it hadn't been spread out for some time. He invited the visitors to sit on the front terrace of the house. Only two of them came on to the terrace; the third was clicking away with a camera photographing the baskets and the hand sieves and the fans, and at the place where the *tingkem* were he examined everything carefully. In fact by then *tingkem* were already not much in use, a bit old-fashioned; nowadays there were lots of cardboard boxes which people used to carry things.

"So, gentlemen, where are you from? I'm sorry I can't properly welcome you."

Getting to the point immediately, the visitors said why they had come. They wanted to invite Grandfather Oleh to Bandung, to perform a traditional storytelling of Sundanese legends.

Grandfather Oleh shook his head at being asked to perform, especially in Bandung. It was true that Grandfather Oleh had a reputation as a traditional storyteller, but it had been a long time since he had performed, a long time since anyone had called on his services.

"Gentlemen, it has been ten years and more since I've given a recitation, and now you ask me to give a performance in town. I don't think I dare. I'd be very embarrassed."

"It doesn't mean you have to recite throughout a day and a night; at the most it would only be for an hour," said one of the visitors.

"What? Only an hour?" Grandfather Oleh was silent. His imagination was picking out stories which could be performed in the space of an hour. There weren't any, he felt; in an hour the most you could do was get through the introductory passage.

"That's right, Grandfather, since the intention is only to give an example of how there still exist oral storytellers. What's needed is that you should describe your experience in becoming a storyteller."

Grandfather Oleh nodded. He didn't know what was meant, but he thought to himself that if he had to describe his experience as a storyteller, he could do that.

After a while Grandfather agreed, only he didn't have the money for a fare to the town, especially if he had to bring his *kecapi* (zither). The visitors expressed their willingness to come and pick him up in a car. No problem there.

Before they left, the visitors looked around at Grandfather Oleh's handicraft, at the small strong baskets, at the sieves and baskets and the steamers. And in fact they bought some things right then, saying that they liked the design of the weave, because it was finished well with the interspersing of the fine outer bamboo bark and it was strong. And they didn't forget to ask Grandfather Oleh his age, his full name, and whether he had had any schooling or not. They said they needed the information for his storytelling performance.

In the evening after the *isya* prayer, Grandfather Oleh reached up to the loft just above the low ceiling to find his zither.

"Leave it till tomorrow," said his wife, Nini Anih, who was weaving a mat.

"I just want to have a look at it. It's been a long time since I unwrapped my zither from its covering," he answered as he stretched out on tiptoe leaning against the cross-beam. He groped for the zither, and pulled it out slowly, taking it down from the loft.

The zither was wrapped in a white calico cloth which was now rather dirty. He opened it in the center of the house, where the light was rather dim. He brushed off the dirt; he undid the string around the cloth.

Then he slid his hand over the zither, which he hadn't looked at in years, and laid it in the center of the room. He wiped it, stroked it, cleaned it. The strings were loose; the ones which were still taut were the smallest ones.

Terum. Without meaning to, he plucked the good strings with his fingernail. The sound rang clear and fluid. How fine the sound was.

The wind blew hard outside the house, whooshing, pounding the leaves, pounding the windows, rattling them as though someone was trying to open them. Grandfather Oleh was silent, keeping still. Inside the house the cold air went through him like the prick of a sharp point. A biting pain. He felt the stiffening of the hairs at the back of his neck, the hairs of his calves, his chest, his eyebrows. He closed his eyes. *Terum.* Again without meaning to, he plucked at the strings. Colors rose up to him, deep indigo, warm yellow, a pale blue. They brushed against his face.

Suddenly there were people all around, from all four corners of the winds. The queen quietly expressed her wish, the king softly issued his command, the courtiers murmured their approval, the sounds reverberated. Mama Lengser, the majordomo, was chatting away to the night-watch. The servants sitting there bowed their heads low. Was this what they wanted to be performed, to be recited, what they were waiting for, what they were all expecting to see? A storyteller who had occasional clear-sighted glimpses of the mystery of the world, who could read the signs: the branches swaying, the dried withered leaves falling, the dew settling, all were portents. There was a sudden gust of wind. Grandfather Oleh opened his eyes.

"Forgive me, forgive me. It wasn't that your servant was neglecting you," Grandfather Oleh said softly to himself. This was the zither that had accompanied him as he went from village to village, town to town. Long ago. Long, long ago. It was with this that he had brought to life kings and queens, legends which had filled the imaginations of those who heard them. Grandfather Oleh looked around each corner of the room. In that corner there was a pile of pandanus leaves ready for the weaving of a mat. In that corner lay a whittling knife, a small saw blade, a machete, a sharpening stone, tools for stripping the bamboo. In that corner were upright baskets, sieve-baskets which just lay there scattered, steamers neatly stacked up, with deep carrying-baskets lying ready. In that corner was a pile of washing.

"Close the windows, Nini. I'll bolt up," he said as he got to his feet to bolt the door.

The zither lay there in the middle of the room. Grandfather Oleh went ahead to lie down on the bed. Nini Anih was still weaving the mat.

That night, tossing and turning, he could not close his eyes, though he tried; he could not sleep, though he wanted to.

The next morning, a little dizzy because he hadn't slept well, Grandfather Oleh repaired the strings of the zither, adjusting them according to his ear, which was not so good as it used to be. There was no getting away from the fact that he was old now. Even though he felt fit and well, it was unmistakable that his sight, his hearing, his senses had lost some of their power. Grandfather Oleh sighed softly. He looked at the instrument and stroked its bright curve. He wiped it, blew on it, wiped it again.

It was thanks to the storytelling that Grandfather Oleh had met his wife, thanks to the storytelling that he had been able to support his family, indeed had become relatively well-off, was able to afford a house, afford some luxuries.

Graceful, that was the best way to describe her, the young girl who had come close up to watch the storytelling performance at Rancoray, wearing a dark yellow dress, with a slightly worn belt and a white scarf around her head. He was pleasantly surprised by the way she looked at him, and taken by the sight of her as she walked gracefully by. She sat modestly; she had a way of tilting her head, and she was slim and tall. They weren't courting for long. Everything worked out perfectly; they were married and Grandfather Oleh thus acquired a wife from Rancoray, Nyi Anih. She was then in her twenties, and they set up house there. From his storytelling they were able to afford a house, from the storytelling they were able to buy land, from the storytelling they were able to do well, put their children through school. Indeed things got better almost by the month, especially where requests for performances were concerned. From their income they were able to save as well as live comfortably. If one counted it up, the storytelling had gone on for forty years, from his twenties to well into his sixties. The high point had been the 1960s until the end of the Seventies. In the Eighties there were lots of people who worked in government who invited him to perform, because they said they wanted to keep alive village cultures. Cassettes were made, videos; stories were written down, lord knows where all that went. What became clear was that storytelling was on the decline. People seldom requested it.

"Will there be offerings made before the storytelling ?" Nini Anih raised her voice from the kitchen.

Grandfather Oleh was startled; he was suddenly brought back from his daydreaming.

"I don't know, I'm not sure about that. Perhaps not."

"It would be very unusual to hold a storytelling session without making a ritual offering first, wouldn't it?"

"But didn't they say that it's not really a storytelling session? The invitation is more that I should describe my experiences as a storyteller."

Nini Anih didn't say anything more about the matter.

"When you have time, would you wash the cloth cover so that it's clean? There's still time to do it, a few more days," said Grandfather Oleh.

On the agreed date, they came to pick him up in a gleaming car. Grandfather Oleh had been bustling about. He had an *iket* twisted around his head in the casual jackfruit-sheath style and wore a black blouson and three-quarter-length loose silk trousers down to his calves. He carried his zither, wrapped in the white cloth which Nini Anih had washed. He also carried a bag slung on his shoulder in which there was a sarong with a head-cap for when he would be praying.

The car moved off slowly. Grandfather Oleh said a *bismillah*, followed by the muttering of a prayer for a safe journey. The car went on its way to Bandung.

When Grandfather Oleh had been at his peak as a well-known storyteller, his voice used to ring out loud and clear and echo and reverberate; and he knew by heart the stories that he chose to recite. If he made the clown figure Old Retainer put in an appearance, there was invariably a lot of joking and the audience used to laugh.

"We've arrived, Grandfather," said the man driving. Grandfather Oleh sat up a little surprised. When they reached the heart of the town in Bandung, he was taken to a tall building, the lecture hall of a university. He was welcomed and escorted and shown to a large comfortable padded chair. He sat there a bit apart, almost disappearing into the chair. And then Grandfather Oleh listened to the conversations around him, people talking about the need to preserve the traditional arts. He nodded. It moved him that now in this modern age the people who showed concern about traditional performances, who appreciated them, were those who wore ties, who wore shoes, were well-dressed elegant people who got into and out of cars. He hoped it wasn't all just talk.

At the appointed time, Grandfather Oleh was invited to begin his recitation, after being told that he had only an hour to perform. He sat on the stage, in front but a little to the side. He sat cross-legged and took out the zither from the wrapping of white cloth. He gave his greetings to the audience. He adjusted the *iket* tightly round his head, then he shut his eyes. It was as though all of a sudden he was silently thinking, trying to concentrate his skills, muttering the incantation that he normally used, saying a prayer softly to himself, not forgetting to say the *bismillah*.

Treng. He strummed the strings. He gave voice and the sound was as rich as ever. The opening ritual incantation to ward off calamity was sung in its special way, slowly and deliberately, as an introduction.

"Humbly I offer my service to mother earth, to father sky, to those who have completed the eight years, those who have completed the twelve months."

It was a long introduction. He took a long time to sing the incantation. Grandfather Oleh was employing his mastery, everything was as it should be. He did not omit one expression of humble apology.

"With humility I ask that, if there is anything I forget to say, anything I say wrong, make any mistake in my recitation, I may be forgiven, by those there, by those here, by you all. And I humbly request your assistance so that we all remain protected and blessed and well."

And then he began at once on the story, the legend that he was going to recite. Grandfather Oleh paused. He shut his eyes, he shuddered slightly and took a long breath There was perspiration on his forehead. There was a tension between the left and the right sides of his head, there was tension between his red blood and his white blood, tension between his flesh and his skin, tension between his bones and his sinews.

And finally Grandfather Oleh completed his recitation of the story: "I ask forgiveness, to those who are here now in this place, to those who are not here but who sit listening at all four corners of the wind. I am not going to talk about the history of long ago, of the deeds that took place in the past, of the stories that I used to tell. Time has its measure, it cannot be prolonged nor shortened, and a legend cannot be extended nor shortened, it must follow its measure. If a name is forgotten, it is forgotten. If a name is missed out, it is missed out. Take care not to shorten things, take care too not deliberately to draw them out. Of course there are books telling these legends, of course these legends can now be read by all."

Treng. He struck the zither again, and straightaway he went into the incantatory conclusion of the recital. And when the incantatory conclusion was over, Grandfather Oleh put his hand over the zither and then spoke with a slight choke in his voice.

"I hope all of you here in this building can witness that now I am going to hand this over to all the important people sitting here in the front. Grandfather Oleh the storyteller has come to an end, Grandfather Oleh the storyteller is no longer, there is only Grandfather Oleh the weaver of baskets. May the telling of the stories long continue and flourish. I believe these important people genuinely love storytelling. My request is that these stories, this zither be preserved, because these stories are what inspire the ideas and hopes of the Sundanese."

Grandfather Oleh looked up, he lifted the zither onto his lap, stood up, and walked slowly, approached the rows of people sitting in the front. He knew for certain those sitting in the front were the leaders of the community, the most important people there. He handed over the instrument; and the people who took it stuttered their appreciation. Grandfather Oleh went back to the stage and sat down as before.

"Please if you have any questions, I shall answer them if I can, and if I can't, please excuse me."

He spoke like this because, once before in the Eighties, he had attended a discussion like this. Perhaps it would be no different now. He thought to himself, aren't discussions just the same as other discussions whenever they're held?

Many people asked questions. They asked: how had he first become so attracted to storytelling, how had he learned, where had his teachers come from.

Grandfather Oleh replied straightforwardly, but at the end of each of his replies he added, "Everything needs dedication and due attention. Don't be troubled at having to support yourself; don't be tempted simply by what you see; don't be distracted by your feelings; don't harbor unkind thoughts about others."

Some asked why just now Grandfather Oleh had said that his days as a storyteller were over; that he would be a storyteller no more. Grandfather Oleh replied, "I am old now, sir, weak in body and in mind. I need to be replaced by someone younger, someone who is fit and strong, who can see properly, sharp-sighted, keen-eared, someone who can sit cross-legged for long stretches of time, who doesn't forget things. As for me, I shall peel and strip bamboo and I shall make baskets and earn my living."

It was time for the *lohor* midday prayer; Grandfather Oleh's session was over. He got down from the stage and made his way to the mosque and said his midday prayers before he set off back to Cangkudu. He made a special prayer, chasing away his thoughts, which were ever turning to his zither. Wasn't it through the zither that he had found happiness, through the zither he had won a name for himself? What he had not said was that as regards being a storyteller today, well, there was not any future in it.

Mamat Sasmita

The Spell for a Dream

After the call to the midday prayer, Kang Sabri went to have a rest in Grandfather Oleh's small shop. He could have a nap there. He wedged himself alongside the things piled up there and leaned back on one of the shop's wooden pillars. The breeze brushed gently against his body, as though it were stroking him to sleep. He half-shut his eyes; if he nodded off, he could sleep till the late afternoon propped up there like that.

He reached out to a new fish-trap which had just been woven and wasn't quite finished yet: there were still frayed ends which had not been cut off. He looked at it carefully. Grandfather Oleh's weaving was especially good and strong. He looked at it again. Suddenly he came to himself. He put the fish-trap back where he had got it from. If he went on like this he would end up wasting time. He went out to the side of the shop; there was a well and a bucket for the water and he could do his ablutions. The water was cold and he shivered. He washed his hands then his elbows then his legs, knees, everything thoroughly. He scrubbed his forehead hard. His skin stung, as though he had scrubbed down to the bone. His sleepiness disappeared once he had done his ablutions. Then he went into the small prayer-house to perform the midday prayer. The prayer-house was not very big, only six feet by six feet, just for the use of anyone passing who wanted to pray.

Grandfather Oleh with his wife Nini Jumsih, were grandparents many times over. Goodness knows how old they were. Kang Sabri only knew that to him they had always been old, but they were still fit and well. Throughout the day they sat by their little shop at the side of the road; they had done that since they were young. They had never moved away; they had always just been there. And before, the road had just been a path, a way to get to the rice fields, to the upland gardens. Now it was a busy road; it was the only road that went through the village connecting it with the town, the market, the mosque, the mosque compound, the village hall, the district office. Their house was combined with the shop.

Grandfather Oleh was one of the oldest people in the village, and so was Nini Jumsih. So Grandfather Oleh knew precisely how the village had grown over the years, the way the houses had been built higgledy-piggledy, the way the population of the village had increased, and the everyday lives of people there. People now lived differently from before; anywhere you wanted to go it was easy, you just had to decide to go. Anything you wanted, that too was easy, all you had to do was buy it and possess it. That was the way Grandfather Oleh talked. But really Grandfather Oleh had worked hard and had made good use of the land he owned beside the road, just behind his shop. Even though it was not a large plot of land, he had been able to plant cassava there and bananas. At the side of the shop there were big trees, *rambutan*, mango, *jengkol*, jackfruit. And next to the well he had planted *sereh*, betel vines, gourds, and *ganyol*. There was also a clove tree; and of course there was a ginger-root plant, and *cikur* which was like ginger, and turmeric. But there were no shallots or garlic. He said it was difficult cultivating them, and anyway if they did not use shallots and garlic in their cooking it wouldn't do them any harm. They had enough rice fields for their daily needs, since there were only two of them. As for something to go with the rice, boiled cassava was sufficient, or boiled bananas or even boiled *ganyol* roots. That was quite filling, and it wasn't as if they lacked strength or felt weak.

What they served in the shop was coffee especially. It was the same price as the price of a small sachet of coffee on which you poured the water. Someone once asked them whether they didn't make a loss selling it at that price. After all they had to make a fire and get wood for it, to boil the water. They said that they did not have to pay anything for the fire: the wood came from the shavings from the bamboo strips which they used for weaving, as well as from the dried twigs and branches they picked up. As for their labor, well, that was readily given; you didn't have to charge for everything, otherwise you would not get the benefit of doing something charitable. Whether there was any justness in what Grandfather Oleh had to say, lord knows.

After praying, Kang Sabri sat crouched in front of Grandfather Oleh, who was stripping bamboo.

"The bottom edge of the fish-trap looks a bit rough," Kang Sabri said, his hand reaching out to the fish-trap he had looked at earlier.

"They're always like that," Grandfather Oleh replied.

"Why don't you do it differently so that the frayed edges don't show?'

Grandfather Oleh looked at Kang Sabri and said, "With any kind of work everything has to be done the proper way; you have to know the right words to say."

"What do you mean by that, Grandfather?"

"That's what the old people used to say, what my parents used to say. When you begin working on bamboo, you have to know the right time to harvest it so that the wood is at its best; when you splice the bamboo you have to know the lie of the grain; for the weaving you have to know how the joint turns, and when you weave it you have to know how to treat the shell of it, the hollow of the wood, so that the weave is strong." Grandfather Oleh paused and took a sip of coffee from his shallow bowl. Kang Sabri was fascinated. He asked Nini Jumsih to pour some more coffee for him. The coffee in the glass seemed to steam, a sign that the glass had been filled with water just on the boil, brought hot from the fire, not poured from water which had been standing.

"As for the principles and the right words to use, what I mean is that you have to say a word of apology, ask permission, because at the least you need to remember that the bamboo to be cut down is also part of God's creation, and so you have to say a *bismillah*, an acknowledgement to God. And that's how it is whenever you make things. There should be an accord between your words and your actions; there has to be an agreement between the two, not a tension. The fish-trap is for holding fish, for harvesting fish from the river. If you look at it carefully, it's like a breast; there's a shoulder, there's a swell. That's something to be aware of when you're feeling a fish-trap, just like when you're feeling the space below a person's rib cage. If the fish you catch is too tiny, the kind that you would catch in a fine net, or it's still a tiddler, it will swim out of the bottom of the trap, it won't be taken, it's still growing. And when it's producing eggs, it won't go into the body of the trap either, it won't be taken because it's too big, it's pregnant, about to produce offspring."

Kang Sabri could only nod.

"All that is just traditional wisdom, encouraging people not to be greedy," Grandfather Oleh finished up. "You must forgive me; I had no intention of giving you a lesson, but it just came out after your question. And that was just as I heard it from the old people; that's what they said about the right words to use."

Kang Sabri was still silent, thinking. He felt ashamed of himself; particularly since whenever he went fishing he was determined to bring back as much as he could, as much as he was able to catch. He felt he did not know anything about the traditional wisdom of the past, although he almost always took a fish-trap with him, because it was a favorite pastime of his to fish in the river.

Kang Sabri had almost forgotten that the reason he had come to Grandfather Oleh's little shop, besides wanting to have a coffee and to pray in the prayer-house, was because he wanted to ask Grandfather Oleh something, not something which was in the way of a general question but something he was afraid might appear rather awkward to express. In the end he stretched out for a small bamboo scoop lying beside the fish-trap.

"And this too: when you weave it you have to make a proper shell?"

Grandfather Oleh glanced at the scoop that Kang Sabri was holding. "Yes, when you weave a scoop, it's especially important that you make a proper shell or hollow it out."

He went on, "In the past there used to be a *lawon* design that was called a scoop pattern."

"*Lawon* is a kind of cloth?"

"Yes, a cloth worn as a skirt. Nowadays one often calls them *sarong poleng*, checkered sarong."

Kang Sabri nodded. He took the scoop outside, so that he could see it in the full blaze of the day. He wanted to see the pattern. And yes he could see it; it was just like the black-and-white of a chessboard, he thought, remembering the chessboard now rather dirty and much used which was kept at the motorbike-rank shelter. It was only as a motorbike taxi that Kang Sabri was able to provide daily support for his family.

"The old people used to say that scoops or nets to land fish were like the hollow of large throwing nets. And when you turned the small boat-like scoops upside down that was like the arch of the sky. They used to say, the old people, that being empty and being full were a pair, just like in life: there is pleasure and there is pain, there is dark and there is light, there is good and there is bad. A person's life is also sieved like that: good with the bad, pleasure and pain. The black and white checkered sarongs were often worn by religious teachers, and were called *poleng puranteng*, the sacred checker."

Kang Sabri just smiled sheepishly when he heard what Grandfather Oleh had to say. He had not imagined that this would be the kind of thing he would hear. It applied to himself. He had been a motorbike taxi man for a long time and he felt that he had more often encountered pain rather than pleasure. There had been a sieving of both.

It was getting late in the afternoon and the other motorbike taxi men were gathering there, as well as those coming back from the rice fields or from the upland gardens wanting to have a rest and drink some coffee in Nini Jumsih's shop.

He put aside his intention of raising something else with Grandfather Oleh. There were too many people; he was embarrassed, afraid of being jeered at, especially by the other taxi men. He said goodbye to Grandfather Oleh and went back to the taxi rank, to see if he could add to his day's takings. He had done quite well earlier in the morning and had had two rides, one trip to the town and one to the market. The man on the town trip was a good fare, because he had asked him to say a prayer for the success of the business in town and had given him a bit extra. He had earned a fair amount, enough to cover the cost of feeding the family that day. He set off on his bike over the unevenly paved road and then came to the village road. It, too, was in bad repair, especially since it was the rainy season and the road was slippery and muddy. If you didn't keep skillful hold of the handlebars, the bike was likely to slither underneath you and you would tumble off. A lot of the agricultural produce could simply not be transported, though there were trucks that tried to get through, and everything was loaded up on them; everything piled up. It made one frightened just to look at them. No one knew when the road would be repaired. If the road was repaired, then the bikes would be able to travel along safely, and there would be no need to be constantly buying new tires.

Now there was no way that tires could be well-maintained; they were always bursting, always going flat. That was certainly the case with the inner tires. And the outer ones were always being shredded, cut up by sharp stones. It was one debt after another; he felt bad towards the repair shop. If there was a puncture in the inner tire, one could repair it oneself, provided one had a pump.

In fact there was another road, a shorter one to both the market and the town; but unfortunately the bridge at the Cikidang river was not in good repair. The upper structure was rickety and the iron frame was completely rusted. Not only could you not get a motorbike across it, even crossing by foot you had to be careful. It was frightening; it seemed on the point of collapsing.

"Yes, well, perhaps!" Kang Sabri suddenly said, but he had other things to think about when he was on this bike, negotiating the steering to avoid the gaping potholes on the road. Perhaps the reason why Grandfather Oleh took this view of things and had that matching attitude—namely that you had to surrender, give in to your fate—was because he was old, his sun was setting, as it were. But Kang Sabri was still young; he had two children, the eldest had just started primary school; there was still a long way to go to fulfill his responsibilities. The authorities did not receive many requests; wouldn't it be possible to repair the road and the Cikidang bridge? With the situation what it was at present with motorbikes going up and down, the surface was very quickly destroyed. And one constantly had to go to the repair shop since tires were bursting all the time every day. The situation meant that one's work was constantly being halted. And this was also the case every morning when he had to take his son to school, the one who had just entered primary school. He took him across the rickety bridge, since he did not want to let him go on his own; he was afraid he might fall from the bridge.

The upstream water of the Cikidang flowed fast under the bridge, and in the rainy season it raced in full spate and it flooded.

In fact the business of the broken bridge had already been discussed with the village head by the villagers, and then the matter had been passed up to the head of the local federation of villages, the *lurah*. And from there to the sub-district head, the *camat*, and then on to the head of the local government department, then to the district head, the *bupati*, then to the provincial governor, then to the minister and then to the president. In a while the decision would come back down the chain, but there was no certainty that the request would be approved. It was a long business, even when it was not a matter of the people responsible being transferred to other jobs in the meantime.

Kang Sabri frequently had to remember to keep his feet on the ground; he had to think of what was feasible, but his thoughts kept turning back to the same issue: if the road was good, if the bridge was good, perhaps the money which he now spent on repairs, the money he used to buy tires, could all be saved, so that they could have something to pay for his children's' schooling.

When he reached the rank, there were several people there in addition to the taxi men, some dozing in the shelter, some playing chess to chase away the tiredness. Kang Sabri sat down with them in the shelter.

"Is it my turn now?" Kang Sabri said.

"It is," said one of those who were dozing.

A few days later Kang Sabri was again sitting cross-legged in Nini Jumsih's shop, having a cup of coffee and eating the snacks: some fried cassava, some fried sweet potato, and fried bananas. He steeled himself; there was something he wanted to ask Grandfather Oleh, never mind that he might be laughed at.

First he moved close to Nini Jumsih, pretending he wanted to share the warmth of the fire, since even though it was daytime it still felt rather cold, as it did at the beginning of the dry season. So he squatted in front of the fire and helped to stoke it. Nini Jumsih was sitting on a low stool pounding cassava roots in a mortar.

It seemed that she was on the point of making some sweet rice cakes.

"Nini, does Grandfather know any secret spells for having pleasant dreams?" he whispered to Nini Jumsih.

"What kind of dreams, lad?"

"I want to dream about meeting... no, not that, but a dream where I meet myself."

"Perhaps he does have something."

Apparently Grandfather Oleh had overheard the conversation between Kang Sabri and Nini Jumsih, since he happened to be sitting at the front in the corner of the small veranda where he was stripping bamboo.

"What's all this about my knowing a spell? Didn't I get it from you, Nini?" he shouted out.

"Hey, don't go around accusing people, it's wrong to do that," said Nini Jumsih no less loudly.

"Come, come, in the past when we were young..." Grandfather said in reply, but he didn't continue, for no reason. Hearing him, Nini Jumsih giggled as she shook the cassava flour through a fine sieve.

"What was that about the time when you were young, Nini?" said Kang Sabri.

"Ask there," said Nini Jumsih pointing in the direction of the veranda, meaning Grandfather Oleh, it seemed.

Kang Sabri left the kitchen and approached Grandfather Oleh, not forgetting to take a glass of coffee with him.

Grandfather Oleh went straight into stories about when he was young, when he was still single. Every night, he said, he used to dream only about Nini Jumsih, and in his imaginings he was being looked after by her and being pampered by her. And then all of a sudden he wanted the reverse too: he wanted Nini Jumsih to dream about meeting him. So he asked those who were older than him about his wish to obtain a spell that would succeed in making her dream about him. And someone did tell him one, but there were the usual pre-conditions attached to it, acts that he had to carry out, as though he had to buy the power of the spell. To start with he had to fast for seven days, and he had to be constantly chanting; and on the seventh day he had to immerse himself in a deep pool in the river for the whole night. And then if he wanted to utter the spell he had to bathe first in seven natural spring fountains.

"And I carried out all these instructions. Whether they were going to be effective or not I didn't know; but in addition I concentrated all my thoughts on her, and there was the proof, my dreams fulfilled, I married her, but perhaps it was because we were courting before that."

"So I was under a spell then…?" Nini Jumsih could be heard calling out from the kitchen. Grandfather Oleh ignored her comment, and he went on stripping the bamboo for weaving. Kang Sabri smiled and chuckled.

That was Grandfather Oleh's story and he ended by saying, "Don't think improper thoughts for a man, lest you're damned for it. Don't use the spell to imagine others; it's better to cherish the ones you have."

"That's right, men who act like that aren't worth anything; you should think of your wife at home," Nini Jumsih called out from the kitchen. Kang Sabri pretended not to hear.

"And how does the spell go, Grandfather?" Kang Sabri looked at Grandfather Oleh as he spoke.

"And who is the person, lad? Someone from here?"

"No, not anyone from here, Grandfather, someone from the town."

"That's rather far away. What precisely do you want?"

"Well, to arrange it so that the person dreams about coming here, so that the person has dreamt about wanting to come here at leisure and look round."

"A woman, lad?"

"Not a woman, a man."

"Some relative of yours?"

"No, a person in authority."

"And this person in authority, who is he?'

"The district head."

Grandfather Oleh was silent. He seemed anxious and looked hard at Kang Sabri. Kang Sabri didn't say anything more; he regretted he'd spoken. Nini Jumsih kept on talking from the kitchen, "That's a foolhardy thing to do. Take care that you don't cause trouble; don't interfere in things you don't know about."

Kang Sabri quickly said what he intended. He wasn't planning anything wrong—he only wanted the district head to come to the village, so that he could inspect conditions in this area. So that the road would be repaired, so that the bridge would be repaired, and a health clinic set up so that people who were ill would not have to die on the way while trying to reach the town, so that the school children would not have to crawl along collapsing bridges. Wasn't that after all what had been promised in the political campaigning?

"Grandfather, never mind if you don't give me the spell for a dream. Since you have already met all the conditions for making the spell work, it should be you who performs the proper ritual, so that the person in authority comes here." As he said this, Kang Sabri was reaching for his wallet, from which he took out a newspaper clipping and a campaign leaflet. "This is his name, his age, his date of birth and the day of the week on which it fell, his address, his photo and the names of his parents." He held out the clipping and the campaign leaflet with the district head's data to Grandfather Oleh.

"But if you just invite him here, maybe he'll come," Nini Jumsih said from the kitchen.

"But if we invite him, we'll have to waste a lot of money entertaining him, feeding him properly, because, so one hears, you have to slaughter chickens and goats, you have to empty the fish-ponds and so on. I feel sorry for the village council. They would have to run around and do this and that. It would be us here who had to do all the hard work. It's better to do it the way I've thought out."

"If anyone wanted to come here, I would just offer them rice cakes," said Nini Jumsih.

"Yes, but it wouldn't just be the man himself; he always has to be accompanied by a procession of people. Those who came with him would probably fill three big buses, and if you offered them rice cakes, you would need about ten trays of them," Kang Sabri replied. Nini Jumsih didn't say anything more, nor did Grandfather Oleh. He didn't say another word, and when Kang Sabri took his leave Grandfather Oleh just said, "Right."

The next day, just before dawn, when the dew was still glistening on the leaves, Grandfather Oleh was still sound asleep, because the whole night he had been tossing and turning. Nini Jumsih was sweeping the yard, sweeping up the shavings and keeping them separate for the fire. In the rubbish she swept up, there were the newspaper clipping and campaign leaflet from Kang Sabri. She collected them along with the other scraps of rubbish, then she put a flame to the pile, and everything was swirled away by the wind, flying off who knows where.

Mamat Sasmita

The Star Spring

The upland garden orchard that his late father had left to him, was large, about four hundred *tumbak*, each of which was over fourteen square meters, it was said. He grew all sorts of things there—nangka trees, *rambutan*, *gedong* fruit, *kadongdong*, *sawo* and lots more. Growing on the sides of the slopes were *muncang*, candlenut trees. They had been there for a long time and now the trunks measured the whole span of one's arms. When Kang Sabri was a boy, if the candlenut trees were in fruit he used to rush around with his friends and gather up the candlenuts. They picked out the biggest nuts and used them for their games of hitting one nut against another. Kang Sabri had a favorite nut, which he called Si Banteng, the Wild Buffalo, because the twists of the sinews of the nut looked like horns; it had never been beaten in any contest. The shell of the nut would become smooth when it was rubbed with the oil from the nut it had smashed, bright and rather black.

There were different kinds of bamboo planted on the slopes: *gombong* and *haur* of thicker bamboo, and *tali* and *tamiang*, which were more slender. The *tamiang* had long thin joints between the nodes and people often came to ask for some; they wanted it to make flutes; others made blowpipes from it. In front of the clumps of bamboo there was a spring. The stream from it gushed out and it flowed in great quantity. This spring bubbled from a huge source the size of a grown man's waist. It was called Séké Béntang, the Star Spring. They called it this because there was no other spring like it in the village. The water burst from it clear and bright, and there was always water there, even when there were exceptionally long hot dry seasons. People used to say that the reason it was a Star Spring was because a star had fallen into it. True or not, who knows.

Kang Sabri squatted down. He sat on his haunches on a slightly raised bank looking at the Star Spring. The water was gushing ceaselessly from within the earth. There were flecks of foam where the water had raced especially fast, as it tends to when it is nudged by strands of grass which spread fan-like into the water. Kang Sabri looked up; where did the water come from? There was no answer. Kang Sabri looked up again; the trees lived from the nourishment they received from their mother soil. Kang Sabri looked up again, and saw Mount Sawal looming high above. Kang Sabri looked down and saw the rice fields stretching away in the distance. Kang Sabri looked down again and saw the house ponds which would be full of fish. Kang Sabri looked at the water-skimmers which played the on surface of the water; sometimes he could see water-beetles scratching at the bottom of small pools.

The stream flowed to towards the east. Part of it was diverted to a rather large tank, plastered and strong. At the front were six spouts, which the people of the village used for washing clothes and bathing and washing plates and glasses.

The water was shared out to the extensive rice fields—to Haji Sobirin's rice fields, to Kang Dana's rice fields, to Ma Inung's rice fields, to Bi Is's rice fields; almost all the rice fields received their share of water. There was one particular stream which had been channeled away specifically, although some of the channeling was in disrepair; this flowed to the *pesantren*, the religious school of Ajengan Falah. The water was for the pupils there and they used it for their pre-prayer ablutions, for bathing, for washing their clothes, and for cooking. All this water came from the Star Spring.

"What's to do," Kang Sabri said to himself as he stood there; then he walked off along the rice field dikes, the soles of his feet soaked with the dew.

It was his mother's story, a story which had been passed down from older generations. They said that in the past, up there where the vegetation was thick with *saliara* shrubs, there had once been a very tall *reunghas* tree. And at the time of the guerilla troubles, when the Darul Islam rebels of the Fifties were fighting for their political ideals, there had once been a group of them, just a few people, scrambling round as if they were disturbed. It appeared that they had decided to lie low in the clumps of bushes below the *reunghas* tree; but they broke out in swelling and they scratched at their skin and were very agitated. They were easy prey for the military, who came and shot them. The *reunghas* tree was known as a poison tree. Its sap could cause itching and a red pimply rash, not to everyone but to those who were susceptible to allergies. The *reunghas* tree now no longer existed. Goodness knows what happened to it, whether it was cut down or just died. The tree which now climbed up to the sky was a *loa* fig tree, and so well established was it that the place where the water bubbled up was sometimes called the Loa Spring; but it was better known as the Star Spring. Mother also said that that there had often been fighting between the rebels and the army there, and there had been a lot of deaths. In fact a lot of corpses had been seen floating in the pools of the spring. And that was the reason that it had acquired the reputation of being a taboo place and people rarely dared to pass by it. It only became popular again a long time after the rebels had disappeared and after the tank and the water spouts were constructed.

The land had been inherited; it had originally been acquired bit by bit by Kang Sabri's grandfather from the profit made from selling coconut oil. It had been just by the spring that his grandfather had made the oil. It had a reputation for being especially good, perhaps because the water used to produce the coconut milk came from the spring, which was so clean and clear. He didn't know where precisely his grandfather had put up the little hut and built the fire on which he placed the coconut milk mixture and slowly stirred. Perhaps it was the place where there was now a small prayer-house. Close to the water spouts, a prayer-house had been built from contributions of people from the village, a place where those who were working in the rice fields could come at the times of prayer, a place of rest for those who were passing and had just come from the town.

Two weeks ago someone had made him an offer for the land—a good offer: the price was higher than the market price for land there. The person making the offer had come along with the village notary. It wasn't clear where the man had come from, but from his clothes he seemed to be a townsperson. Why a townsperson should want to buy land in a rural area was a mystery, but the village notary seemed to be pressuring him to sell the land. Kang Sabri didn't immediately give the matter much thought, since he had to discuss it first with his younger brother and his mother. Even though he was considered the head of the family, he still could not make decisions just like that, even though his brother and his mother left it up to him.

His mother's words were still in his mind. "Mother leaves it up to you, Sabri, because you are in a position to judge what is for the best and what is for the worst. Only bear this in mind, that you don't let the money you receive from the sale of the land just be spent up all at once. You have to think of your brother's schooling, and even more you have to think of the expenses when it comes to getting married. That money has got be the capital." As for his brother, he just said it was up to him. Listening to his mother and his brother only confused him more. He was reminded of so many examples of people who had sold the land that they had inherited and who instead of prospering from it had found themselves living in worse circumstances. Perhaps that was the result of suddenly coming into a windfall which you hadn't worked hard for; the consequence was that you just squandered it.

Kang Sabri flicked off the dew which clung to the hairs of his calves and quickly made his way home. When he changed his clothes he put on his best shirt, not the everyday shirt he used when he went out on his motorbike intending to use it as a taxi service. He put on a jacket too. The sun had just risen and was now hot. He started up his motorbike, and warmed up the engine, then he set off, not to the motorbike taxi stand, but to the *pesantren*. He wanted to visit Ajengan Falah.

He went into the *pesantren* first, and not directly to see Ajengan Falah. He went to the wash room, to the toilet cubicles, and looked around rather furtively as though he were inspecting the place. He didn't feel awkward; it wasn't as though he was a visitor, since he too had once been a pupil there. He looked at the water which was flowing freely, bright and clear from the fountain, then he did his pre-prayer ablutions. He wanted to say a prayer in the mosque, but he drew out the time looking at his watch. The water was crystal clear, and all from the Star Spring. There were tens, perhaps hundreds, of pupils who bathed there, who did their ablutions, who did their washing using the water which came from the spring, including his brother who, did he not, prayed there every afternoon. After he had said his prayer, he approached Ajengan Falah's house; he had deliberately chosen to come early before the teacher began his lessons.

"Seeing you rather startled me," said Ajengan Falah.

Straightaway Kang Sabri explained what was troubling him, in particular that someone wanted to buy the land where the Star Spring was located and was willing to pay a lot for it. He finished by saying, "I have been thinking, about what my late father said to me, always reminding me that the water that flowed down to the *pesantren* had to be maintained and that there should never be a time when the water ceased to flow."

Hearing what Kang Sabri had to say, Ajengan Falah shifted in his chair, moving back a little. For a moment he didn't say anything; he was silent as though trying to compose himself. After a bit of time he spoke at last: "I shall speak just as it comes to me. We derive a lot of benefit from the water that streams down here; if there was no stream I don't know what we would do. We would have to do something because the pupils will still need to do their ablutions, still need to bathe and to do their washing. They mustn't get skin sores because they can't wash, or their clothes smell because they can't wash them, or worse still be unable to perform their ablutions."

Kang Sabri quickly apologized and said that he had had no intention of worrying Ajengan Falah, that he had wanted to meet him only because he had reckoned that this was the best way to get his worries off his chest and at the same time ask what the regulations were about selling something one had inherited.

Ajengan Falah replied, "I am grateful, my son, that you have asked me to discuss this issue, and I also appreciate it that you still regard me as a parent." And then Ajengan Falah moved quickly on to giving Kang Sabri his advice. First of all, he should respect his parents; and as for selling what he had inherited, whether this was land or anything else, there was no problem about it, only he should be sure that the share that he got and the profit from the sale was used in a beneficial way, in other words, was used for good purposes.

Next Ajengan Falah prayed that Kang Sabri's plans would come to fruition and that no problems would arise. "And, my son, when you decide to get married, don't forget to let me know."

"Of course, sir, who else could I ask for advice?" Kang Sabri replied.

After his meeting with Ajengan Falah, Kang Sabri went straight off down the south-leading road with the intention of meeting Haji Sobirin, who had the most extensive of the rice fields that were irrigated by waters from the Star Spring.

He didn't speak for long with Haji Sobirin. He only wanted to inform him that someone had made him an offer for the land where the Star Spring was, someone from the town.

"I wanted to warn you that if it comes to it and I sell, then there is a possibility that the water supply for your rice fields may be cut off in the future."

Hearing that, Haji Sobirin did not say much, but he certainly seemed worried. That day Kang Sabri didn't go off and try to earn something by using his motorbike as a taxi. Instead he went off to meet everyone whose rice fields or whose ponds were irrigated by water from the Star Spring.

A few days later, everyone in the village knew about it and was talking about the Star Spring being sold. The story buzzed about, and as usual a small thing was turned into something big. There was a lot of speculation. What would happen if the communal fountains were closed, what would happen if the water to the *pesantren* was cut off, what would happen if the rice fields dried out? And there were those who said quite openly that those who owned rice fields and those who owned ponds that received their water from the Star Spring would now have to give something to whoever provided the water. There were those who said that the people who wanted to buy it were townspeople, important people, and that in the future they would take away the water in big tanker trucks for the purpose of turning it into a business, selling drinking water. They would sell it in bottles and plastic cups; and if this was true, then they would discuss with the villagers about making a donation to compensate for buying it. Townspeople, everyone said, were greedy and thought that everything had a price and was for sale.

Kang Sabri's sweetheart also asked about it, because although her house was not in that same village and was rather far away, she had heard about it from some source or other.

"Kang, is it true that you are going to sell the land where the Star Spring is?"

"I haven't completely made up my mind. I'm still thinking about it."

"What do you want the money for?"

Hearing the question Kang Sabri looked at his sweetheart in reply, as though he wanted to see into her thoughts.

"So that we can get married," was Kang Sabri's reply. There was a sudden silence as though a noisy cricket had suddenly been squashed underfoot. Only it seemed as though a gust of chill air had passed over. After rather a long silence, Kang Sabri spoke as though he had made up his mind to express his thoughts.

"Yuyum, after my father's death, when I became the head of the family, I had to come back to the village to look after Mother who as you know is now old, and I had to give up my place at university. I was ready to become a motorbike taxi driver to pay for my brother's school fees. You, Yuyum, were fortunately able to continue, although it was only for a diploma, and now you have a job. Yum… would you be willing if I asked you to work hard with me, with all the pain and difficulty we would face, to set up house together so that our children might have a future?"

She replied with simply a nod and twisted her fingers.

"Yum, let's go now to the Star Spring, while it's still light."

When they reached the Star Spring, there were a lot of people there bathing at the waterspouts. And when Kang Sabri with his girl came up, they all jokingly called out that a heavenly spirit had come to make an annual inspection of the stream. Kang Sabri and Yuyum just carried on and excused themselves for disturbing them.

"Look at the water-boatmen enjoying themselves together. When will I be a water-boatman and swim in the water together with you, Yuyum?" Yuyum only smiled and pinched him affectionately. Kang Sabri pointed out his mother's rice fields and their boundaries, and said that it was from those rice fields that they were able to have food on their table every day. The rice fields were not extensive but enough to provide for the needs of the three of them for a season. "Yum, when we have children let's bring them up so that one is a general, one a scholar, one a risk-taker, one a wanderer, one who can measure the extent of the earth, and one who can measure the extent of the sky. We will make the Star Spring the place where they begin their lives and dream of their futures."

"Just like in the advertisements," said Yuyum.

"Different, Yum. The future doesn't come from a tin of milk powder, but from its mother's milk, from the its birthplace, which we will look after. Look at that clump of bamboo, look at that clump of *saliara*. That's what will provide them with their future."

He took her through the undergrowth up the hill. There was the upland garden, with its *jengkol* trees, its *rambutan* trees, its jackfruit trees, its mangosteen trees, its *peuteuy* trees, which would provide for the futures of their children to come, as well as pay for the schooling of his younger brother.

After that, Kang Sabri couldn't stop talking about how they would plant water-spinach in part of his mother's rice field, and stagger the planting so that each week some of it could be harvested and sold at the market. And near the house they would plant lots of gourds which they would also sell at the market. And in front of the large trees they would make beds for seedlings, for trees of many different kinds, *huni*, *sawo*, *samolo*, papaya, mangosteen; he wanted all the fruit trees that could be found here in Sunda, in the west of Java. He would plant the seeds of them all, and they would sell the fruit to people in the towns.

The news that the Star Spring was to be sold and that the proceeds of the sale were going to be used for wedding expenses spread fast. Especially so after it was said that several visitors from the town came to Kang Sabri's house, ten of them in two cars, and expensive cars at that. The visitors were all taken to the Star Spring. Kang Sabri did not say much; in fact he kept to himself. If anyone asked, he would simply reply that he didn't know, and add that he was feeling confused by everything. And then once Kang Sabri and Yuyum had walked together to the Star Spring, the rumors grew more intense that Kang Sabri was about to get married, and that meant that the Spring was about to be sold.

The person who was most agitated was Haji Sobirin, because if the Spring was sold and the water carted away in tankers to town, then it was likely that his rice fields, now so fertile, would dry up, would become impossible to cultivate. So one day he purposefully set off to visit Kang Sabri. He let it be known that after each harvest and after each emptying of the fish-ponds, a share would be given to Kang Sabri. He said that this had been agreed by everyone who had rice fields and fish-ponds. Kang Sabri was a bit puzzled hearing this and said, "Thank you for your kindness. This promise is only between the two of us; only we two are party to what you have said. And the real truth of it, the essence of it, has of course been witnessed by almighty God."

"Yes, exactly so. And I fully agree to it. Only I just hope that you do not sell."

Kang Sabri quickly replied, "It's just that I am caught in a difficult position because Yuyum's family have been asking how much I will be able to afford for the wedding."

And it was true, Haji Sobirin's promise came good. After the harvest, several sacks of rice were sent to Kang Sabri's house, and there were several carp—not big ones, just a kilo or two. Quite a decent amount, you could say. After a time the rumors that the Star Spring was going to be sold died away. There was a whisper that the buyers were getting permits, and they were told this was something that could not be done in a hurry. Right up to the time when Kang Sabri was getting married, the Star Spring had still not been sold. The wedding had taken place all of a sudden because Yuyum's parents had pressed for it, saying that there was a danger that a long engagement could lead people to say that the two had already been intimate. It was not known where Kang Sabri had got the money for the wedding; nobody knew. The celebration lacked nothing, the baskets of rice kept coming in from here and there; there were those who contributed chickens, some even gave goats, and of course there were lots of fish. The pupils from Ajengan Falah's *pesantren* were directed to go together to collect firewood for the outdoor fires where the food would be cooked. Indeed there was no need to buy rice. Many of the chickens and the goats were not slaughtered, and much of the firewood remained piled up in store.

During the celebrations, the village notary was asked about the Star Spring and he replied without hesitation, "The sale is not going ahead. The buyers have withdrawn because of the condition."

"What was the condition?"

"They had to sign an agreement in front of a lawyer that none of the spring water, not even a plastic cupful, could be taken away." Hearing this answer, the questioner nodded.

As for Ajengan Falah, it was as if he was aware right from the start that Kang Sabri had exaggerated the news of the Star Spring being sold, because he had devised a little plan: that those whose rice fields were watered by the Spring would help out with the wedding arrangements, as Kang Sabri required. He was a sly one, asking in this indirect and unforceful way. That's what Ajengan Falah said to himself, but he quickly asked divine forgiveness lest he be considered to have thought ill of someone. When the bridal pair were relaxing together after the wedding, Kang Sabri put his arm around Yuyum and whispered, "Now then, Yum, let's carry out that plan of ours to have a child who'll be a general." Yuyum gave him a meaningful look.

Usép Romli H.M.

Somewhere to Get Away from it All

The rain clattered down without stopping. Sometimes it went on throughout the night. It started at *maghrib* and then petered out around *subuh*. Sometimes it rained throughout the day. It started when it became light and then only stopped around *maghrib*. And indeed sometimes it had been known to rain throughout a day and a night. It put a stop to all work. Well, that was the rainy season for you.

The rain was falling on the village of Kondang. It was nestled in the valley below a hill which stood out exposed on all sides. Only to the east of it was there some space lying between Honje Hill and Hanjuang Hill. And there was a waterfall there. It cascaded down pouring water into the Cipamarakan river. And there the sun's rays glinted off the water, gradually brightening up the village, which every morning was shrouded in mist.

The main livelihood of the people of Kondang was farming. They scratched away at a living. They planted what they could harvest quickly, such as maize, yams, gourds, as well as different kinds of pods and runner beans and things like that. They also planted other things which took longer to grow before they could be harvested. Things that you could forget about and leave to themselves. They counted on those things to see them through during the difficult season when the rains were few. Things like cassava especially. Besides that there were *gadung* tubers and *suweg* herbs and things that grew wild. Different crops required different kinds of attention. But there were a lot of advantages. Some things were for one's own consumption, some things were for sale.

There was no separating them from the land, that was the philosophy of the people of Kondang. Seven generations of them had been there since lord knows when. From the time of their fathers, grandfathers, great-grandfathers, great-great grandfathers stretching right back.

And were they not people of the soil, would they not return to the soil? It was these sentiments which made the people of Kondang unwilling to move from the land.

But lately, from the time of the big landslide at Sereh Hill to the south of the village, there were many people who were becoming alarmed about their farming. They were afraid of being buried by a landslide. Especially when flooding was followed by boulders tumbling down from the hills. The Cipamarakan had been blocked off by the landslide just by Abah Sahro's rice fields, and the diverted stream from the river had flooded, swallowing up the rice fields and nearby vegetable gardens. It was fortunate that the village itself had escaped the flooding.

The water receded after the mud which had blocked the Cipamarakan was dredged away. It had taken the villagers of Kondang a week of working hard together to clear the mud and boulders. And then the stream had started flowing again down the hill, leaving thick slimy mud in the terraced fields and the gardens. They had had to wait two or three seasons before that land could be used again.

"If there was anyone who wanted to buy it, I should be happy to sell my rice fields," Abah Sahro said, grumbling a little. He was sitting around with others on the veranda of Kang Marjuk's house at the time. They were watching the cassava porridge cooking in the steamer. The steam was still curling off from it.

"Who would want to buy our land?" replied Jang Suha to Abah Sahro. He reached for the scoop and scooped out some cassava. Then he ladled some out on to a large leaf which lay to hand, using it for a plate.

"Yes, you're right. People want land that lies by the side of a main road." Kang Edon also helped himself. "Next to the Cibatok market place, they say, the land is worth four million a *tumbak*. Even more in Koropeak, because there are luxury houses there and so the price of land has rocketed to seven or eight million a *tumbak*."

The others sitting there were silent. They were chewing their food. They could taste the flavor of it. It had been made from cassava which had been steeped in water, then steamed, then dried, until it was like rice.

It seemed that everyone thought the same. The land, their livelihood from farming, was in all their minds. The more time passed, the less their land was producing. Because it had been exhausted by factory-produced chemical fertilizer. It had seemed a simple matter when they had started using it, chemicals like urea and sodium chlorate. It had been more effective than chicken droppings or manure from the stable or compost. You just had to spread a kilo of urea once and your rice field square would quickly thrive. It was quick to spring up. The more you attended to it, the better the rice grew.

So things took less time. It was easier to handle. If you needed the fertilizer, all you had to do was go to the shop. You didn't have to work all out shoveling and carrying. And it didn't stink.

The only damn thing was the pests. They were small insects, weevils. Some were black in color, others were brown. They settled on the plants in droves, just as the ears of rice were beginning to swell, and then the ears turned yellow as though they had been singed.

And you were forced to get rid of them with the chemical pesticide, which you had to buy. It wasn't enough to chase them away with the smoke from burning rice husks or the bark of *suren* trees at the edge of the fields That method only worked on butterflies or caterpillars. For the weevils, since they had come from the use of chemical fertilizer, you had to kill them with chemicals, too.

You sprayed them. There was a strong pungent smell to the pesticide. It hung around everywhere. It settled in the water of the paddy fields. The result was that the animal life there all died off. Things like dragon-fly larvae, water-beetles and other water creatures. There were corpses of dead insects floating about everywhere. And it was the same with the dead ants, which stuck to the leaves of the rice plants.

And then there were other animals that were affected—crabs, eels, all were caught up in it. They did not die straightaway as a result of the spraying, but, because their food supply was gone, in the end they too died.

"It was during our grandfathers' time; that's when we began to use chemical fertilizer and pesticide." Hadma broke into everyone's thoughts. The others looked at him and were silent for a moment. Then they all added their scraps of information.

"That's right. It was about fifty years ago. I was just eight at the time. An instruction was issued by the government: the kind of rice seeds we used had to be changed. And the time to start planting had to be the same for everyone. I remember, Mama Haji Kodir's field had just been planted with transplanted seedlings, and they had to be pulled up. They were the kind of seeds known as *sengon*, tall and thin. The rice from them was soft but firm. The people in the government office said that that kind of seedling was out of date. It took six months to grow before you could harvest it. The new seed however, only took a hundred days from the time you transplanted it."

"Yes that's right; it was called super seed," Kang Edon chipped in. "The only trouble was that you couldn't grow the seed yourself. You had to buy the new seed. It wasn't like Mama Haji Kodir's *sengon* seed."

"And you couldn't get away with doing things on your own," interrupted Abah Sahro, who was the oldest there. "At that time I had just set up house. I was working on Mama Komar's rice fields, three square plots. I had just sown the seeds, and one of the village officials came up to me. He told me that I mustn't begin the sowing too early. I had to wait for the rice seeds which the government would be distributing. As for the seeds we already had, we should just use them for cooking, he said, because we were not going to use them as seed. We had to wait around for almost two months. The paddy fields had just been ploughed, the nursery beds been made ready, but there was no rice seed. Our stock was finished. After all, we had eaten up the rice we had and the seed, and were depending on the new seed to be handed out. That was the time when we had to eat dried sliced cassava and *onggok*. The only thing we didn't have to resort to was the banana trunk pith, like they say people had to eat during the Japanese occupation."

"What happened, did the seed eventually come?" Kang Edon asked.

"It came and we sowed it quickly. Then transplanted it quickly. And we waited to harvest it after a hundred days, just hanging about. We were really starving. But the village official said we weren't starving. There was plenty of food, he said. Because that's what those high up in the government were saying…" Abah Sahro flicked his lighter. He lit the cheap hand-rolled cigarette which had been hanging from his lip for some time.

The fact of the landslide, together with the talk they had while eating the cassava mixture on the veranda of Kang Marjuk's house, seemed to have influenced the Kondang villagers. Many now felt reluctant to go to the rice fields or to their small-holdings. Many tried different jobs in succession, working as porters in the town, trying a bit of street-selling, or simply any other way of earning a living rather than through farming. The rice fields and the upland gardens were abandoned and left to grow wild.

"If anyone wanted to buy my land I'd be happy to sell it," someone said.

"Who would want it?" another answered.

The whisperings of one or two started to spread and became the common talk. They all agreed that that was what they wanted to do.

To start with, a land estate agent came round, a broker. He looked at the land in the valley and up the hill to the foothills of the mountains, to the pastures. An agreement to sell was reached. There was the haggling over the price. And then payment straightaway. The price was few hundred thousand rupiah for a *tumbak*.

So it was that almost all the land and the rice fields in the village of Kondang was auctioned off, as it were. What was left was only the land on which houses stood, the mosque, the fish ponds, and the field on which the children played.

And even the land up in the mountains, above the village, was sold. To a conglomerate in Jakarta. Cash down. Because the money offered was higher than the normal price, the owners of the land had no objection to selling. Especially when the ones brokering the sale were the village head and his staff. Half the people were a little afraid, because they felt rather intimidated.

Most surprising was Pudin's land. A hectare and a half. There were clove trees there and *sengon, jabon,* and other kinds of trees grown for their wood. It was just the land that was bought. The trees could be felled by the original owner and he could keep the profits. It was said that the buyers were only concerned with the surface area of the land in order to build luxury villas. All that land was flat and faced east. The view from there was magnificent. Towards the valley, to the rice fields which stretched out as far as the foothills of Mount Penclut.

Of course Pudin was overjoyed. He was getting money for the land and money which he would earn from selling the wood. He was able to fulfill his dream of buying a pickup vehicle which he could use to bring goods to sell back and forth from the town.

As for the others, some sold tens of *tumbak*; others as much as two or three hundred. Including Oji's land on the mountain slope. Every year it had been left uncultivated. But because there was a source of spring water, there it was bought for five hundred thousand a *tumbak*, and of course he was very pleased. In fact he would probably have let it go for only one hundred.

The village head and his deputy, the village secretary, as well as their staff were overjoyed. Besides the money they earned from cajoling those who owned the land to sell, they also earned extra profit in other ways. According to rumors, they got about two or three hundred per *tumbak*. From three or four hectares they were probably getting five hundred million. It was no wonder that the village secretary was rebuilding his house. The village head, it was said, had bought a "Mio" motorbike for Neng Santi, the substitute teacher, whom his wife disliked so intensely. In fact she had even bawled her out. She had screamed at the woman for prostituting herself to her husband.

A month after the sales had gone through, the names on the titles changed, and the new property certificates made out, a convoy of trucks and diggers arrived. They flattened the land for the construction of the villas. It wasn't only Pudin's land which was bulldozed; other land was too. But not all of it. There was land which was completely flattened but there was other land which was deliberately kept apart. That area was for flower gardens and lawns.

Not even a year had gone by and the appearance of the village of Kondang had changed; it was now something else. It was a haven of tranquility. It was full of flowers of all colors and different kinds of plants.

What stood out was a huge tall building. Modern and the latest in design. It faced the village. A massive building. It stood out, impressive, surrounded by beautiful gardens.

The parties and prayers to celebrate the completion of the building took place over three days and three nights. The villagers of Kondang were invited on the first evening. They were asked to give a *barjanzi* recitation. The gift bag for them to take home was quite good. Besides the food they received in their party boxes, they were also given envelopes: each received fifty thousand rupiah. On the closing night, it was those like the officials of the district and sub-district government who were invited. The district head couldn't come himself, because he was having a meeting with the governor, so it was only his deputy who was there. But it was still an enjoyable occasion. Especially since it was enlivened by a zither and flute performance. It had been organized particularly to please the district head, who was fond of such entertainments. But the deputy seemed to be able to show quickly that he, too, liked that sort of thing. He was especially pleased to be offered something that made his pocket bulge.

"Pa Janur is a top man. A self-made businessman, close to those at the center of power in Jakarta. He's often invited to the palace." That was what people were whispering. As for the person called Pa Janur, no one knew him. No one had met him. Not even the village head or the secretary were clear about who he was, since the business of buying and selling the land had all been transacted by subordinates.

A week after that, some news spread abroad. Pa Janur, it was said, was very happy with his house and its location and everything else. He had decided to set up a challenge. Anyone who could find any flaws or anything wrong with the building and its location would be given a reward, a fully paid trip to Mecca, on an *umroh* visit.

First of all it came from the security man who was on guard there all day. And then it was passed on by the newspaper delivery man who delivered the papers every day. And eventually it reached the villagers of Kondang, whose houses were simple structures on stilts—to all the world, if one saw them from the big house, stretched below like piled up bits of cardboard.

The man referred to as Ajengan, the religious scholar of the village, whose house was equally decrepit, also heard the news. And so did all the village officials and all the people in the highways and byways.

"If you want to find the money for the cost of an *umroh*, just go ahead and earn it; no need to find the answers to riddles and puzzles first," said Ajengan, whom the villagers respected, but who, even though he was a well-known scholar, had not yet had the opportunity to visit Mecca. He smiled quietly to himself.

"Yes, indeed," the others commented.

But who doesn't want to go on an *umroh* all expenses paid? Only how was one to find the flaw in that huge house? The colors were lovely. The walls were strong. The location was ideal. It compared well with the palaces of sultans and kings anywhere. It really was perfect.

But there were nevertheless people who took up the challenge and wanted to have a go at finding a weakness. It wasn't just a question of *umroh*, but the satisfaction of being right. It would be a triumph. And if one was wrong, there were no unfortunate consequences. It wasn't like competitions in the time of legendary kings. If you were right you won the hand of a beautiful princess, but if you were wrong it was off with your head.

Aki Samun, who daily cleaned and looked after the village mosque, wanted to try.

Having made up his mind to do so, he went up the hill, straight up to the guard's post. He explained that he wanted to make clear what the flaw was in the building, exactly as stated by the owner in relation to the competition.

"I have a condition. I must be allowed to stretch out first and relax on the terrace while I wait for the owner of the house to arrive," said Aki Samun.

The guard didn't know what to do. Especially since Pa Janur was about to arrive that afternoon. If he allowed Aki Samun to stay there, he might be doing wrong; on the other hand if he didn't, what might happen? There might be an unpleasant outcome to it all.

But Aki Samun was insistent.

"If I am to know what the flaws are, I have to see the building from close up, it's not possible to see them from a distance. It is supposed to be a fair competition, not just a brag, isn't it?" Aki Samun looked hard at the guard, who was fidgeting uncertainly.

After discussing the matter with his fellow security guards, he eventually allowed Aki Samun to come in. He put him on a sofa on the terrace just behind the kitchen.

"When the master arrives, make sure you behave properly in the house," said the guard, inviting Aki Samun to enter.

When Pa Janur arrived, Aki Samun was relaxing. He was sitting in front of a plate of different snacks that the guard had ordered for him from the kitchen.

"What's happening here? How does this old man dare to sleep in my house?" Pa Janur said with anger in his voice. Before he had even taken off his jacket and tie, he immediately telephoned the guard on the intercom. Then he nodded once or twice.

"So, old man, you want to have a go at the competition? Want to go on the *umroh* eh?" His voice was mocking.

"Oh, it was just because I heard the story; they said there was a competition to find the flaws in this building. As for *umroh*, however much one may want it, it's up to God, isn't it? God decides who can go to the holy place. However much one has for the fare and the costs, if the Great One doesn't allow it, then it won't happen," replied Aki Samun equally tersely.

"So, old man, you know what the flaws in the building are?" This time Pa Janur spoke a little more politely.

"Yes, I know them," Aki Samun replied quickly. "Among other things, a great drawback of this building is that it is going to disappear."

"Disappear? Disappear where?" Pa Janur said looking closely at him. His personal assistant and his bodyguard were on the alert.

"Wherever. It could be carried away by a landslide. Or carried off in a flood, for example. Or its owner could disappear first, leaving the building behind, empty. In this world nothing lasts forever."

"A building like this, so carefully built, so strong, disappear?" Pa Janur shook his head in amazement.

'Well, that's what's wrong with it. That's the flaw. This building is going to collapse and be destroyed, however much the owner is convinced that it will last forever. Much of the proof of the flaw can already be seen. It's as I just said just now. More evidence will be seen in time. It could be now, it could be tomorrow, the day after tomorrow or in the more distant future," replied Aki Samun as he walked away, leaving Pa Janur and his staff open-mouthed.

And after the space of a week, a crowd of people descended on the house. They were officials of the KPK, the Anti-Corruption Committee. They put up a huge board which announced: "This building and all its contents have been seized by the KPK."

Pa Janur, everyone said, had been put into a prison cell. There was no question of paying Aki Samun the *umroh* fare as promised.

He was probably thinking only about himself at that point, though no one in fact knew what he was thinking.

He may have been thinking about the village of Kondang and how it had been transformed and become a flat wasteland. Almost all the agricultural land had disappeared, because it had been turned into buildings, all of which had many flaws.

Yus R. Ismail

The Neighbor

The orchard, which was about fifty *bata,* 750 meters square, was being razed. The trees were being cut down. *Sukun,* cloves, banana trees, *sengon*—all just became so much waste wood. And everything in that orchard, even if no one gave much attention to it, grew well. To say that the Ambon bananas, for example, were as big as the forearms of a child is no exaggeration. Simply looking at them gave one a sense of wellbeing. It was unlikely that ever again would one see such a profusion of bananas hanging from such a profusion of trees.

The person who took care of it was Mang Warja. I don't know who owned it. I had never met him in any of the neighborhood meetings. Mang Warja only referred to the person who owned the orchard as the "Man from Town." And I didn't ask any further. It didn't matter to me who owned it.

But in truth after the trees had been cut down, I had an excellent clear view. It was just by my house, separated from it only by a small patch of land on which *sedap malam* flowers had been planted. Normally the sun clearing the tops of the trees would just reach the window of my bedroom around ten o'clock. It was now seven and it was warming my mattress and pillow, which had been hung there to air. And in the evening there was no sense of uneasiness as one looked out at the yard.

A week after the trees had been razed, the boys were playing football there, every afternoon, and on Sunday from the morning onwards. They also played badminton, catch, marbles; it was as though they had a new playground, and in fact one afternoon Pa Atan and Mang Aep added to the fun by joining in the football. From when I was a boy, I had liked football, so I had itchy feet when I watched them. I enjoyed it. They were laughing, shouting, jostling each other, tripping each other up, suddenly falling, playing with other boys; it made me feel young again seeing them. But since I was old now, I didn't play football. All I could do was take part by standing at the side of the playing field (that was what we ended up calling the orchard), looking on and chatting with others. Mang Dadan had made special bench out of thick bamboo and had brought it there from the bamboo clump by the stream.

We enjoyed it there having a mug of tea together, hot with broken lumps of brown sugar, and sometimes there were slices of boiled sweet potato or boiled cassava. It was wonderfully relaxing, feeling the breeze wiping away the sweat as one drank the hot tea. We split up after we heard the voice of Mang Malik, who was acting as the *azan*, giving the call for prayer in the distance.

Unfortunately it was only for a month that the orchard, or rather the playing field, was available for football and to bring the old folks together. After that they began to put down the foundations for the what was going to be built there. The earth was dug up and the reinforced concrete was laid down. Trucks bringing building materials came and went. There were also ten of them on site at the back. And there were several foremen. There was even a qualified civil engineer who, they said, was there to make drawings and design the building.

Of course putting up a building like that was a strange sight for people in the village. So it wasn't surprising if every afternoon there were a lot of grown people looking on, observing the men doing the construction work. There was all sorts of banging and tapping. The wood used was all teak, and the fixtures and decorations were all brought from faraway towns. A month after they began working, a huge tall building stood by the side of my house. When it was evening there were hundreds of lights blazing like a fairground. At the front along the border, there was a garden full of flowers neatly laid out, in matching colors and sizes, the different colors carefully selected by a gardener. Every morning and late afternoon the garden was watered. There seemed to be five servants, with various tasks, watering the garden, sweeping and putting clothing of different kinds out to dry.

I first made the acquaintance of the owner when he held a thanksgiving feast to celebrate the completion of the house. Inside the house it was vast, with high ceilings and terraces, and it was full of people. It seemed that almost the whole village had come, and some people even brought their children. I suppose everyone wanted to see what a rich man's thanksgiving meal was like. And, well, you would be missing something if you didn't go. In addition to the special strange-tasting small cakes brought from town, there was something to take away and boxes containing a meal with rice. The contents left people who hadn't been there with a feeling of regret for a month. There were slices of stewed beef, grilled chicken, hard-boiled eggs, curried liver, and sweet-sour *gurame* fish, and there were envelopes containing a hundred thousand rupiah.

Pa Kalang, he said his name was, I don't know from where. His refined appearance matched his standing as a wealthy man. He face was smooth and unblemished and he spoke easily; his clothes glittered like the host of a television show. There was a pleasant fragrance about his person, coming from I don't know what perfume. He didn't have time to talk since he was so busy. He was doing nothing else but shaking hands with guests when they arrived and when they were leaving.

One, two days passed, then a week, two weeks, and I didn't see him again, Pa Kalang. Occasionally I felt I'd like to meet him, talk about this and that while introducing myself, since I was his nearest neighbor. But every time I asked one of the servants in the house, Pa Kalang was away. And I could see from the comings and goings of his car that indeed he went off very early in the morning at *subuh* and came back late in the evening. Perhaps that's the way of wealthy people; every day they're very busy doing their work.

In the end I just gave up the idea of getting to know my rich neighbor. It didn't matter; it was quite usual not to be close and intimate with one's neighbors. There was nothing wrong in that. And didn't he keep on sending things to the house as gifts? One morning a servant came round with a plate of some special papaya *dodol*, a kind of fudge, because he said that Pa Kalang had just come back from Palembang where that was a special sweet delicacy. One evening the servant came round with a bowl of *gudeg*, a vegetable stew, special to Yogya, from where he said that Pa Kalang had just returned. But I just wanted to get to know my neighbor, not receive gifts which he sent round. Whenever I had the opportunity, I too sent round things. When my son-in-law, Kang Yana, harvested some *sawo* fruit, I sent round a basket of them. And when I went to Sumedang to take part in a training session for substitute teachers, I brought back special *tahu* from there.

My acquaintance with my wealthy neighbor was limited to these exchanges. Lots of people asked me things about him, but I only smiled in reply because I didn't know anything.

"So where does Pa Kalang work?" said Pa Lukman when I met him in the village hall.

"Where's his wife? How many children does he have?" said Ceu Dini when I was having a *lotek* salad in her food stall.

"Will it be all right if I send him a proposal requesting help for the Independence Day celebrations on the 17th of August?"

said Jang Dipa, the head of the village Karang Taruna youth organization, who liked to put on a play to celebrate Independence day.

I only smiled in reply to all these questions. And eventually the questioners would smile back at me saying, "Well, you are the closest neighbor...."

After the Friday prayer I didn't usually go straight back home. Ustad Wahyu used to give us a Quran recitation lesson. But on this occasion Ustad Wahyu couldn't manage it, because he had to visit his grandfather, who was ill in Kuningan. So I contemplated the view across the yard. I sat on a wooden bench in front of some bougainvillea flowers that shaded the area.

I felt a bit embarrassed looking at my own house. It had been built on land measuring eight *bata*, about 115 square meters. There was one bedroom, one bathroom, a sitting area in the center of the house, and a kitchen hidden away at the back attached to the house in a makeshift way. There was a light with a twenty-five-watt bulb in it in the center of the house and a ten-watt bulb on the balcony just outside the house. I felt embarrassed when I looked to my side and saw the huge building looming upwards with hundreds of lights, with a neat garden and its flowers. Perhaps others would have smiled at the comparison. But this was the first time I had taken things in. But it didn't matter to me. I didn't feel put out. Or envious at someone else's good fortune. If I remembered how my own house had been put up, I could never stop feeling content with the way things had turned out. I had saved to buy it, or rather I had given some money in exchange to obtain it from Abah Doni, who had had the goodness to take only the cost of fifteen *bata* for what was in fact a larger plot than that. I had saved enough for the foundation, then I had constructed it bit by bit. I'd taken years to build the house to look as it did now. And the garden, all of it was my own work helped by friends. There were bonsai trees which I had searched for high and low in the forest with the help of Jang Nanang, and lots of flowers which I had got from the garden of Jang Agam, the man from Lembang.

I was idly standing there when someone greeted me. I turned round to answer. To begin with I was a little alarmed. It was Pa Kalang. God be praised. From the start hadn't I wanted to get to know him better? But I had not expected this. After chatting about this and that and asking polite questions in the usual way, Pa Kalang sighed.

"I moved here initially because I wanted a place for retreat. To relax. But it hasn't turned out like that."

"Perhaps you should cut down on the amount of work you have, Kang," I said. I addressed him as Kang because he said that was what he wanted me to call him.

"I haven't been thinking about my business enterprises for some time. I am just rushing about here and there in fear, avoiding things."

"What are you afraid of?" I was smiling as I replied to him. I didn't really believe in his anxiety.

"The thing is that I have a lot of debts that must be paid off."

"Something you owe?"

"Yes, debts."

I smiled weakly at him then, hearing this. I thought he was joking. A man like him who was so generous with his giving, worried about debts. Or was he indirectly referring to me? I was worried about a debt. I had not paid the installments on my motorbike for two months now. I didn't know what to do; I was afraid the bike would be seized by the dealer, but I couldn't pay yet, since my monthly pay which I had just received had been used to pay for the doctor's expenses in town for my son.

"Akang, you don't need to be anxious about your debts. I am sure you have enough to pay them off."

"It's not that, Yi. The debts that I have are not simply financial debts. I have many kinds of debts. Debts arising from my behavior, from my thoughts, from my feelings. How can I pay them?" he said letting out a sigh. And now he looked to me as though he was ashamed. In the fading light his expression was drawn as though he was fighting against some great sadness. I didn't say anything to him, and then he took his leave from me. I was at a loss. I didn't understand.

In the morning, after the *subuh* prayer, I saw his SUV leave the mansion. Usually Kang Kalang left before *subuh*. Who knows, perhaps he wasn't going off because he had some business to do but because he was avoiding his creditors. For almost a month I didn't see him again; he was probably worried about his problems.

One day when I was looking out at the view after the *maghrib* prayer at the mosque, someone again greeted me. The first time I had been surprised, because I hadn't thought that it was Kang Kalang. But now I was surprised by his appearance. His face was yellowish as though wasted by disease. His frizzy hair was white. He was all skin and bones like a dressed scarecrow.

"Akang, how are you?" I said inviting him to sit down on the bench.

"I'm not well, Yi. I'm not well because of the debts," he said, trying to suppress a sob as though he was in pain. I put an arm round him. When he had calmed down a little, he carried on.

"I've gone here and there trying to pay my debts. I have more than enough wealth. I could pay my debts ten times over. But when I meet someone to whom I have once owed money and I want to pay, the person just replies, 'Don't worry about it. I have happily forgotten about it; it doesn't mean anything to me. Consider your debt paid.' But that doesn't make me happy. I feel that that just increases my debt. And when I feel a sense of shame because I have hurt someone in the past, and I admit my fault to the person and ask what I can do to make amends, the person says, 'It doesn't matter; I just considered it bad luck that I had in the past. I've got over it.' Hearing that I scream even louder inside myself, Yi. I am in even more pain, the pain caused by my own behavior. I am a creditor to myself. How can I pay off my own debts?"

I didn't reply; I didn't know what to reply.

Initially I respected my neighbor's confidence. It was his guilt. But eventually I wasn't able to keep it to myself. One afternoon I said to my wife, "I feel sorry for Kang Kalang. He's lost so much weight and he's all wrinkled. His face is pale, and it looks quite serious. What's the use of being rich if that's what happens to you?"

"Who are you talking about?"

"Our neighbor, the owner of the mansion with the five servants and the deluxe SUV. It cost a fortune, they say."

"Our neighbor is a small banana plantation, dear. Now you understand why you shouldn't always be looking at yourself in the mirror in the afternoons: the devil uses his opportunities. Come on quickly go to the bathroom and do your ablutions. Mang Malik has just made the call to prayer."

I shook my head and repeated the religious formula *istigfar* to overcome my shock. Was this true? I put away the mirror I had used while combing my hair and I went to the bathroom. My *maghrib* prayer was disturbed, because someone was repeatedly knocking at the door. I couldn't concentrate on any of the words of my prayers, but went straight to the door and opened it. It was Kang Kalang. He was even more haggard, alarmingly so. He hugged me tightly.

"Forgive me, Yi, if I am disturbing me you. I have come to say good bye. Don't be like me, Yi. You have to be good. Don't get yourself into debt. And the debts you have now, pay them off one by one as much as you can. I'll pray that you do," he said. I went with him to the yard. He said goodbye and then walked off, weaving his way head down.

My wife was right. There was no mansion. In the plot of land stood a frangipani tree, and in front of that there was a tree stump. It was there that Kang Kalang was heading.

Aan Merdéka Permana

Corrupt

Yesterday Pa Wahyudi was put in handcuffs by the KPK, the Anti-Corruption Commission. It was said that he had been caught red-handed giving a wad of notes as a bribe to a government official.

"Could it be true? What will it mean?" said Mang Kayum. He was perplexed.

"What do you mean, what will it mean?" Jang Udi asked in turn.

"Think about it, Ujang. If the man is arrested by the KPK, that will mean he won't be able to continue fighting the cause of the poor street-sellers."

"So what? I'm not a street-seller; I'm a *tukang ojeg*, a motorbike taxi. I don't remember Pa Wahyudi making any promises to *tukang ojeg*," replied Jang Udi.

"Oh, come on. Yes, it's true he didn't make any specific promises to *tukang ojeg*. But just last month, weren't there several meetings in the village hall where Pa Wahyudi said that he would repair the village roads, that he would build a junior secondary school for our village? And he never failed to give donations to mosques all over the place. But with this, now, all those plans for construction projects will just die. Just imagine, if the village roads were levelled and finished, then traffic would flow smoothly, and *tukang ojeg* would benefit." Mang Kayum sighed, apparently saddened by the thought that with the handcuffing of Pa Wahyudi that would be an end to all the development in the village, because all of it was in the hands of Pa Wahyudi.

"If the village roads were made good, then there would be more *ojeg*. And then it's likely that small village minibuses would come on to the scene. And villagers would start owning their own vehicles, and that wouldn't be of any benefit to *tukang ojeg* at all." Jang Udi pulled a face, because, as he said, the livelihood of *tukang ojeg* lay in roads being full of potholes which became water-buffalo hollows during the rainy season.

Pa Wahyudi was an important figure in a well-known political party. Besides being a party figure, he was also a businessman. As such he was the contractor for all sorts of construction projects. He constructed market places, he constructed bridges, he constructed mosques. He was friends with the small man in the street and with people high up in the civil service. That was perhaps why many government projects fell to Pa Wahyudi. According to government regulations, any business contractor who wanted to receive a government construction project had to go through the process of tendering. But in the case of large projects, they were always won by companies owned by Pa Wahyudi. In the first place that might be because it wasn't just one or two companies that he had set up, but a number of them. In the second place it might have been because of his friendships with officials in high positions. It's natural, isn't it, that everyone wants to help out friends.

Pa Wahyudi was now asking for the support of the people, because in the coming general election he wanted to be elected as a member of the national assembly in Jakarta. At the moment he was a member of the regional assembly, from which he hoped to move up.

"It won't be difficult because, after all, Pa Wahyudi is the kind of chap who opens up employment opportunities for people who are now idle for lack of a job," said Mang Kayum.

But now why had this man, who was so good to the man in the street, a man who had done so much for him, been put in handcuffs by the KPK? Of course if he had been arrested by the state, then it must be something to do with embezzling government money.

"It's as far from the truth as the sky from the earth, Pa Wahyudi robbing the state," said Mang Kayum, determined to defend Pa Wahyudi.

"Well, it's happened, Mang. The officials concerned certainly know more about it than we do."

"Do you think so? I think we know better. It's a fact that he has promised to support the street-sellers so that they are not harassed by police patrols. And he has said that he will build a new market place that will be kept for the occupancy of street-sellers."

"Only they will have to pay for their kiosks there, and it will be expensive, won't it?"

"Yes, it will be expensive; in fact very expensive. But you will be able to defer payment and pay in installments," said Mang Kayum.

"So it's true what Jang Cepit said," said Jang Udi.

"Who's he, then?"

"He used to be a student, but he didn't finish his degree. Then he became a member of some organization or other, and now gets involved in national protest demonstrations."

"And what did Jang Cepit say?" Mang Kayum wanted to know.

"He said Pa Wahyudi made under-the-table deals to win projects. Because if you wanted to win a contract you had to bribe officials, and the result was that the cost of the project became expensive. The proof is there in the business of the street-sellers' kiosks. You have to buy them and they're very expensive."

"But it's common to buy things on credit," said Mang Kayum.

"Well, I don't know," said Jang Udi jumping up.

Pak Wahyudi had promised a lot. He'd made promises to the street-sellers, to parents of schoolchildren to whom he had promised he would build a junior secondary school. He'd even promised the boys who kicked a football around that he would build a public football field. Now many people felt frustrated and disappointed because Pa Wahyudi had ended up being arrested by the KPK.

When Pak Wahyudi was put in prison, many others went there with him. Among them were several important government civil servants, because they had long been receiving bribes from him, so that they would use government authorizations in ways to benefit Pa Wahyudi as a businessman. There were judges, policemen, lawyers, and there were even village heads who were caught up in business deals, because it was through them, it was said, that permits were issued allowing village land to be used for fertilizer factories, as well as for pasturing cows, although that land was rice-field land.

When Pa Wahyudi was brought before the corruption court, the common people demonstrated.

"Free Wahyudi. Don't slander the people's champion."

In another corner there was also a crowd of young people waving bits of paper.

"Get rid of corruption."

There was no shortage of people who yelled and shouted abuse at the KPK. They said the KPK was arrogant, they said the KPK was biased. The KPK were the sycophants of people in power. But there were other groups who were shouting, "Long live the KPK."

Jang Udi was also at the court. But he only went as far as the front courtyard. He didn't participate in the demonstrations. But although he didn't take part in the demonstrations, he earned some money taking there people who did.

"The money's not bad, I get 10,000 rupiah a trip," said Jang Udi laughing.

Nina Rahayu Nadéa

The Election Promise

Edi was marking the pupils' exercise books when Mang
Epul, the school porter, gave him the invitation.
"It's an invitation, sir. Compulsory attendance, so they say."

"Who's it from, Mang?"

"I don't know. The person who delivered it rushed off on his
motorbike. There was no time to ask him."

"OK, thanks, Mang."

He slit open the envelope and read the contents carefully. It
was a letter for *honorer* teachers, who only had honorary status in
schools and did not receive salaries that were in any way adequate,
but who worked because they hoped one day to be appointed as
proper fully-paid teachers, members of the civil service. The point
of the letter was that all honorary teachers were expected to attend
this meeting.

For a moment Edi was silent. He regarded the prospect of
taking part in the meeting with a heavy heart. He could guess from
the letter what would take place. But he had been an honorary
teacher now for almost twenty-five years. A feeling of depression
came over him. Especially when he thought of all his colleagues
who had become civil servants ahead of him. And him? He had
had no luck. But in terms of trying he had done all sorts of things.
For example, recently going to that famous *dukun*, known for his
magical powers, to ask him to arrange it so that he would be made
a civil servant. But what he had found was a fat *dukun* who had

asked him a few questions and then pocketed his money. And his status had not changed; he continued to be an honorary teacher. One thing he had not tried was paying out some money. But where could he possibly get the amount of money for the agent who said he could arrange things? According to rumors, you needed about ten million rupiah.

As for that, never mind having ten million, he had never in his life even seen that amount. He had once been invited to go along to meet someone who could help him achieve his goal, but if it was only to meet someone and there was no firm guarantee, what was the use?

So he thought he might go along to the meeting and see what he could. Who knows, he might have some luck. That's what he said to himself. And he was encouraged when he asked the headmaster whether he might go, since the headmaster had been eager to give him permission. So in the end Edi and some colleagues who were in the same position as himself, that is, all honorary teachers, went off to the place arranged for the meeting.

There were a lot of people in the room. The immediate agenda was to hold a discussion about the new leadership candidates in the upcoming election. The campaigners of a certain candidate had come to that forum so that they could see about having their candidate elected. They could guarantee, they said, that their candidate, if elected, could be trusted. There would be no cause for anxiety in the future in terms of raising the standards of education. That is what they said.

"Make sure that you vote for candidate number two."

"Hold on. The other day the special allowance from the local government for honorary teachers only amounted to twenty-five thousand rupiah a month, and even that is only paid out once every several months," interrupted a voice from the back.

"That's not going to be the case from now on. In this 'Reformation' era, we have something to make you happy. The government policy is that the allocation for education should be set at twenty percent of the total government budget. The salaries of civil servants will be raised. And for honorary teachers, make no mistake about it, there will be an equality of welfare provision, by means of 'in-phasing.' So those who are not civil servants will have no problems, thanks to the 'in-phasing.' The salaries of honorary teachers will be the same as the salaries of those who are civil servants. Just look at what has been planned for the future. If our candidate is elected again, all honorary teachers will receive civil servant appointments. And allowances will be raised too. And even the functional allowance relating to the specific job you do, which was previously set at two hundred thousand a month, will be increased if we are elected. This is what our candidate, who is concerned about what happens to people, will do for you. There are no other candidates who think about these issues at all. So remember: number two."

"Number two," all the honorary teachers then shouted out.

"Don't forget, all of you, that the day before the local election you should all meet here early at ten o'clock. There will be something we need to discuss."

And after that, the meeting—which had been attended by almost a thousand teachers—broke up. And they all remembered to take back home the little packets of food which were handed out to them.

"Good news. Number two has won."

"Thank God. Our votes counted after all," said Edi, joining in the celebration.

"And what did they say about the future?"

"Now all we have to do is pray that we all become appointed civil servants."

"Particularly me. I'm already rather old. I'm forty," said one of the female teachers.

"Don't worry about it. The older teachers will be the first in the line for the appointments."

"Thank the Lord."

All the people who had been at that meeting were pleased and happy that their candidate for the local leadership had won the election.

As they went home they were in a buoyant mood. Their hopes for the future were in each of their thoughts. Their long journey to this point no longer presented any hurdles or difficulties.

All this time, the work they had had to do was no different from that of the civil servant teachers. But what had not been the same was their welfare. In this matter there was an enormous and conspicuous difference that separated the status of honorary teachers from civil servant ones. With the election of the new local head, they hoped that he would be more attentive to educational standards and values and would properly value the honorary teachers and, who knows, might be prepared to give them the same status as civil servants in the matter of money.

In the teachers' common room there was a prominent announcement.

"To All Honorary Teachers. You are advised to open a personal bank account in your own names as soon as possible."

"What's this about?" Edi wondered, reading the announcement.

"It's for the functional allowance, which is going to be made available soon, this month or next. Now the money will be paid directly into the personal bank account of each of us, not as in the past when it went into the school's bank account," Wawan explained.

"That's excellent, if it goes into our personal accounts. If it goes through the school's bank account it's not clear what happens to the money. Last year a lot of it was sliced off, almost a half. We had to accept it. It wasn't any good not accepting it, they said, because the money had been automatically sliced. So there was nothing to be surprised about when the money we received turned out to be less than the money we had to sign for. Word was that the money sliced was to be given to those who hadn't received any functional allowance and to those who worked in the school office administration. Someone else said that the money was for the local education department. That would be fine: in fair weather or foul, we would all be in it together. But it wasn't acceptable when it turned out that those who were supposed to receive their share from the amount cut from the incomes of others had received only a paltry sum, enough to buy a bowl of noodles and that was all. Just so that someone could say that some money had been given out of the functional allowance, whereas most of that money went lord knows where. Just as well, perhaps, for some, that no one knows where it went. A lot of doubtful people seem to have been involved. And we still don't know who they are. Now, hopefully, if the money is put directly into our personal accounts the amount won't be cut."

"Hopefully."

"But what about people who don't have enough money to open a bank account?"

"That's true. I'm in that position. Yesterday I had to pay my electricity bill; one hundred and fifty thousand gone just like that."

"So what can we do?"

"Everyone was suddenly silent, pondering.

"Let's borrow money from the school cooperative. They're sure to lend it to us. It's not money just to have a good time, but to open a bank account. Later when the functional allowance has come through we'll pay it all back."

On the spot they all went off to the treasurer of the school cooperative.

"How much does each person want to take out?"

"Two hundred thousand, just enough to open a bank account."

"It won't be for long, just until the functional allowance money comes through, then we'll pay it back immediately," someone said.

"All right. Here, count out the money."

"But why is it four thousand short."

"That's the commission for the cooperative. If you don't pay the money back within two months you have to pay the cooperative four thousand each month for its services."

"All right then. It's not going to matter. We'll be reaping our harvest soon."

They didn't dawdle, but went off to the bank straightaway to open a savings account.

"Have the functional allowances come through yet?"

"Never mind the functional allowances. Even that money used to open the bank account is less than it was because of bank charges."

"Really? But it's almost three months now."

"I know. I get a headache thinking about it. Not only are there bank charges but there's also the money that has to be paid to the cooperative for the loan. Headaches."

"Announcement, announcement. Everyone needs to have their deposit accounts ready, the functional allowances will be available in a week's time."

"Is that true? Who said so, Wan?"

"Someone said that they'd heard there was some news. But I don't know if it's true or not."

"Idiot. We're being serious."

"Wan, why don't you go to the bank and ask? You're usually the one who's keen on asking."

"The bank people are fed up with me. Even the doormen now are offhand in the way they treat me because I go there so often. It's your turn now."

In the end Edi gave in and went to the bank to ask whether the money had come. But the answer was the same: not yet.

Everyone was quiet when the headmaster explained that the number of people who were due to receive functional allowances had been reduced from what it had been the previous year. The number of people who had received them last year had been fourteen, but this year it was only going to be seven. This was not what the school wanted; but the names of the people to receive the allowance had already been drawn up by those in authority. The school knew nothing about it. But they had been told that the criteria for selection were the number of children in the family and the number of hours a person taught.

"That's rotten. How could we not be eligible; doesn't the number of people who get the allowance increase from year to year? And now it seems that the office administrators who usually don't get it are going to get it. It looks very much as though people here in the school are fiddling it somehow."

"Yes, I'm in a mess too. There's the money I had intended to pay back my in-laws for a loan; now I can't do anything and have just got to bite my knuckles. Just my luck. I've got to pay a service charge each month to the cooperative for the loan. And the money which I had gone to such trouble to find to put into a deposit account is being whittled away with bank charges. It always seems to happen to me."

They all marched off to see the headmaster in his office. But the explanation was still the same. The school had no authority to question or decide or select the teachers who would receive a share of the functional allowance allocation. The names of all the honorary teachers in the school had been registered by the headmaster and had been sent on to the Education Department. But this had been the outcome. The numbers had now been reduced, and it was not just this school which had been affected but all schools that received functional allowances. Only half the number of teachers of the previous year were going to receive the allowance. It was all in the hands of the new administrative head. Their school was one of the lucky ones, said the headmaster, because some other schools received no allocation at all.

And the matter of the school administrative staff receiving allowances? For some time there had been plans afoot to help them out, said the headmaster, especially those who received nothing at all from the Education Department. He felt that at least once a year they should feel they were getting something for the work they put in. But where could the school find money from its own coffers to do this? But if this was thought unfair and caused problems, then in the future he would not propose it.

In the end, the headmaster made a decision which made those who were going to receive nothing happy, although it was at the cost of those who were slated to receive an allowance. All the money allocated for functional allowance would be totaled and then distributed evenly to all the honorary teachers. In this way he said, they would all be in the same boat, sharing together their mixed fortunes.

In the staff common-room there was an announcement.

> *To all honorary teachers. You are required to collect together all your documents relating to your teaching contracts, right from the start of your service to the present as well as your pay slips so that registration for in-phasing can proceed.*

"What's all this data for?"

"Here's something now that will bring a smile to the faces of the honorary teachers. All of them are now going to receive salaries which are at the same level as those received by civil service teachers. That's what in-phasing means. We will be on the same grades as civil servants. Those who are graduates will be on Grade 3A. Even those who are not graduates will be graded, provided that they meet the conditions. Look here are the regulations," said Edi handing out a book.

"At last something good. Let's hope this time it's true. Never mind about the business of the functional allowance. Now we've got in-phasing."

"Come on then. Let's get all our documentation ready."

"Apparently it's all done."

"How do you mean all done?"

"The people in the office have made photocopies for us all and put everything in personal files. I think we each need to give them twenty-five thousand. Do you agree?"

"Ask the others if they agree."

Edi, who was the oldest honorary teacher, collected the money from all his colleagues to pay the cost of the photocopying. In fact the office staff had not asked for anything. Only it was the custom if any business like this occurred, then people were sure to give the staff a little something. Everything was reckoned up and there were no problems.

A week later when the honorary teachers asked about the matter, they were told it was being processed; two weeks later when they asked they were told that the information had been passed on to the Departmental treasurer; and a month later it had been forwarded to Jakarta. And then after a year there was no news; right up to the present no one knew anything about it. In the beginning everyone kept hoping and asking each other about it. They grew tired of looking out for news. Every time colleagues came back from visiting the Departmental Office questions would unfailingly be put to them. But it was always the same; just rumors. No one knew anything.

Another time there was an announcement in the newspapers that the allowance given by the local regional Department was going to be raised from twenty-five to a hundred thousand a month, but the sum would not be given on a monthly basis but would be totaled and given in a lump sum. It was nine months since then and the sum would be nine hundred thousand. Everyone was making calculations, imagining what they would buy, dreaming of this and that. After all, they would be getting a sum of nine hundred thousand. They asked the department that was meant to be processing the money what the situation was. Other towns such as Cimahi had already received their allocations by that time. So the teachers were on tenterhooks; how was it that other towns had their money but theirs not? So they straightaway asked the Department about it. The official reply was: "The budget allocation has been made, but we have been given no proper authority to distribute it, because there is no available legal procedure under which we can distribute regional functional allowances to honorary teachers." That is what they said.

Those concerned were taken aback: why did the regulations differ from town to town? Local allowances had been given out in some places but not in others. Perhaps it was something to do with what they called "Regional Autonomy."

Edi was very pleased one day when he heard from the headmaster that he and some colleagues had been deemed eligible to come under the new regulations for the certification of teachers, which if it went through would mean a considerable rise in income. His data had already been sent to the local Department. So he was very happy about this and felt that he now had something new to hope for. And he was further encouraged by the headmaster.

"God willing, you will be summoned for the certification process since you have been an honorary teacher for so long."

"I see, but if I may ask, doesn't it matter that I am not yet a member of the official Teachers' Foundation?"

"Never mind about that. God willing, I should be able to help out there. Just say a prayer that it works out."

"Yes, I will. Thank you, headmaster."

Three months later came the news that the information about who would be the participants to be called for the certification program was available at the Department Office. One just had to pick it up. Edi was very surprised. There was only one name in the list of those who had been selected, and it wasn't him. He felt sick. The person called up for the program was Nurdin, who had only been an honorary teacher at that school for two years. How had that happened? And Yeni's situation was even worse. Her application had not even been officially recorded. It appeared that her name had been replaced by Anwar, who taught under her but in the same subject. What awful luck for Yeni; even if she continued to wait for further news, it was certain now that she would not hear anything, because right from the start her name had not been put forward.

Edi and Yeni went immediately to the Department Office to enquire. The man in the Office said that "the data which we have received is exactly what has come from the school and about which I know nothing more." So the Department was processing the data in accordance with what they had got from the school. Edi had not been selected because he was not a graduate and the quotas were full. They said a lot more, but it was very unclear. Edi and Yeni were confused simply trying to follow it all. They were used to facing disappointments like this.

"It's strange that your name was not on the list that was put forward, Yeni, though Anwar's, who is under you, was."

"It looks as though my name has been replaced by his. If you look at his year of entry into service it's the same as mine. So my name wasn't recorded but his was."

"That seems to be it. All we can do is be patient, Yen."

"Yes, that's our country," said Yeni with a wry smile.

Edi's patience was really tried by the Almighty. For two months he had received no honorary payments from the school. The reason given was because the BOS, Special Operational Help, funds from the government had not been distributed. If he had had money, the headmaster would have bailed out the payment of honorary teachers from his own pocket, but it so happened that just the moment he was out of funds, so Edi and his colleagues had to tighten their belts and cut down on what they ate.

But daily needs can't simply be put off to some future time. The kitchen stove has to be lit. The more those daily needs grew, the more Edi was unable to find the wherewithal since he was only an honorary teacher. Market traders made no difference between those who were honorary teachers and those who were civil servants. They were like spies who knew when civil servants received a rise in salary. Like this month, as soon as it was announced that the salaries of civil servants would be raised, prices went up even before the money had been received.

For those who were civil servants, this wasn't perhaps a problem, because they had money, and there was no talk about the government only paying them in installments. But for their colleagues, the rise in the cost of things was like needles digging into them. For although they could accept that their salaries be paid in installments, there was no coming to a compromise with the price of things.

Edi let out a long sigh when he met the school treasurer and wanted to borrow some money, because he was immediately told there wasn't any. He was now sitting back in his chair in the common room thinking what steps he could take so that he could light the kitchen stove and cook some food. He remembered Wawan, who was now the Deputy School Secretary of an SMA, a senior secondary school. He would try to borrow some money from him and at the same time ask whether he could teach at that school next year. In this way he wouldn't be so dependent on the honorary salary which he received from the SMP, the junior school, which was now the cause of so much worry. His salary could be paid in installments. And perhaps by teaching at the SMA he would not have so many headaches to worry about, he thought. Then all of a sudden the person he had been thinking of came in, as though he knew that Edi had been wanting to see him. Edi opened his mouth to say something, but he saw that Wawan's brow was furrowed and he looked unwell. So Edi didn't say anything. For a time neither of them said anything. The heartbeats of both of them seemed to be running in unison as each of them tried to cope with their problems.

"What's up, Wawan?" Edi finally decided to ask first.

"Problems, problems."

"Problems?"

"Next year it looks as though I won't be teaching again at the SMA."

"What? What's happened?"

"No one is registering for the school. Only seventeen pupils. And there are a lot of civil servant teachers. I have just been called in to see the headmistress. She said that I should take leave next year, but if the numbers of pupils increased then God willing I would be called in again."

"Really? So much for..." Edi didn't finish his sentence.

"So much for what?"

"I was going to ask whether I could teach at your school. To make ends meet. You too must have felt it here, two months with no pay because the BOS money hasn't come through. So. Perhaps as Deputy School Secretary you are in a better position than others. You're more fortunate, aren't you?"

"The Deputy's honorary payment means nothing. If they don't have any use for you, they just chuck you out."

Just then Pak Andreas and Ibu Tina appeared with beaming faces.

"Well, what are you going to use the certification money for then, Tin?"

"If I am lucky and see the money, then I intend to buy a car. Yesterday I looked at some with my husband. An old second-hand one will do, provided it's usable. I'll teach myself to drive. Civil servant teachers have to keep up with the times, don't they? It's not like in the Old Order period when teachers weren't respected at all and a month's salary was used up in a week. There was even an Umar Bakri song about it, wasn't there? What about you, Andreas?"

"I'm going to buy some land back in my village. It'll be part of my pension plan. I'm intending to go back there again."

"That sounds a good idea. I hope it works out."

Edi and Wawan exchanged looks. It was the difference between heaven and earth. These others could look round for ways to enjoy life, whereas they had to swallow their tears and find a way to make ends meet.

Edi remembered how he had participated at that meeting where all the honorary teachers had been present. The allocation for education was going to be raised to twenty percent of the total government budget in order to provide for the welfare of teachers. But where was this welfare? He hadn't been the beneficiary of any of it. The promise had been just a promise and had not been kept. He felt angry seeing what had happened to him. However stupidly he might act in the future, one thing was certain: he would never again pay any attention to politics. The talk of politicians was only for their own benefit. He felt again the pain and hardship that he had had to suffer for twenty-five years. But those in authority, those in government, didn't understand the lot of people like himself.

"Vote for number two. Vote for number two."

"Damn the vote," he said to himself.

"Vote for number two. Vote for number two."

"Damn the vote," he said to himself with even more feeling.

Yus R. Ismail

The Rented House

All day I had been going around looking for a house to rent, but without finding anything. I mean not finding anything that suited what I wanted and could afford. Both in terms of the house and the cost. There were some which were spacious, just the thing, and would have been fine for our three children and my small handicraft business, but the cost was beyond what we could afford. There were others which I'd seen which were within our budget, but either the house was cramped or the well had been blocked off. I sighed to myself. I had been going around for a week.

I parked the motorbike, the installments of which I had not yet paid off, near the small mosque. It was just by the side of some rice fields. Clean-looking. Trees had been planted all around. The flowers made everything seem fresh; there was a cleanliness in the air. One felt relaxed looking at the view. There, too, there were some mango trees, the sweet-scented variety, laid out in a row with some orange trees as well. The bougainvillea were bordered with *bakung* flowers, which stood out in all their whiteness.

Behind the mosque, a little way distant, there was a house. Perhaps it belonged to whoever owned the mosque; perhaps it was unoccupied, since I had never seen the owner. Perhaps it was a holiday house, a villa, which was occupied once a month at that.

Every time I came to the mosque to pray, after I had performed the ablutions I used to look at the house. Whose house was it, and what was it like inside? In fact you could only just see the outline of it. There were bushes hiding it, and plants growing wild formed a screen the height of an adult. The trees, too, grew in abundance. There were *rambutan* trees, and avocado trees, *sawo, jackfruit, sirsak*, papaya, all planted at random, it seemed.

Inside the mosque, a group of old men were performing *zikir*, rhythmically and without pause, repeating the same religious formula. There was no time for talk as everyone got ready for the ritual prayer. Hands were raised to the side of the head in the first movement of the ritual, and then praying began. After the communal prayer, individuals said their own private prayers as they felt inclined, and then they sat back, stretched out their legs, and eased their limbs. I was a little taken aback when I turned my head to the right and the old man at my side there stretched out his hand in greeting.

"It's been a long time since you were last here," he said.

I smiled. "That's right," I replied. "I haven't worked as a laborer for some time now. At the moment I'm learning how to set up my own small business, so I don't go around as before. You still remember me, then, old man?" It was true; fourteen or fifteen years ago when I was still a boy I often used to stop off at that little mosque. At that time, when I was peddling packets of coffee, noodles, and spiced vegetables, I used to rest a while at the mosque. After prayers, I used to sit on the terrace outside counting my takings. There was always a breeze. And I had an unobstructed view of the rice fields, which stretched out far in front.

"Aren't you the person who looks after this mosque and the house behind over there?" I said, pointing out the house behind the mosque. And we began to talk of this and that. He said that the person who owned the expanse of rice fields there bordering the mosque and behind the house was one and the same. But the old man wasn't entirely clear explaining who the owner was or where he came from or when he had come there and other details. As for me, I simply rattled off my stories of going around looking for a house to rent. The house we were living in at the time had to be vacated in a week's time.

"Well, if you need a house, have a look at this one then. I don't know how many times the owner has said to me, find someone to occupy the house; it'll just be cold and deserted if it's left empty," the old man said.

Of course I was happy to go and have a look. What wonderful luck, I thought. But when I went into the house behind the mosque, I took a deep breath and gasped. A house like that was beyond our means. The house was roomy. It was a tall building, its frame apparently was of light steel. Its floor was made of wooden teak tiles, shining, clean, properly cared for. The sofa was soft; its color matched the brown of the teak. There was a display cabinet, an aquarium, anthurium flowers with elephant ear leaves. The person who owned the house clearly had good taste. There were four rooms, all very spacious. There were two toilets, clean both of them. At the back, what appeared to be trees planted at random turned out to be a beautiful garden, well-arranged and carefully looked after.

I could only smile to myself. The old man had perhaps not known that my funds would not stretch to renting a house like this. But never mind, I said anyway, "How much does he want for a year's rent, Ki?"

"If you want to take it, please do so; there's no need to worry about the cost. That's what the owner said. Here's the key. Please go ahead and move in. I've got something else I have to attend to."

Strange. Life is strange. For a moment I was taken aback. I

couldn't think of anything to say, though all sorts of things were churning in my head. Even when the old man said goodbye and put out his hand to shake hands, I could only reply with a silent nod. Yes, life had always been strange; it wasn't only now. It wasn't just this business with the rented house.

I quickly rushed home. That very day I asked my wife and the children to come and see the house, and straightaway they wanted to spend the night there. The children jumped about here and there. The youngest, who had just learned to walk, kept falling over noisily trying to follow his elder siblings. The children, too, were perhaps beginning to feel that this was their ideal home. My wife and the children didn't go out again from the house the following day. I took care of the bringing of all our things and arranged the formalities to do with the children moving schools.

We were settled. No more complaints. The business, too, was now on a sound footing and could expand. It felt as though we were finding our feet at last. At first we used to make handicraft items and sell them in the Sunday market. Then we were able to place things in one or two stalls, and we obtained contracts in one or two schools for teaching practical skills. And finally we won a tender from the Local Education Department (LED) to supply all schools in the residency. We had to register our company and obtain all the relevant documents. And that was the beginning of it all and how we were swindled by Pa Sutar, the head of the history division in the LED.

My company, before all the relevant documents were complete, was "borrowed" by others so that it could be registered with the history division of the LED. But then things got stuck, because the documentation was not complete. It couldn't go forward and it couldn't go back. If the company pulled out, then the project would be cancelled, and of course that would be a great embarrassment for Pa Sutar as divisional head. And that was why one of the members of his staff, Rudi, along with Pa Sutar himself, went on and on about needing to be helped. They telephoned, they sent sms messages, and they even came round to the house.

"Please, please help. Please would you get the documentation finished. And as far as sorting out the profits, you can speak to the head of division himself," said Rudi, who it appeared had just been appointed to his civil service job but was already an expert in scooping out money from projects. I don't know where he was from, because he spoke Indonesian and not Sundanese to me, and he worked in the residency office in Bandung. I gave in. There was no need to discuss the sharing of the profits first; I just went ahead and sorted out the documentation, going here, there, and everywhere. And this required some capital; that it seemed was the way to do it. There was nobody who didn't want a little something, a little help they said, when doing this or that.

By the time I completed the documentation I was almost sleep-walking. Because everything had to be done quickly, "gifts" had to be given to this person and that. An experience which I had never gone through before. But because everything had to be signed and sealed quickly, I had to do it. And then, after all the documentation was complete, all the project administration conditions met, and the money was at last in hand, suddenly it was another story. After the money had been received, it was as though Pa Sutar didn't want to meet me again. He only sent three hundred thousand; to pay for expenses, he said, and even that was cut by fifty thousand by Rudi for Jabar bank charges.

At first I was angry, disappointed. I felt I'd been badly treated, and so I forced Pa Sutar to see me. In the end, this head of division, a *haji* to note, was willing to repay the expenses of the cost of the documentation and the cost of the "gifts." "But really the documentation was not my concern; but never mind, I'll repay the cost," he said, as though he were doing me a favor. He didn't acknowledge that the borrowing of the company, the borrowing of the name, the borrowing of the bank account, should all have been paid for. What's more, he had forgotten that the completion of the documentation had been done to help him get on with a job which had stalled, which he had said would be would cause him a lot of embarrassment if it was cancelled.

Thinking about that experience was also strange. Pa Sutar must have felt that he had come out of it well. In fact he was only deceiving himself, corrupting his own conscience. It is the case, I think, that possessions can corrupt one's conscience, when one is greedy, when one has trampled on the feelings of others. And as for me, it's true that in the beginning the experience made me feel disappointed, but then it became a spur for the business. The documentation which had been obtained through "gift-giving" was put in a cupboard, safely stored away, and became a sort of talisman reminding me that good fortune didn't come to one whenever one wanted it; it wasn't at all like looking for it, which one could do at any time.

My ambitions for my business grew even stronger after the shabby way I had been treated by Pa Sutar. I rushed here and there, I was never tired. The small stalls where I placed samples of our items grew in number, some of them even went to wholesalers. There was more work than could be handled by myself and my wife and so we brought in people we knew, and in fact we even sub-contracted work to the houses of such people. The work of buying the raw materials, taking them to people's houses, taking the items to the stalls, that was all done by someone else. In the end, my job was only to do the accounts, make the payments, and increase our sales.

After that our good fortune was like water in a ditch: it seemed to flow as though there would be no end. The strange thing was that after we had bought a car and one or two expensive things for the house, sent the children to schools where the fees were very high, managed to go on a little outing every school holiday, put money away in various accounts and bought gold, we didn't think of buying a house or building a house for ourselves. It was as though we were unwilling to move from the free rented house.

In fact I had kept trying to contact the owner for the first few months after we had moved in. I tried for a couple of years. But because nothing came of my attempts, we then happily accepted the situation. In the back garden of the house we built a fish-pond, since there was a stream there which welled up from below a *pisitan* tree. In the middle of the pond we erected a *saung*, a small covered platform on stilts, from which we could look out over the rice fields as far as the eye could see. Or we could sit and chat there with friends. The children often invited their friends there to study together or to roast cobs of sweet corn. And when we were all gathered together there sitting in the *saung*, it was as though we never wanted to go back.

I was at my most content when I was simply tending to the plants around the pond. But when it came down to it, it was Mang Maman, the gardener, who arranged the garden. He was a manager of an ornamental flower business in Cihanjuang. Not only were there flowers around the pond, but in the front, too, there was an ornamental garden which was lovely. "It's because the soil is so rich and open and spacious; it makes it easy to arrange things," said Mang Maman.

Almost every day my business partners, friends, acquaintances, and their children and wives, came there and seemed not to want to go home. "Wonderful. Once we've arrived here we forget about going home," was what they tended to say.

And so it was that every day I was there looking at the view, either in the front garden or in the *saung* in the pond, and I was never bored. I never noticed time passing. Days went by in the wink of an eye. The months followed one another in quick succession, the annual calendars too. The children who had played hide-and-seek were suddenly adolescents, and then they'd finished university. The time for their weddings came and there was no thought of looking out for a big hall that we could hire. The house with the gardens was space enough. And after the ceremony was over, guests used to talk about it in their little chats, when they met at *arisan*, and on the internet. They were full of praise, clucking with approval over this or that aspect of things. And there were even one or two people who came to visit after the occasion. They liked it so much they said, the house was so beautiful. I felt very content.

And therefore I was surprised when one day, when I was strolling in the Carrefour, I was stopped by someone.

"Excuse me," he said politely after offering me his hand, "Aren't you the man who lives in number three Surga Street?'

"Yes, that's right."

"How is the owner of the house?"

It was though a sudden gust of wind had hit me.

I don't know how it began, but people who said they knew the owner of the house where I was living kept cropping up here and there. When I was taking my grandchildren to the shops to buy toy guns, when I was meeting my business partners, visiting a friend who was ill, just walking to get some exercise, there they were, stopping me, saying they knew the owner of the house and asking how he was.

From that time on I became unwell thinking about it all. My thoughts kept turning in my mind. I felt sad, but I didn't know why. Sometimes, when I was by myself, I cried, and ended up sobbing. And the situation grew worse when one afternoon there was a knock at the front door. The visitor said that he was the owner of the house.

There wasn't much talk, nothing he asked for. He just said, "I'm pleased that you like the house." And then he said he would have to go. I can't describe how painful it all was, and I don't know why there was such pain. When I went to my wife overcome by the emotion of it all, she simply stroked my cheek.

"However things are, our home is not here, this is only a rented home, however nice it is," she said, and there was a choke in her voice.

"You're right, I know. And we have always been aware that a person's home cannot be bought with money, and it can't be built with possessions, however much one has."

My heart was bursting.

Absurditas Malka

The Whirlwind

I had seen the boy who was chasing the wind do seven circuits around our house. Almost every day he just leapt and jumped about, never tired of shooting off, rushing around, hunting the wind whose breezes never took shape, whose gusts never took form.

Whoosh!

He went off like an arrow, running hard to chase the wind which went off on its own way, goodness knows where.

"Sadun. It's already mid-morning. Come and have something to eat first!" Ma Inoh called her grandson, who was now beginning to look unsteady on his feet. The boy was Sadun, Ma Inoh's grandson, Nyi Irah's son.

Sadun looked pale and his face was running with perspiration. It was hardly surprising; he hadn't stopped leaping about, rushing hither and thither in every direction; wherever there was a breeze, there he ran.

"Kang, what's the matter with that boy, he looks as though he's not all there?" asked Marini, my young sister, who had just arrived back in the village three days ago.

"No, there's nothing wrong with him. Sadun is a good lad. He's just become like that since the whirlwind of three months ago."

"What happened?"

I didn't reply immediately but looked closely at Sadun, who was now staggering towards the bamboo-floored veranda of his grandmother's house.

"Kang…." She dug her elbow into my chest while I stood silent looking at the boy panting heavily on Ma Inoh's veranda.

"Whoa, no need for the elbow."

"Well, quickly then. What is the matter with the boy? Why is he like that?" She was itching with curiosity.

"Sadun wasn't like that before. It's only since the hurricane destroyed his house three months ago that he has become like this."

"A whirlwind destroyed his house? How did it happen?" she asked.

"I don't know how it seemed to arise from nowhere; it was an extraordinarily strong wind coming from the west. Trees were uprooted, water buffalos lifted off their feet, sheep sent flying. And besides that, the wind tossed up Sadun's house and all its contents. Everything was torn up and flew off."

I could still picture it flashing before me, how it happened, when the whirlwind that had come out of nowhere carried off Nyi Irah's house. It was only her house that was torn up by the wind; all the other houses were saved, including ours which was just in front, not far from her house.

"Was the house empty at the time?"

I glanced again at young Sadun, who was gulping down a drink. From afar I could see him stretching out for the kettle and pouring water into a glass till it was full. He drank, gulping it down until it was all finished. Then he poured some more water, and drank again.

My thoughts went to Sadun's late mother, Nyi Irah, who had been caught up by the whirlwind.

"Kang, you shouldn't stop when you're telling a story. Come on, continue."

"Don't say that. It's not a story... It really happened. It pains me when I think of it. It pains me deeply."

"Well, how did it happen?" She kept badgering me.

"At the time, Sadun's mother was in the house. There was nothing I could do. I couldn't help her. I was just able to lie flat in a ditch holding tight to the roots of a tree. I only heard the noise of the scream, mingled with the screeching of the whirlwind..." I didn't go on with the story. I felt a pang of grief as I was speaking and thinking of it all.

"Oh lord.... How awful for Sadun, that that should happen."

Her voice was sad, full of sympathy.

"Nyi Irah...just disappeared, carried off into the sky. And from that moment, Sadun has been without his mother. There has been no news, no trace, not a single person has seen his mother since."

It was as though a blade had twisted even deeper into my chest. I was churning with emotion.

Tik. A cold tear fell from the corner of her eye, and she held fast to my wrist. Who would not have been affected hearing of an incident like that? Never mind my sister, a woman, not remaining unaffected—I myself, a so-called man, felt the wrench in my heart if I remembered the whirlwind of three months ago.

"Now, I understand. What the boy must be going through!" she said with a long sigh.

I nodded, taking a deep breath. It made no difference, the pain did not go away. The wind which blew and carried off everything with it was still clear in my memory. I saw it still, Nyi Irah carried off into the clouds and me not being able to do anything, only stare hollow-eyed, my buttocks clenched tight. I was trembling as though I was lying next to death there close by me.

"Then the whirlwind just vanished without a trace. It was as though someone had come deliberately just to look for Nyi Irah to invite her to take a trip into the clouds. Of all the things that were sent flying by the wind, nothing fell to the earth again. They vanished together with vanishing of the wind. Without a trace."

"Unbelievable. Was it really like that?"

"That's exactly what happened. I wouldn't have believed myself if I hadn't seen it with my own eyes. And it wasn't only me that saw it, many others saw it too."

"Isn't it possible that Nyi Irah could have fallen back to earth somewhere far away?"

"That should have happened, but no trace has ever been found. Almost every day, for the space of a month after that, the other villagers and myself looked for Nyi Irah, but we didn't find a thing. Nothing."

"How strange, how strange that there should be a whirlwind like that. You don't think it could have been a supernatural wind?"

"I don't know. I don't understand it."

She was suddenly silent. She and I looked at young Sadun a short distance away. Both of us tried to stifle our emotion with a long deep sigh.

"Mother… Mother… I want to come too."

Sadun shouted out loud holding his hands out in supplication to the sky.

*

The sun was declining, and it would not be long before it set behind the tips of bamboo clumps at the west end of the village. Sadun was not following its progress, not caring what time it was. If he wasn't called in by Ma Inoh he would surely continue leaping about, chasing the wind till he had exhausted himself running along the path; this was just the time of day when he would rush off.

"Mother… Mother… I want to come too."

It seemed that these were the only words that came from Sadun's lips. And they were uttered with a tremble of his voice which, when

I heard it, went right through me. A voice sharper than a knife plunged in my heart; a shuddering, piercing sadness.

"Kang, Kang. Run, Kang. A whirlwind!"

I felt myself being shaken by my sister, as from the west, without anyone noticing it, a whirlwind was now blowing hard, twisting in a spiral, catching up everything in its way, a wind that had come from nowhere.

"Sadun, lad, a whirlwind! Run here," I said. I yelled as I tried as quickly as I could to reach him, since I thought he was going to be carried off by the pull of the wind.

Crack.

I held fast to a clump of long grass. The wind, twisting, was beginning to tug at me. In the blink of an eye, in the cloud above I saw a boy tumbling there, twisting, taken by the wind.

"Mother... Mother...."

Then in a sudden flash I saw Sadun walking, striding along going towards a woman who was floating in the clouds. They were not being tugged by the wind, they weren't being tossed about, they seemed to be quite unaffected by the turbulence. Although it was only a flash, although the dirt and the dust hid my view, I saw her clearly; it was Sadun's mother, Nyi Irah.

I couldn't look for long, the dust and sand were making my eyes smart with pain. I was able to shut them, one hand protecting the eyes, the other holding tight to the tall grass.

"Goodbye, Sadun, we'll miss you. Fare well."

I took a deep breath, happy to let Sadun go off to meet his mother in the clouds. Then suddenly the wind disappeared without trace. I blinked; all the darkness had vanished. The wind had vanished. Sadun had vanished. Nyi Irah had vanished.

Miss Maya

When I got to the river it was late. The sun, as round and as big as the lid of a rice basket, was beginning to set. When it touched the horizon, the sun seemed to sink into it. As it slowly went down it was clearly visible. The color which had been breaking up a moment before was now deep red in the sky. The leaves stirred by the evening breeze seemed to flash, reflecting the rays of this dying sun. The sight of the water running through the river was so pretty. The deep red seemed to catch on it, and played on the surface for a great distance.

I looked on, my eyes wide open in wonder. When I had stretched out by the bank of the river just now, everything had been so peaceful. I had wiped away some of the perspiration that was drenching me. And now what I had come to was so much more than just peacefulness. I felt a sense of joy just looking round. If a request to God were permitted, I would wish this picture of nature, the sun setting here, be kept forever like this. The wellbeing arising from watching this beautiful sight would not then be only a momentary thing.

"There, everything looks beautiful. It's not like here, where there is litter and dirty sewage water and piles of rubbish all over the place." I could still hear the anger in her voice, Miss Maya's voice. That had been last week when we had met on the bank of the Citarum river. These weren't quite the exact words, but this was what she meant when we met face to face. She had been my friend on Facebook. We had spent all our time chatting. We had talked about everything.

"Come and spend some time in my village, Maya's home," she said referring to herself. "And if you like it, you can stay there forever." That's what she said. I don't know how the conversation had arisen, but then, all of a sudden, out came those sentences. That was how I had come to make my promise when we had met face to face on the banks of the Citarum. Then she told me where she lived and gave me a map she had drawn.

"When you have reached the Ciwening river you should cross on the raft. But you should get there after dusk so that it's easier. Just ask the ferryman and say that you want to go to Maya's village."

That was what she had said. Why hadn't I straightaway asked her why I had to arrive after dusk? I was so full of conflicting emotions. Miss Maya who was sometimes so fierce, sometimes so pouty, sometimes flirtatious, sometimes egoistic, sometimes atheistic— that's what I felt when we were chatting—now when I had actually met her my heart burst with love for her. I had originally intended to ask this and that and raise this and that objection; but I wasn't able to. I only smiled and nodded. And that was Miss Maya. I had never met someone so attractive. Her smile, the twinkle in her eye, the way she looked, her hair, her face, her voice, it seemed impossible to describe them. I didn't have enough words to say how beautiful Miss Maya was. In fact I only met her briefly. Just like now, my wonder at the setting sun. It left one with a feeling of great content but that quickly disappeared.

After the sun had sunk into the horizon, it quickly grew dark. I looked around for a flat stone on which I could say the *maghrib* prayer. I was not sure what to do, going along like this after dark. It would be better to pray first and get it over with. And wasn't that the raft for crossing the river tied up motionless there? The ferryman was nowhere in sight. What I noticed first was a small hut in a hollow. Some smoke was curling from the roof and it seemed someone was cooking there. God be thanked I could at least pray there. And perhaps I could offer something in exchange for a bite to eat, a small plate of rice or some cassava: there was sure to be something. My stomach was rumbling now.

To my surprise, it turned out to be the hut of someone making *surabi*, small pancakes, for sale. What a piece of luck. They had been a favorite food of mine ever since I was small. I loved them.

"Well this is very fortunate, Bibi, I'm hungry and I see you have some *surabi*. But actually I'd like to pray first."

"Whatever you like. You could have the *surabi* first. I have just made some *oncom*. Or you could pray first. At the back there is a washing place with a bamboo water spout that you can use for ablutions."

Because my stomach had only once that day had its rice quota, it seemed better to have the *surabi* first. What was it that Ustad Wahyu said? Instead of praying and thinking about food all the time, it was better to eat first and while eating think about praying. The *surabi* were delicious. I also helped myself to the fried peanuts. Without realizing it, I had gobbled up five *surabi* in a trice. They were washed down with strong hot tea, unsweetened and refreshing.

"And now that my stomach isn't growling anymore, I'd like to pray, Bibi."

"Go ahead, go to the back. The prayer mat is there; it's laid out on the floor."

After I'd said the prayer, I felt fully invigorated. My stomach had been filled, the perspiration had been washed away because I had taken a quick shower at the spout at the same time as I did the ritual ablutions. I wanted to take my leave straightaway before it became too late. But the lady who made the *surabi* was nowhere to be seen. The fire was no longer burning. The embers of the fire, however, were still glowing and hadn't been doused.

"Bibi, Bibi ...." I walked around the hut to see if perhaps she was at the washing place, then I looked inside the hut because the door was open. But the *surabi*-seller was not there. Should I wait? Where had she gone? She might be back very late. Not knowing quite what to do, I took out some money from my pocket. There was a fifty thousand note and a five thousand one. The five *surabi* and the peanuts would be at the most seven thousand. I put the five thousand note next to the *surabi*. I didn't worry about the fact that this was two thousand short. I would pay it on the way back from Maya's village.

The water of the Ciwening was extraordinarily bright and clear. The fish swimming around were of all sorts of colors; they seemed to be carp, darting here and there. The reflection of the moon bobbed about in the water, broken by the movement of the fish or the lapping of the raft.

"Is this the right way to Maya's village, Kang?" I said for the sake of breaking the silence. The ferryman smiled and then nodded.

"Do you know, Miss Maya?"

The ferryman smiled again and then nodded. I smiled too. Why each time he was asked something did he simply reply with a smile and a nod? My attention was still held by the fish who looked as though they were chasing each other around the raft. A thin mist seemed to dance gracefully around us, changing shape with the motion of the raft. In the distance I could just hear the sound of a *tarawangsa* and a *rebab*; the plangent notes stirred me. An experience like that was something to be felt, something to be contemplated, not something to talk about.

On the other side of the river, I jumped from the raft and the ferryman smiled and nodded and then poled away on the raft to the middle of the river. It moved off slowly cutting through the mist which had thinned now, broken by the moonlight. Now I was standing on a path which led to I didn't know where.

This wasn't an ordinary path through the forest or through an upland garden; it was like a well-tended path in a flower garden. The borders of the path had been planted with *bakung* flowers, conspicuous in their bright whiteness. I just followed the path wherever it led, since I couldn't see properly because the mist still hid things from view.

The path was not very long. It came out to a flower bed of *bakung* flowers and then went round the garden. In the middle of the garden were roses of different colors. The perfume of *melati* flowers hung in the air, and the flowers followed the line of the fence. The air was wonderfully fresh and the garden so beautiful. Clearly it had been carefully tended by someone who knew what they were doing. It couldn't have been imagined, couldn't have been pictured, a garden like this. I rested a moment before pressing on through a grove shaded by giant trees.

At the end of the garden a clump of bougainvillea curved down as though making an arch to the road in front. And there to my surprise stood a small picturesque-looking house in the dell. In front of it was a fish-pond, the surface glimmering in the moonlight. By the side of it were some sweet smelling mango trees loaded with fruit. There were *sarikaya* trees, too, planted in rows, and there were orange trees. And in the center of the pond were water lilies which took one's breath away. You could hear the sound of water pouring from water spouts. To the eastward side there was a small rest hut just above the fish-pond. A hanging lamp cast its swaying beams into all corners. There seemed to be a meeting going on.

"Hello, may I introduce myself?"

"Yes, please, of course."

The people sitting there all got up, men and women. There were about ten people. They all welcomed me. They were very friendly and shook my hand, and there were even one or two who bowed to me.

"Please excuse me if I interrupt you a moment. I am on my way to Miss Maya's village. Is it still far from here?"

"This is Miss Maya's village. Please come in. You have been expected," said a man wearing an *iket* around his head.

I was surprised. What? I had been expected?

"Allow us to introduce ourselves. All these people here are Miss Maya's older relations. I'm her uncle. And that man there who is wearing a *kopeah*, that small white hat, and that woman who is wearing a white *kebaya*, those are her parents," the man with the *iket* began to explain. "And the man on the far right, that's her elder uncle and his wife. And all the others are Miss Maya's uncles and aunts."

I was shocked. I hadn't imagined it would be like this. I hadn't thought her parents would be waiting for me. And where was Miss Maya? This was all turning into something very serious.

"And here is Miss Maya," said the uncle wearing the *iket*.

Miss Maya came out of the small house led by the hand by a woman. Her long *kebaya* was also white; in her hair she wore a bridal chaplet of *melati*. A garland of flowers came down to her feet and she swayed slowly as she moved. I looked away, saying under my breath a "God help me" and a "My God" one after the other. In all the times I had looked at the photographs of show people and actresses, I had seen nothing like this. No film star from Indonesia nor Hollywood nor Bollywood had ever been able to cause me the amazement that I now felt. This beautiful girl now sat down between her parents right in front of me, her legs tucked modestly under her. She glanced at me a moment and her eyes twinkled; she smiled and then looked down again. My heart started beating nineteen to the dozen.

"My boy, Miss Maya speaks a lot about you, and is so excited every time she has finished talking to you. She used to tell us that there was someone she was in contact with on the internet who was constantly fun to talk to: sometimes he was good to her and praised her; sometimes he criticized her; sometimes he seemed very fond of her; sometimes he just seemed to be in a world of his own. Could it be then, my boy, that you have the gift of saying exactly the right romantic phrases to a woman?"

I kept my head bowed. I felt that perhaps there was some truth in this, because indeed I had once gone to learn about this sort of thing from the master, Dhipa of Galuh Purba.

"So we the elder relations of Miss Maya came to a decision. We wanted to invite this Arjuna to meet him in person. We want to ask whether you are seriously interested in Miss Maya or whether you are just amusing yourself. So, lad, you can see Miss Maya as she is. If we say she is pretty it's not that we want to boast, but I have never seen her equal."

I stole a look at Miss Maya, and going through my mind was what her uncle had just said. But I was in turmoil. I hadn't thought it would come to this. I had just been casually having fun.

"What do you say, my boy? Have you come here just for a bit of fun or are you really serious about Miss Maya?"

I nodded. "I will do whatever her family want of me," I blurted out. My lips seemed to speak without giving me time to discuss the matter first. Those present looked as though they were thinking deeply about what I had just said. Miss Maya smiled.

"If that is the case, then the family will not raise any objections. But there is something that needs to be made clear; a condition that has to be fulfilled."

"A condition?"

"Yes, that's right. Since in this place here everything is beautiful, everything is charming, everything is calm, everything is carefree, compared to what is found in the human world, the condition is, my boy, that you leave behind your human nature. You may never again cross back over the Ciwening river. You must never again desire it. Because if you do not leave your human nature behind, this will be a source of great danger. Think carefully, my boy, is there anything that you are likely to find yourself wanting? Your mother or your father, for instance?

"No, there is nothing. I am an orphan and a bachelor."

"If that's the case, all that remains is to go ahead and make a start. Parents of Miss Maya, are you prepared for this event?"

Then I suddenly thought of the *surabi*-seller. I still owed her two thousand rupiah.

"Can I just interrupt a minute? I don't have any desires which might pull me back, only there is one thing. Before I crossed over the river I ate some *surabi* and I still need to pay two thousand rupiah which I owe."

The relations looked at each other. Miss Maya looked down.

"Oh, you don't need to worry about that. It's only two thousand rupiah. Here we have millions, money is no problem."

"Because it's not a big issue, I just want to ask permission to go over for an hour. I would like to go over at this very minute."

I felt sorry. It was regrettable. But my feelings told me that this small matter had to be taken care of quickly.

"I want to excuse myself now, I'll only be away a short time."

I stood there. The relations looked at me closely. So did Miss Maya.

When I got to the flower garden I turned around. Why did Miss Maya look on the point of collapse? The roses didn't seem so fresh, the *melati* flowers looked sad, the bougainvillea were wilting, the *bakung* were hanging their heads.

"Akang, Akang, do you really want to leave us?" the people were saying, and some of them were pleading.

"I regret it, deeply. But this matter has to be settled. Just wait a short while."

Miss Maya looked at me. From the corner of her eyes I saw the tears flowing and wetting her cheeks.

I jumped out of the raft and went straight off to find the *surabi*-seller. But although I looked high and low, I couldn't even find the hut. I stood still for a moment. The stars were swimming in the sky. The moon was nowhere to be seen. Across the river, Maya's village seemed hidden, there was not the slightest trace of it. I heard indistinctly the *azan*'s call to prayer. There might be a problem here. It would be better for me to say my prayers first before I started asking around.

Quickly I went off to find a mosque. I wasn't in time to join those who had congregated there for the prayer. After I had said the final words of the ritual prayer, I added some private prayers. Some gray-haired men were waiting until I finished. The other members of the congregation had already gone off.

"Where have you just come from, lad?" someone asked rather anxiously.

"I have just come from Miss Maya's village."

The old man stared open-mouthed. I heard him slowly exclaim, "God be with us."

"I had intended to stay and make my home there. Only there was something I had to do. Before I crossed over the river, I had eaten some *surabi* and I was in debt to the *surabi*-seller for two thousand rupiah. So I came back across to find her again. But unfortunately she doesn't seem to be here."

"Not unfortunately, but thank God. The *surabi*-seller came to your aid. If you had settled in Miss Maya's village, you would have been in torment forever. Miss Maya's village seems modest and ordinary, but in fact it is full of pain and sorrow. If the people in Miss Maya's village see others in difficulty, they rejoice; if they see others encountering misfortune, they take pleasure; if they see others hungry, the people of Maya's village laugh out loud. Don't worry too much about the *surabi*-seller, since that was no ordinary *surabi*-seller. How could anyone possibly be selling *surabi* in such a remote place. Who would be the customers?"

I stood and stared. I was confused. But I just looked down at the floor. Suddenly I felt a spasm of sadness. I was saddened by own behavior; I had been tempted by something that would have been of no good to me at all.

"Come along now to my house now. You're very dirty."

I got to the house. It was small but tidy, and the man invited me to sit on the porch. On the table there was a large jug with a lid, full of tea. And there was a plate, also covered.

"Mother, some cups. We have a visitor."

Soon after that the door opened. What was this. I was again confused. I knew this person. No, I wasn't mistaken. This was the *surabi*-seller.

"What a surprise, a visitor. Poor boy, you're probably tired," she said, while she took the lids off the jug and the plate. "Now just try these. These are my *surabi*. And here is a jug full of tea, too."

And not long after that someone came out from the house carrying a tray. What? I was even more confused. Wasn't this person the image of Miss Maya? Only this person's head was covered and her eyes were cast down as though she were embarrassed.

"This is my youngest. She's on holiday at the moment; she's still a student at ITB."

Déni A. Fajar

Ramal, the Foreteller

Father was taking down the lamp hanging on the rafter when the door banged and was suddenly slammed open with some force. I hid behind Mother, who was folding up her *mukena*, her prayer cape, having just said her *ashar* prayers. In the frame of the open door stood Ramal, chest out. His eyes were burning bright, like the bright flash of lightning out in the yard. The rain was pouring down. The wind was blowing hard. The noise of its clatter was depressing. At one moment it seemed close, at another far away, as though it was deliberately making a tour of the village.

Hiding behind Mother's back, I stole a glance at Ramal, who was standing like a statue in the doorway. His hair was dirty and knotted, and his scalp was black from the rain. The rain was dripping from his shorts, falling on to the bamboo plaited floor, washing the mud down his legs.

Although he was shaking with cold, Ramal looked rather wild. He was panting like someone who has just climbed a steep hill. In his right hand he gripped a large stick. That was just like Ramal, he never came out without something. His hand had to be gripping a stick, a bamboo staff, or whatever could be used as a cudgel.

"Make up a packet of rice and something to go with it," Father said to Mother as he approached Ramal.

"I don't want anything to eat," Ramal said.

Father looked surprised, but he continued walking towards him. Mother, however, hesitated and didn't go straight to the hearth. As for me, I trembled even more looking at the man in the doorway, staring at him standing there, chest out, for all the world as though issuing a challenge for a fight.

"What do you want then? Cigarettes, to keep off the cold?'

No reply.

"If you're asking for money, you won't get it. There's none to give away here. Ridiculous, you behaving like a spoiled child wanting his own way. Lord knows how you would use the money," Father said again.

Ramal was like that. When he came, if it wasn't food he was after, he was pestering us for money. But he was only like that with Father. Others, as soon as he approached them, shooed him away.

"I don't want any money. I want to be called a *pahlawan*, a war hero," said Ramal, facing Father.

He didn't exactly shout his request, but nonetheless it took Father aback. He looked wide-eyed at Ramal for a moment. Then he and Mother exchanged glances. They were both open-mouthed. In fact Mother muttered a God-help-us to herself.

"I did my share of fighting for independence at the time. I was there fighting the enemy, the colonial army. I'm a hero, too, aren't I?"

Silence. There was only the sound of the rain outside was coming down heavier.

"It's right that I should be called a hero, too, isn't it?" Ramal said again.

"Yes, 'Mal, you're a hero," Father replied.

"Then I have the right to be buried in the heroes' cemetery. When I die I want to be buried in the heroes' cemetery. Can I be buried in the heroes' cemetery?"

"Of course, 'Mal. Heroes have the right to be buried in the heroes' cemetery," answered Father.

He sounded like a parent placating a child. He was pacifying Ramal so that he would go quickly.

Just as a peal of thunder shook the yard, Ramal moved from the door. Father saw him out. He looked at Ramal, following him with his eyes as he went down the steps and crossed the yard, walking swiftly towards the village. The rain showed no sign of letting up. The thunder claps were growing more frequent.

"Why did you listen to him?"

"What do you mean?" Father said looking at Mother.

"Ramal. Why did you agree with what he was saying, saying yes that he had the right to be buried in the heroes' cemetery?"

"Don't worry about it. I was just pacifying him so that he would go. You know what he's like; if I hadn't acted like that he would have made himself at home," Father said as he hung up the lamp and lighted it.

"That's all very well, but he asked to be buried in the heroes' cemetery, of all things. Usually if he comes, he's happy with a meal and a cigarette. But this—I'm afraid how it will end."

"Don't worry about it, Father said again. "There won't be any consequences. Tomorrow it will just be the same as ever: he'll walk around the village and the children will follow him laughing at him. Just forget what he said he wanted."

"What if he comes again tomorrow asking for your promise to be made good?"

Pressed like that, Father was silent for a moment. By the light of the hanging lamp I saw that he seemed to be thinking.

"What would be the problem if we agreed to it? Ramal does in fact have a right to be buried in the heroes' cemetery. He is, isn't he, a hero? He did fight during the struggle for independence."

"Agree to it! What do you mean? The heroes' cemetery is already full. There's just room for one more, in the corner there by the *berenuk* tree, and that has been reserved for the *lurah*, the village head."

Father was silent again.

"What's going to happen if Ramal insists on his right? The *lurah* is not going to give in, he's not simply going to smile and agree to his place being taken by someone else. Especially if the person claiming it is someone like Ramal. You can imagine what he would say. Everyone remembers what he said. 'That's my plot in the corner of the heroes' cemetery. It's not just for anyone'."

Father did not say anything. The noise of the thunder claps shook the sky with even more frequency. It was even blacker. The rain continued to pour down as if all the heavens were being emptied out. When Father had finished securing the windows, there could just be heard the call of the *azan* announcing the *maghrib* prayer, muffled as it was by the heavy sound of the rain.

The next day Ramal did not in fact come. In all likelihood he was as usual going round the village. But there was someone who did come to see Father. The *lurah*. He came in an official capacity, accompanied by the village secretary and the village security guard.

"I heard that loon Ramal visited you yesterday?" the *lurah* said.

"That's right. Yes, he came here and was polite about it," said Father.

The *lurah* looked at the village secretary. He looked unhappy with Father's reply.

"Apparently he made an unusual request to you, Akang."

It was surprising that the *lurah* addressed Father with the polite "Akang."

Father took his time replying. I saw him looking out of the corner of his eye at me. I felt that Father must have thought that I had told the *lurah*. I couldn't hold his gaze; he seemed so angry. I looked down at the floor. I didn't dare to look him in the face. With my head down I heard the *lurah* say, "Apparently the fellow wants to be called a hero and all."

"That's right. In fact he even wants to be buried in the heroes' cemetery," said Father.

"And, Akang, you said that was all right and you agreed that he had the right to be buried in the heroes' cemetery. It's almost as though you didn't know what sort of person Ramal is," the *lurah* said, raising his voice.

"You're right. Ramal is not quite all there. But we all know, don't we, that Ramal played his part in the struggle to get rid of the Dutch. We shouldn't forget Ramal's courage at the time. How many of the enemy ended up as corpses floating in the Cisalak river, when Ramal stood in front of the truck and stopped it when it was full of soldiers who had come to take our village? Only Ramal didn't have the good fortune to come out of it intact. When the Revolution was over, his mind suddenly went."

The *lurah* didn't reply. All of a sudden he looked thoughtful.

"And because Ramal played his part risking his life when he fought against the enemy, I think he has a right to be buried in the heroes' cemetery," said Father again, unwilling to back down.

"So you're happy, Akang, if Ramal is buried in the heroes' cemetery. Even though he's not got all his wits," replied the *lurah*.

"Yes, he's not got all his wits, but that doesn't change the fact that he has the right to be buried in the heroes' cemetery. If he insists that that he wants to be buried there, then we shouldn't say no."

Hearing this reply the *lurah* let out an exasperated sigh. Then the visitors turned on their heels and left Father, trying to hide their annoyance. Very different from the look and step of Bima when he was defeated in magic by the small spirit, the *lurah* went off in a huff followed by his staff, the secretary, and the guard.

A week after showing his anger, the *lurah* held a meeting in the village hall. It was no small meeting: everyone in the village was summoned. Even the small children had collected there. Those who usually went off very early to their small-holdings and their rice fields to do some weeding or get on with other jobs, left their houses this time to come as summoned.

And in fact all those who were invited to the meeting could not fit into the hall. There were people thronging about outside, a larger number than those actually inside the hall. While waiting for the meeting to begin, the older people were exchanging news and views. A number of them were nodding to each other in the shade of the banyan tree which hung over the yard of the village hall. The children of my age were overjoyed by it all. There were plenty of one's friends there. No one stopped us playing catch. And as we chased each other about we shouted happily. The village hall, which on an ordinary day was usually as quiet as the grave, was now all of a sudden humming with noise.

"It's just like the *lurah* to hold a meeting at an inappropriate time. He has no consideration for people's needs. He's no leader," said someone to the others round him.

"Yes. He just thinks of himself. It's only his feelings that are important. If he wants to call a meeting, he summons us to the village hall. If he says that we have to clean up the irrigation channels after a flood, then we have to get down to it and plunge into the mud," said someone else.

"It's not democratic, that sort of behavior."

"We should take a stand now and again. Not let ourselves be treated like doormats. Show that we're not *wayang* puppets who can be shoved here and there by the *dalang*, the puppet master. Anyone who is a 'Cepot,' a servant, wants occasionally to be a hero like Arjuna, and not be a clown all his life. Wasn't that Astrajingga's fate? It's all the work of the *dalang*."

"Yes, that's right, if you think about it. The *dalang* isn't fair," someone else remarked.

"If the *wayang* puppets didn't follow what the *dalang* wanted and revolted, the whole *wayang* world would collapse. The *dalang* would be out of work; there would be no one attending to him. And if that was the case, we'd be the ones to lose out, because there would be no more performances."

"Stop the talking about the *dalang*. Listen; the meeting is about to begin," said one of the old men who was sitting next to the doorway of the village hall.

"I don't hear anything."

"How do you expect to hear anything when it's drowned out by all the noise coming from your throats."

"Sh! Sh! Silence. Listen. Listen. You children stop playing around."

There was a sudden silence. There wasn't a sound outside in the yard or inside in the hall. The only thing that could be heard was the voice of the *lurah*.

"Pay attention, all. I became the authority in this village not because I wanted it. I became the *lurah* because all of you in the village asked me to stand and voted for me. But why is it that now after I hold the title, many of you seem envious, many seem to begrudge me the position? And as the days go by, many of you, while on the surface are happy with things, in your thoughts you are actually against me."

Silence.

"I frequently hear that there are those who would like to lead a protest against me and accuse me of being undemocratic. I frequently hear that I am a *lurah* who is greedy to get his hands on this and that source of funds."

Silence.

"I know many of you would like to force me to resign."

There was not a sound.

"And in fact recently there have been those who have expressed their disagreement with me being buried in the heroes' cemetery… uh, that is when I'm dead."

"If he wanted to be buried now, no one would object. In fact I'd be quite happy to carry the bier," said Igong whispering.

"Hey, quiet you. Don't just talk for the sake of it."

Igong didn't say anything more. The hall was silent again.

"It's for that reason that I have called you all here to this meeting. I want to show you that I am not an undemocratic leader who has no affection for the people."

The sound of murmuring began to be heard, the sound of people buzzing like bees. They were muttering to each other.

"As for the right to be buried in the heroes' cemetery, I have the right to be buried there, not because I hold the office of *lurah*. My right comes because I fought during the Revolution against the Dutch. So let no one begrudge it—including Ramal, who also has the right to be buried there. Many of you do not know that Ramal is a hero. You only know that Ramal as someone who has lost his wits. Nothing else. But in fact he took part, risking his life staring down the muzzle of the enemy's rifle…" said the *lurah*.

"But there's just room for one more in the heroes' cemetery," said Aki Ije.

"Couldn't you just fit them both into the one grave? After all that's the kind of fate heroes are used to, isn't it?" said Igong again.

"So listen all of you. I want to testify that if I die before Ramal, bury me in the heroes' cemetery. On the other hand if Ramal goes first, then the place is reserved for him, the man who's lost his wits." The *lurah*'s voice was clear as though he was answering Igong's question.

When they heard the *lurah* say this, a murmur broke out then among those who had come to the hall.

And then would you believe, a few days after the meeting in the village hall, Ramal fell ill. The man who every day used to wander round the village followed by a troop of children was now laid out in the guard post hut. He was shivering as though with cold, but the sweat poured from his body.

He just looked at the food that was offered to him. The body of the madman looked as though it was shriveling away. His eyes, which usually had a wild look about them, now looked lifeless with no spark in them. He simply groaned all the time. The children thronged quietly past the guard post where he lay.

As the days went by, Ramal's condition gave more cause for alarm. He was just skin and bones. When his body was feverish, he became delirious. Everyone in the village was nervous and tense, it was as if they were afraid that this man who had lost his wits would die on them.

"It seems as if that remaining plot of land in the heroes' cemetery is going to belong to Ramal then," Igong said.

"Watch your talk. It's bad luck to claim you know when someone's going to die. Who knows, tomorrow or the next day Ramal will be as right as rain again," said one of Igong's friends.

"The *lurah*'s going to be very angry if Ramal gets his wish to be buried in the heroes' cemetery."

"Yes. Especially since he had counted on that remaining plot being his."

"Me, I'm quite happy for it to be filled by Ramal rather than being for the *lurah*. The *lurah*'s no hero in my eyes anyway, the way he tries it on with fellows' wives. Didn't he try to get round my girlfriend," said Igong.

The business of Ramal being ill eventually came to the *lurah*'s ears. Every day the sick man's condition was reported to him. And the strange thing was that every time he heard that Ramal's condition was worse, it was as though the *lurah* himself had caught the illness. If the report was that Ramal showed no signs of getting better, he despaired.

"It seems that Ramal is past all help now, sir," said the guard.

"Have you sent him medicine?"

"The madman won't even take bread, let alone any medicine, sir."

"If that's the case, fetch the district doctor, take him to the guard hut. Perhaps he'll show some reaction to the doctor."

The next day the doctor carefully examined Ramal. It was strange; the sick man seemed not to get any better. His illness was daily becoming worse. Everyone in the village was uneasy because the sick man seemed to have no hope of recovery.

Hearing that Ramal had reached that stage, the *lurah* now became dispirited himself. He was even more constantly absorbed in his own thoughts. And indeed at times he could be seen muttering to himself. He became thinner. His eyes were sunken. His face was pale and bloodless.

No one could see him. He had no inclination to go to his office by the village hall. The guard and the village secretary took up posts in the *lurah*'s house. And even that was just having coffee on the veranda, because the *lurah* kept to his bed in his room.

The *lurah*'s behavior became the talk of the whole village. But no one could say what was happening. The village became anxious.

Till one day just before *lohor*, from the mosque loudspeaker, Guard Udin made the announcement:

"*Inna lillahi wa inna ilayhi raji'un*. May the dead rest in the peace of Allah. The *lurah* has passed away," he said pursing his lips and wanting to cry. He was strongly affected by the death of a master to whom he had been very close.

The village was in commotion.

"What did he say about the *lurah*?"

"He's dead."

"Yes, I know he's dead, but I didn't even know he was ill."

"He killed himself. He hung himself in his room."

The next day when the whole village turned up to follow the *lurah*'s body to the heroes' cemetery, Ramal got up from the guard hut. Staggering at first, he set out with quick small steps westwards. He was leaving the village.

Déni A. Fajar

The Swine

It was the rainy season. It had been bucketing down the whole day and flooded pools of water still lay everywhere. And it was now *isya* and it was drizzling again. The sky was black and the roads were sodden and muddy. It killed off any desire to go out. A lot of people had decided not to set foot outside. In the mosque, the mosque attendant was wandering around aimlessly; there was nobody there. People had decided that the best thing to do was to stay by the fire and warm themselves, every now and again roasting some sweet potato or cassava in the hot ashes. Those who weren't satisfied with just one nipa-leaf roll-your-own cigarette were smoking continuously while waiting for sleep to come. The whole village seemed to be as one.

To tell the truth, I was reluctant to leave the house, but I'd made a promise. This evening I had to meet Ramal, the Foreteller. I stepped down from the house, wrapping my sarong around my shoulders to keep off the cold. It was as though there was not a soul living in the village; no one was outside. There was just the sound of the goats bleating to one another from their stalls. They hadn't had enough to eat.

"Where are you going, Kang?" my wife said.

"This evening it's my turn to help do the rounds with the village watch patrol."

"But it's still early and you're already dressed for it. Usually you don't leave until you've been called for at the door. But now?"

"I've promised to see someone. I've got to go there first, to the corner of the street."

"Eh? To the corner? You've promised to see Darsih, the coffee-seller's widow, haven't you?" My wife's voice had an edge to it. "I hope that each time you do the rounds it doesn't mean you're going to the corner."

"And if it does, what of it?" I said to tease her.

My wife pulled a face. As though she was really angry.

"I'm going to the corner because I want to meet Ramal."

"To meet Ramal?" My wife frowned, as though as usual she didn't believe me. "That's a bit out of the ordinary isn't it, arranging to see someone who's not right in the head? People keep away from him. But you're going to see him. I hope you haven't been infected by something."

"Whoa, whoa, don't just talk for talk's sake."

I set off for the corner. It was quiet. I reached Darsih's small coffee hut. There was no one there except the hut owner dozing at the counter with a radio close to her; the sound of a *dangdut* song reached my ears. Where had all the ghosts who stalked the corner disappeared to? There was not a sign of Darja and his pals. Much better to be in one's house on a cold night like this. Sleeping soundly, huddled together, rolled up in a ball.

I shone my flashlight at the foot of the *sawo* tree. There sitting on the barber's chair I saw Ramal. He was waiting for me, I thought, the loon.

"Hey, you're dazzling me!" Ramal shouted.

"It's me, 'Mal!"

"If it hadn't been you, your honor," I heard Ramal say softly, "I would have sworn."

I didn't reply. I went and sat down facing him. Feeling in my pockets, I brought out some cigarettes. The loon, smiling stupidly, bent deferentially and took out four cigarettes. I didn't make any remark. I was speaking inwardly to myself. Trying to reckon how to get at the "secret" which Ramal wanted to pass on to me. Perhaps there was something in it for me, this information, even though it was coming from someone who was not quite all there.

I waited, but still Ramal didn't speak. Giving up, it was me finally who spoke first.

"Come on, 'Mal, wasn't there some story you wanted to tell me?"

"What was that?" Ramal stared blankly.

"The secret."

The loon was silent again, as though he was thinking about something.

"Provided your honor promises first."

"Promises what exactly?"

"Your honor won't get angry with me."

I nodded quickly. I wanted to know what it was that he wanted to pass on to me. What Ramal then said seemed to explode in my ears.

"Your honor's wife, she's having an affair with the *kuwu*, the village head. I've seen them at it, often." He didn't hold back on what he said. Then he giggled to himself.

The anger welled up inside me. I felt he was making fun of me. But then I thought, it was my own fault, believing someone who was not right in the head. So I didn't vent my rage on him—it wasn't his fault. I walked away. Ramal was smoking a cigarette, and I didn't even glance at him again. I was scared that if I heeded him, he would think I was like him.

As night pressed on, the rain came down heavier. The wind was blowing hard and, in the river at the lower end of the village, there was a confused rushing and rumbling of water. The night was as though in the grip of a spell. There was no one about. It made one uneasy. The rain was excessive; it was very likely that by early tomorrow the rice fields would be awash and the dikes would have collapsed and the fish-ponds would have spilled over. Not to mention all the trees that would have fallen down. That was what commonly happened when there was rain and wind together.

My thought of joining the patrol that night eventually took me to those who were in the watch-hut, talking about this and that.

"Light a fire, Emed," Aki Jahro said, rousing himself from sleep.

Emed didn't dawdle. He went to the side of the hut and looked for coconut fibers and thin dry branches. He had purposely gathered the fibers and the dry branches there, in anticipation. Now he lit the fire. Everyone immediately crowded together wanting to be near the fire.

"What about Kuwu? Where's he then? Isn't it about time he was here?" I looked at Ki Jahro.

"Oh, it's just as usual; Kuwu's always late," Emed answered quickly. He was still drowsy. "That's his character and no one dares to say anything. He treats the business of doing the watch just as he likes. When it's raining like this, if he even just thinks of the patrol duty that's already progress."

"It's like that when someone has a bit of authority, Med," said Adun.

"Look, it's not 'like that', it's just become a habit of his. A good leader doesn't behave like that," Aki cut in. There was irritation in his voice.

In this instance there was good reason for people to feel irritated or even angry with Kuwu. Not only Ki Jahro, but a lot of people, including myself. There was a strong feeling of resentment and disapproval at Kuwu's behavior. We could have made a lot of complaints about Kuwu. He always wanted things cushy, always wanted to get the best for himself. He was an "*egois*," to use the word that young people use nowadays. This matter of the night watch was an example; Kuwu felt no embarrassment before Ki Jahro. Here was an old man conscientiously doing his duty, but Kuwu was the opposite, the height of laziness and always getting out of what he should do. This was unfair. Especially since it had been Kuwu who had insisted on there being a night watch.

"All men are duty-bound to ensure the safety of the village. Duty-bound, I say. No one is exempt or to be treated differently, and that holds for me, too. We all benefit from the night watch, don't we? We all sleep soundly if the village is protected," said Kuwu when he spoke to the villagers gathered in the village hall.

That led everyone to applaud. It was just like him to say this in the speech he gave after he was appointed *kuwu* for the second time. It was as though he had bought the villagers' sympathies. And so for one or two months he proved himself, coming down in the evening and doing his night-watch duty. But it didn't last long. And now he frequently neglected his duty and reneged on his promise. The villagers had begun to feel disappointed and spoke behind his back. There was the matter of the community fund, the money one paid to be exempt from villagers' community service, and it was also being said now that Kuwu had a fondness for women; he was even ready to try it on with those who had husbands!

Crash! The sound of thunder broke off my thoughts. I wiped my hand across my face. I looked at Emed and Adun, who were grinning foolishly.

"It's a good thing you didn't fall flat on your face, Kang," said Emed, laughing with Adun.

'Perhaps he's thinking of the person he left back at the house," said Ki Jahro, his eyes half closed in the corner of the hut. Emed and Adun laughed again.

"This rain's too much," I said changing the conversation.

"It's Ramal's fault," Adun said.

"Why blame someone for it like that, Adun?" Ki Jahro glared at him. "There's no connection between the rain and wind and that loon. How could there be?"

"Because he was praying that this evening there would be this wind and rain."

"You idiot, you believe someone who's not right in the head. It's a sin, you know, being superstitious like that."

"But now it's been proved, Ki," I said looking at Ki Jahro. It wasn't that. I didn't want to defend or support Adun. But suddenly I felt a sense of shock. I kept thinking of my wife in the house. Strange, I suddenly felt disturbed. I remembered Ramal; I was afraid that his words would come true.

Emed and Adun were in their element talking about Ramal. The talk about him revived. It was the usual thing—the loon liked to talk rot, foretelling things and the like. The funny thing was that a lot of things he said came true, and that was why he was called Ramal— the Foreteller. No one knew his real name. He wasn't originally from my village. I don't know where he came from originally.

Two weeks ago, people had gathered at the stall where Mang Udin kept his goats. They had come to see and wait while a nanny goat was having a difficult labor. And then out of the blue Ramal turned up and spoke to those assembled there. Of course the labor's difficult, he said, because she's expecting quadruplets. And after he had said that, he left. Among those who were waiting for the goat to deliver, not one of them believed what Ramal had said. But then after the delivery, everything that Ramal had said was proven true. Mang Udin's goat gave birth to quadruplets. There was no one there who didn't shake his head in amazement.

When the mosque clock was stolen, Ramal said who the culprit was. According to Emed again, the mosque attendant had specifically gone to ask Ramal. Ramal said that it had been taken by so-and-so and sold to so-and-so in the village of so-and-so.

Consumed by curiosity, Mang Merebot had gone and followed up on the person who had bought it. And there the clock was. The clock that had been reported stolen was recovered. The culprit had almost gotten away with it, but he'd been caught.

"It is also Ramal who has taken to talking about Ceu Awang, your wife, Kang!"

I glanced up and looked at him intently.

"What did he say?"

Emed and Adun looked at each other. They looked as though they had a bone stuck in their throats; they both gaped. It seemed they wanted to reply, as though perhaps they wanted to get something off their chest. Eventually Adun braved himself to speak.

"The Foreteller says that Ceu Awang is in the habit of doing you know what with... with Kuwu."

"Adun, you idiot, what are you talking about," Aki Jahro stared at him angrily. "Don't believe him, lad. These two are just teasing you."

The rain was still pouring down. I could hear thunder claps pounding in my head. My mind was in turmoil between believing and refusing to believe. My wife's face appeared before me, followed by Ramal's, grinning foolishly, and then the face of Kuwu dripping with sweat like someone tired but satisfied with the pleasure he'd had. There was a flash and a crack and a peal of thunder and the three faces disappeared.

When I left the hut I didn't look right or left but walked quickly ahead, not caring about the rain which was coming down heavily. I heard Ki Jahro talking to Emed and Adun.

"Stick to him, Emed, Adun. It's your responsibility, you two idiots. You see what you've caused because you couldn't keep your mouths shut."

I was driven by anger blazing inside me, and I walked quickly on to the western end of the village. Emed and Adun shouted to me, asking me to wait, but I didn't listen.

"Where are you going, Kang?" Emed said. He was now at my side. He was panting from running to catch up with me.

"I'm going to grab the swine."

"Where's the swine? Even the swine are sleeping soundly in weather like this."

"At my house."

There were no more questions. We reached the house. It was dark. In the middle of the house there was only the illumination from the light of an oil lamp. On the steps up to the door of the house were some shoes covered in mud. Everyone on the night watch knew whose shoes they were.

"Look, those are Kuwu's shoes," Emed and Adun said together.

The rain seemed to be coming down even harder. There was a black banging in my ears, the fire of my rage was flaming inside me, blazing. My hand went to the hilt of my machete. Emed and Adun trembled when I jerked it from its scabbard.

"Kuwu, you bastard. Come out, you swine."

Lugiena Dé

The Orange

I was sitting with him in a row right at the back. He was an old man, the kind of man you would address as "Grandfather" if you knew him well. He was wearing long black baggy trousers and a white collarless shirt. He wore an *iket*, a bandana around his head. For shoes he was wearing casual flip-flop sandals.

If we had been in a village somewhere, it would have been quite natural and no cause for surprise. A lot of people in my village dress like that. And like him they are elderly folk. But this was Jakarta. It wasn't a common sight. It was even more uncommon that he should be here dressed like that at this time of the year, when people were busy traveling back, *mudik*, to their home villages for Lebaran. Furthermore, everyone was laden down with parcels and bits and pieces, but he wasn't carrying anything. All he had was a simple bag of woven pandanus leaves hanging from his shoulder, and even that looked very light; there couldn't have been much in it.

But what was curious was that his lips wouldn't stop mumbling. In his right hand he held an orange, and as he mumbled holding the orange in his grip, he kept moving it about with his thumb.

There were absolutely no seats left, but the bus still had not started off. One could hear the revving of the engine but nothing else. For a time I didn't ask any questions. We both kept to ourselves.

But I kept stealing glances at him from the corner of my eye. He seemed oblivious to my stares. He maintained the same pose as before. He didn't want to turn and look at me at all. He just went on mumbling. Occasionally I heard him mention the word Allah. "Alloh, Alloh," he said. I allowed myself a quick grin.

Then the bus began to move off. It crawled along because of the heavy traffic. Outside the sky was turning a deep yellow in the late afternoon.

If at first I had kept to myself, now he began to attract my attention. He seemed to be normal, sane. I thought there would be nothing wrong in just making a general remark, an opening question. After all I was a journalist, and it would be quite proper if I made the acquaintance of someone like him. It would be like doing some investigative reporting.

"Where are you off to then, Pa?" I asked with a smile.

He turned round and returned my smile. "To Ciamis, young man," he said.

"*Mudik*, Pa, going back to Ciamis?" I followed up with another question.

"Well, yes and no," he said after pausing a second.

"How do you mean?"

"It's like this. You could say it was '*mudik*' because it's true that I am returning to where I come from, but on the other hand it's not *mudik* because I haven't been away a long time; it's not the annual return. If I am not going back specially for Lebaran it's not really *mudik*," he laughed.

I laughed with him, nodding my head.

"But you, young man, you seem to be properly '*mudik*'?"

"Yes, that's right. I work in Jakarta getting by with casual jobs, a laborer. You can earn a living in Jakarta."

"It doesn't matter what you do. It's the same everywhere. What's important is that you have enough and that you are in God's favor."

"Amen to that," I replied.

We became less awkward with each other.

I thought at that moment of Kang Muhtar, a person I knew from Bandung who was active in theatre circles. He, too, wore long baggy trousers and an *iket* every day. It was expected of him; he was into the world of performance. And so was Mang Amid, who also wore baggy trousers and an *iket*, but with him it was because he wanted to be traditional. And in that respect he wanted to be considered as both typically Sundanese and typically village-mosque educated.

"And if I may ask, have you, too, just come from Jakarta?"

"As a matter of fact, I've come from Serang. Then I stopped off in Tangerang and then went on to Jakarta."

"Wow, in the fasting month you've still wanted to go traveling despite it being so tiring."

"Yes, while I still can. While I'm not suffering from too many complaints. Because then when the time comes and I do start suffering from this and that, it'll be difficult even going to ease myself." He laughed.

"That's what you call good health. That's not something I see every day," I said picking up his good humor again.

"True. It's good of you to say so. Especially since I am now an old man. It does feel a rare privilege. Others my age all have something the matter with them. So I never stop praising God and thanking him. By the grace of God I am still allowed to go on my travels."

I nodded. The impression that he was a religious man was confirmed. Especially since he was old. I was sure that he had had a lot of experience and acquired a lot of wisdom in the course of his life.

"You certainly appear to know a lot," I said half-complimenting him.

He smiled.

"What else is there, lad? I'm old. There are not many years left to me. Before I am summoned by the Almighty, I want to turn my thoughts completely to Him. That's what I want. But I'm sorry, I didn't want to preach. I am no religious scholar." He looked down as he spoke.

"That's quite all right," I replied.

"I don't want to appear as though I'm praising myself. Pardon me. But that's just me. That's my way." He laughed.

That was, I suppose, how modest people behaved. You could say that he was a humble sort.

The bus got on to the toll road and was soon speeding away. The other passengers seemed uninterested in our conversation; they were lost in their own thoughts. The old man was still holding the orange, only now he wasn't fiddling with it; he was gripping it tightly.

For a time neither of us said anything, but I still felt curious about him; he was definitely a character.

"And may I enquire, at present what do you do?" I asked him hesitatingly. I suppose, thinking about it, it was not particularly polite of me to probe like that into someone's personal affairs.

"Oh, this is all I do, lad. Traveling about."

"I can believe it. That's perhaps what you should be doing at your time of life, enjoying yourself."

He just smiled and scratched his head.

"As you say, lad."

"I imagine that if you've reached a certain age there are no further burdens to bear. All that's left is to enjoy yourself, the hard graft of life is something of the past. Different for a young person like myself. Something like that?"

He didn't immediately reply. He looked idly out of the window as though thinking about what to say.

"You're right about you've just said, lad. Especially with respect to life's burdens. Only your words can be interpreted in two ways. May I ask what your name is? You don't mind if we talk and exchange stories?"

I told him my name and he told me his.

"So how has it all come about?" I asked quickly.

He smiled vacantly again. "Yes, just like the young, want to rush at it. Why are you so curious to know everything?"

I smiled an embarrassed smile. He could see through me.

"Yes, you're right. I am curious. Because from what I can see so far, you're rather different from most old people."

"Because you saw me mumbling some prayers?"

"Well, that was one thing. Pardon me if I'm being presumptuous." I felt guilty.

"It doesn't matter. It shows you care and you're not indifferent to what's happening around you. That's the way it should be, isn't it?"

I nodded.

"If that's the case then let's talk. Rather than suspect the worst of each other."

Once more I had been caught out. And because I was embarrassed, I half-turned away.

"To say that I don't have any cares and that I am free to enjoy life is quite wrong. I am not a rich man. I, too, have to scratch away to make a living. But it's true that now I don't have many worldly cares. Thanks to God I am happy with what I have. That's the truth of it. You understand?"

I nodded again. "So you are a Sufi?" I asked casually. Put to him just like that, he almost seemed to acknowledge it, but he quickly drew his left hand across his face.

"No, lad. I'm just an ordinary person," he said.

I grinned at him again then.

"I see. But from what I've learned, people who put worldly matters second are Sufis," I said once more.

"I don't know anything about that. I'm just who I am, as you see me, lad."

There was silence for a moment.

"It's like this. Since you're so curious, I'll tell you a little. If I do tell you a bit, who knows it may be of some benefit to you, mightn't it?"

Just like an old man, I thought. Before he starts on a story, he has to make a big thing of it before he gets to the point.

"I hope so. Who can tell?"

"Indeed that's true. Whether a certain thing is of value or not is something only God knows. But a person like me is required to make his own way. Excuse me, I didn't mean to preach. But isn't there a *hadith* that says that the fortunate person is the one whose next day is better than the previous one? No? By the way, are you fasting?"

"God willing," I said, making my reply deliberately vague. Again, again I was caught out. Before setting out I had had some instant noodles with Mang Ihung at the office.

"Thanks to God then that you are. Now let's see what we can talk about to while away the time that remains before breaking the fast," he said adjusting his position. "I am not, lad, one of those people who is desperate for the material things of the world. Provided I have enough to get by on daily basis. I have, as it happens, a small, a very small, rice field in the village. And in between getting a living from farming, I weave mats and things from time to time. But the rest of my time I spend in looking up my friends here and there. And that's how I come to say that what I do is just to travel about. You see?" he said.

After that the old man went on to talk at some length. I just listened attentively and nodded my head. Sometimes I asked a

question. I didn't pay any attention to what was going on in the
bus.

It seemed that he was the member of some *tarekat* sect, but he
didn't want to say which one. And he was going from place to place
to meet fellow-members of the *tarekat*. Of course, I said to myself.
And he had studied at a *pesantren* too. So it wasn't surprising that
he should have a deep knowledge of religion. And I could also
understand why he frequently peppered our conversation with
religious quotes. I don't know whether they were from the Quran,
or the *hadith*. I didn't always understand. I tried to make a reference
to Haji Hasan Mustafa. He suddenly broke out into chanting one
of the latter's verses. And then he explained the meaning of it.

But it was a different matter that I found most interesting of all.

"Happiness in life, lad, is living simply. Because in that way
possessions become one's slave. The way to happiness is meeting
one's needs. Imagine if it had been given to me to be rich. I would
now be the slave of my possessions. I would have been driven by
my desires. What I mean by needs is having enough. But in relation
to desires there is no end to it. You want this and you want that.
Isn't that right?"

I nodded.

"But our religion doesn't forbid us to become rich?" I took him
up.

"Yes, that's quite true. Indeed it does suggest it. Since if we want
to go on the haj we have to have the wealth to pay for it. But, if
I may, I want to ask, if you were rich, lad, what would you want?
Would you perhaps want to do good with your money or not,
especially as far as others are concerned?"

I said nothing.

"Among my friends, lad, many of them became merchants, but
they couldn't be said to live luxuriously. In fact a substantial part of
their wealth is given to religious causes. Just look now at countries

of the Middle East. Aren't they rich? But why do they find it so difficult to help Palestine? They simply enjoy themselves by being surrounded by luxury. Is that doing good?

"That's why I have had quite enough of all that, thank God. And excuse me again; I don't want to appear to be giving you a nice pious religious lesson, it's just that I know myself that if I was blessed with riches it's not certain that I would want to do good with it, either for myself or for others."

I was silent again. What he said applied to me. The more I thought about it, the more embarrassed I became. After all hadn't it been the case that all the time I had been earning a living in Jakarta I had often neglected my religious duties? I had often skipped praying five times. And during the annual fasting, I was always sneaking away somewhere for a quick bite. But I had always felt that I was not earning enough.

And now it had been fated that I meet someone who was thankful for whatever he received. Maybe it was true that I was as I was because I was insufficiently grateful for what I had.

"It's not a matter of how rich or poor one is, whether one has a little or a lot, but how a person practices their religion. Because it's in that way that one meets with what is called God's grace. More than a few poor people experience the joy of life even though they have only salt and chilies to eat with their rice, compared to rich people who dine on all kinds of food," said the fatherly man.

I nodded again.

I had been so engrossed in our conversation that I hadn't noticed time passing and now it was coming up to *maghrib*. The old man was getting ready to break his fast. As soon as we had heard in the distance the *azan* calling the faithful to the *maghrib* prayer, the old man recited some religious verses. Then he swallowed some water. And I did the same, as if I, too, were breaking the fast. So did the other passengers; each one dipping into their own food that they'd brought.

After he had broken the fast, the old man said his *maghrib* prayers in the bus sitting on his seat. But I just knit my brows slightly, not knowing that one could pray like this, since I thought that in circumstances like that one simply doubled up at the next prayer time. My conscience troubled me. Yes, I felt that religion did not play a sufficiently large role in my life.

After the prayer it was time to eat the rice the old man brought out. He offered me the orange which he had held in his hand. At first I refused it, because I couldn't take it, but he pressed me.

"You brought this; it's part of your meal," I said.

"It doesn't matter. Consider it a token of our new acquaintance. And besides I hope that from the gift of this single orange I shall obtain enormous blessing. And anyway I have got some more in my bag," he said, fumbling in his bag for one more.

So in the end I took it. Then I peeled it. The old man went on taking big mouthfuls of his food, not forgetting first to offer me something. I looked on; he seemed to be making a good meal.

The bus was going along very fast.

After he had finished his meal he yawned. And eventually I, too, felt tired.

"Excuse me I am going to drop off to sleep. I'm very tired," he said.

I just nodded. I yawned a few times. And then I fell asleep, too.

I woke up in the bus terminal in Banjar. And that was only after being shaken awake by the conductor. I didn't recognize anything; there was no one about. Even more worrying was the fact that the rucksack which I had brought from Jakarta and which I had held on to had disappeared. Dazed, I looked in the luggage rack. It wasn't there. I looked in the space under the seat. Not there either. I looked under all the seats but I couldn't find it. There was a digital camera belonging to the office in the bag. What had happened to it? I felt around in my back pocket. Again nothing there.

Finally I threw myself down on the seat. I was confused and annoyed. I couldn't understand how I had come to sleep so deeply. I thought of the orange. It couldn't have been that, could it?

I went straight off to the conductor. He just shook his head and said he didn't know. Then I asked something else.

"That old man, the grandfather type?" said the conductor. "He was the one who got off at Cileunyi, wasn't he?"

"Was he carrying anything?"

"Oh yes, he was carrying a big rucksack."

Lord!

Yus R. Ismail

The Horse Trap

It was drizzling with rain. The *azan* had just made the call for the *isya* prayer five minutes ago. But it was exceptionally quiet. The only noise you could hear was the sound of cicadas and crickets, grasshoppers and mole-crickets responding to each other. But that only seemed to make it even quieter; there was no sound of human voices. I pushed myself to go out on the balcony of the first floor; there was only the faint flickering of the light at the front of the house. The nearest houses were some distance away. The village night watch must have been shivering with the cold. It was like this in the village.

"But if truth be told, it's not like this in the village," said Mang Dipa, my closest neighbor about two hundred yards away, when I had met him this morning before he went off to his small-holding.

"I've been here three days," I said, "but every day it seems quieter—really, really quiet."

"Well, usually the nightwatchmen make a lot of noise. It's more like that in the village; when people are on the night watch they're not simply on the night watch. Sometimes they're eating a meal of rice and vegetables together. Or something boiled, cassava or sweet potato or peanuts, there's always something to be found. Sometimes even when it's not their turn to do the watch, people go round carrying flaming torches to the paddy fields. And they do their rounds while warming themselves around a fire, eating a meal, having a spicy dish of eels they've caught, and they chat and talk about this and that."

"And why hasn't it been like that as usual since I've been here?"

"It's been like this for about a month now. There's someone or something going around the village. No one dares go near whoever it is. The watch takes to their heels when they hear it."

"Who is it that's going around?"

"A horse trap."

And until now, standing here on the balcony after *isya*, I still didn't understand what Mang Dipa was referring to. But after I had closed the balcony door and gone into my room to work on the story I had not yet finished, then I understood what Mang Dipa meant.

I could hear, not very distinctly, the sound of a horse trap. The clip, clop of the hooves, the whinnying of the horse, the clicking of the cabbie's tongue as he encouraged it, and the tinkling bells becoming clearer and clearer. The hairs at the back of my neck stood up. This wasn't an ordinary horse trap. This village lay perched at the foot of a mountain, the road went steeply up and down. It would wear you out if you tried to use a horse trap for transport.

Tinkle, tinkle, huss huss, neigh, neigh. It was becoming clearer, more alarming. And the noise of the crickets and the cicadas, the mole-crickets and the grasshoppers, where had they disappeared to? The animals seemed to feel that there was something strange about what was happening. I quickly switched off the laptop which I had just turned on. Then I dived under my blanket and listened.

Tinkle, tinkle, huss huss, neighhhh. The horse trap seemed to be slowing down just outside the house. My heart started pounding even more. After a while the sound of the horse trap became louder again. *Tinkle, tinkle, huss huss neighhhh.* The noise of someone going round the village.

I wanted to have a peek, to see whether it was in fact a horse trap. But far from doing that, I hid myself further under the blanket. I felt I had been at fault. I regretted now that I hadn't learned from Ustad Wahyu the spell to ward off evil. The more so because Ustad Wahyu had often warned me. "The evil spirits in league with the devil are always circling around you, Kang," he said when I met him just after he'd given a Quranic reading.

He was right. This horse trap was a kind of supernatural thing. Weren't there stories of horse traps that used to cart off people who worshipped the devil? Those people who had given into temptation and had been given riches as much as they wanted? The devil came for their souls at the appointed time. And then, didn't they say, the souls of these people became servants, messengers, and even foot mats. It made your hairs stand on end. Who was it that this spirit was coming to take away from this village?

This was the story told, a story which was told really only to frighten children who whined a lot. And wasn't I a storyteller? But I didn't understand that story. From the time of my grandparents and my parents, there had been hundreds of stories of spirits using horse traps. But if the spirits were rich, why hadn't they swapped them in for Lamborghinis which cost billions of rupiah? But if the spirits that came to take you away drove deluxe cars, who would be afraid? On the other hand, the whole point of stories of evil spirits, like this short story, is to frighten the audience.

A little while later the sound of the horse trap, which had moved off into the distance, came nearer again. Clearer. And then the sound of it was just outside the front door. It seemed to grip the house, shaking it, all two floors swaying as though in an earthquake. The hanging oil-lamp swayed. There was a noise of knocking at the door.

Tok... tok...tok.

I had no intention of opening it. I just wanted to leap out of the window and rush off to Mang Dipa's house. The door opened with a creak. I trembled. What had I done wrong? I hadn't made any promises to an evil spirit, had I? The only promise I could remember was one to Mang Dadan, the peddler who sold glasses of *cendol*, who had given me credit. I'd told him I would pay him when I had some money, but I hadn't seen him again.

Creak.

Someone was opening the door of my room. But I had locked and bolted it. But this was an evil spirit, wasn't it, and it was easy for an evil spirit to open doors that were locked and bolted. I pulled the blanket over my head. The sweat poured off me.

"Get uuuup, you. Don't hide, fool. I'll burn you like a flaming torch." The voice was shrill and high-pitched. What sort of evil spirit had a voice like that? It wasn't terrifying, it didn't scare me.

I drew aside the blanket a little and peeked out. I had a shock—but it wasn't a shock of fear. I wanted to laugh. This evil spirit had all the required paraphernalia. He was wearing a crown, and in his right hand he was holding a spear and in his left a shield. But in size he was only as big as a small mug and the spear was only as big as the rib of a palm frond and the shield as big as a *baluntas* leaf. I threw off the blanket. Stupid of me to be afraid like that, I said to myself.

"Come along then with meeee. You have made a promise to my maaaaster. You will become a foot mat in my master's kingdom. Heuh, heuh heuh."

"I'm not afraid now," I said sitting up on the edge of the bed. "What sort of thing are you?"

"I....I....I.... am an evil neejie."

"You mean jeenie."

"I said neejie, fool. It's my step-brother who's the jeenie."

I wanted to laugh. But because he spoke so rudely and with such vulgarity I was angry with him. "Speak like that to me once more and I'll kick you hard," I said standing up, like Andik Vermansyah about to kick the ball for a penalty.

"Hey, hey, friends, come here; this one wants to resist." The spirit sang out imitating an evil giant in one of Asep Sunandar Surya's *wayang* stories.

"Come on all of you, surround him..."

A host of jeenies, that is, I mean neejies, thronged into the room. Thousands, if not millions. All of them quite bonkers.

Five minutes after that, I was in the horse trap. My hands and feet were tied up. The regiment of neejies, millions of them, were lined up behind the horse trap. The drizzle was still making it feel cold. The horse trap was moving along a flat road; it must have been in the heavens.

Tinkle, tinkle, huss, huss, neighhh.

I need to explain the story a bit here in case anyone reading gets the wrong idea and starts spreading it about that I worship neejie spirits. The truth of it is this. I am a storyteller. I roam around the countryside, wandering all over the place, and that's not just a manner of speaking. In my opinion, our times need stories. So that we don't lose our way in life, going nowhere in particular. In each village I'm welcomed and surrounded by people. And those legends of Umar Maya, Lutung Kasarung, Dadap Malang Cimandiri, Mundinglaya Di Kusumah and even modern tales in the form of short stories, novels poems, I tell them over and over again and reshape them. But all these stories are now exhausted in the telling, so in the end I have been forced to make up my own stories.

"Why don't you use my house as a place to write?" said a good friend of mine when I told him that I needed someplace where I could write my stories. I am not going to mention the name of my friend; it could cause embarrassment. But I can say that he held various positions here and there. In government offices he was the head, in political parties the leader, in organizations he was always on the advisory board, and he held shares in various companies.

As for his wealth, no need to say much about it. In Bali, in Java, in Sumatra and in Papua he had hectares of rice fields, not to mention plantations and numerous houses. He once asked me what my bank account number was so that he could transfer money there on a regular basis every month. But I didn't accept his offer. How could I repay him? I would get money out of the deal, but what would he get? He said that he liked my stories. Well, if he liked my stories it was enough that he gave me the time to write them; no need to transfer money to my account every month.

I am not going to tell you about my experiences in the supernatural world, in the kingdom of the neejies, because it's not important. Of course they had got the wrong person. What the King of the Neejies had said about the details they should look out for was all correct: a house with two floors in a village and in the front yard a banyan tree, but the king knew very well that I wasn't the person that he was after.

When I got back to the house it was late at night, almost time for the *subuh* prayer. Without waiting a moment, I telephoned my friend. He was worried. The whole night he had been unable to sleep. He was uneasy.

"Come here now quickly," I said, "there's something important I have to tell you."

While filling in the time waiting for my friend I opened my laptop. I was a bit taken aback: the story which I was in the middle of writing was finished. Who had finished it? When had it been typed out? Never mind if I couldn't answer these questions; the main thing is that the reader enjoys the story. Because that's the important thing for a short story, isn't it? At seven in the morning my friend rolled up in his SUV, a car that also cost billions.

Straightaway I told him what had happened the previous evening. He was silent and he stood motionless.

"So my goddamned advice to you, mate, is that you cut down that banyan tree so the spirits start going wrong when they look for you," I said. I could speak to him in this offhand way since we had been friends from childhood. It didn't matter that he had done so well at this and that, and that he had the figures with lots of zeros behind them stacked up in this and that bank account, because I had never once asked him for anything or made a request to become this or that. "You should go straightaway to Ustad Wahyu so that you can make amends, be penitent. We can both go and be penitent, because I've got a lot of sins on my conscience, too."

My friend was deep in thought; he said nothing. His face looked overcast like a dark cloud in the rainy season persisting from one day to the next. A minute, two minutes, three minutes. He didn't say anything for almost an hour. And I, too, was silent. Occasionally I looked at him; lord knows what he was thinking.

"If that banyan tree is cut down, it will be the end of me. All the wealth that I've got from the spirits will be taken away again," he finally said with a big sigh. "The houses will be burned down. My girlfriends, the other women on the side, my mistresses, they'll all disappear. The car, the plantations, the companies, they'll all be confiscated by the KPK."

"The KPK, the Anti-Corruption Commission? What's the connection? The spirits aren't hand-in-glove with the KPK are they?"

"It's not that. But after I had made my pact with the spirits, I suddenly became the head of the history division in the Department of Education. And that's when the money began to flow in my direction. This tendered project and that tendered project for the supply of books and materials to all the schools in the region put money in my direction. I cheated and tricked the businessmen who supplied me with wads of money. I had them in my grip and I just took the money. I went on getting promotions and the contracts got bigger. My wealth was enormous. The companies rattled along, companies that only tendered for government work, and the political party struggled on with the money there was. After the companies had been lined up, the party came under my control. I became popular. Whatever I wanted, I just had to mention it to those dealing with the administration of the paperwork."

I nodded, not understanding.

"If that banyan tree is cut down, all my wealth disappears. I'll become poor, and I'll probably end up in prison."

"But it's better to be in prison, alive in this world, especially if you're sorry for what you've done and continue on being sorry. If that banyan tree is not cut down, the spirits, the neejies, will eventually track you down. You'll become a doormat, stepped on all the time, treated like dirt. Disgusting."

He said nothing. Then he left; he said he was going to Jakarta to meet a presidential candidate. He didn't say anything more about it. I, too, began to make ready; I was going on my way through the countryside, visiting villages along the route telling people my new story.

One morning when I was walking along a country road, a posh car went past. A Lamborghini in the countryside, I thought to myself.

Tinkle, tinkle, huss huss, neighhhh.

It was the old noise, the sound of a horse trap. The driver was wearing a tie and his hair was oiled down and sleek.

The passenger—imagine! It was my friend, looking vacant, staring into the distance, his thoughts miles away. Just like the damned spirits, the vehicle to take away their worshippers had been changed, but they had forgotten to do anything about the sound.

After that, there were no more questions asked about that government official who had money in these shares and money in those companies. Although one kept bumping into him in one of the national storytelling festivals. Of course he's no longer my friend now. It's true you can still see and hear of his corporal presence walking about on TV programs and in the newspapers and on the radio and the internet. But as for his soul, that's been taken away by the neejies, and he's now a doormat in the kingdom of the other world.

Fitria Puji Lestari

Birthday Tomorrow

She looked hard at the dates on the calendar. Then she looked at the date circled with red ink, February 20, 2014. "Time's rushing by very quickly," she said to herself.

She looked at the date for a long time. And the longer she frowned at that figure 20, the more she began to doubt her convictions. The figure 20 filled her thoughts; she felt as though it was cutting off all the hopes she had nourished up till now. "Oh, Go-o-od," she cried to herself. A tear dripped on to the calendar, and that tear became a flow, staining all the dates, which seemed to be dissolving into one another.

Tomorrow was her birthday. The whole day would be a happy one, as it always was on her birthday. A lot of people would be congratulating her; she'd receive presents from her parents and her close friends.

But the closer her birthday came the more she was assailed by worrisome thoughts. These days a birthday, which was something one should be glad about, only seemed to cause her pain, body and soul. Every birthday that passed seemed to increase the worry and the fears of the people around her. Her mother, her father, her sister, her relatives, all her neighbors were wondering.

Every time there was a wedding, the comments were always the same, "And when will it be your turn? Don't take too long about it, if there's somebody there waiting."

She only acknowledged these comments with a smile. But inside she felt as though a hundred needles were pricking and stabbing her. It was very painful. Left and right, people were always talking about her. The things they said were like sharp slivers cutting her heart to pieces.

"Nining is very choosy about men; she shouldn't be so proud. There was a good opportunity for her, so I've heard, when Wawan proposed to her. She should have accepted him and not come out with this and that excuse for turning him down. What does it matter that he's divorced; she's of the age when she should get married," said her aunt Enong when she rejected Wawan's proposal.

"Parents can only pray for the right outcome, Ceu. It's up to Nining to make the decision; she's going to be the one who has to go through with it," her mother had replied.

It wasn't that she did not want to get married. And she didn't mean to be so choosy, whenever she found herself rejecting men who were prepared to take care of her. She was very aware that she was not the kind of person that men fell instantly in love with, but when she thought about the person who would be her companion for life, she wanted someone who was sincere. What was important was not how he looked or how wealthy he was, but whether he was a person of integrity, someone who would conscientiously undertake his responsibilities. She didn't care that Wawan was a divorcé or that he wasn't handsome and was rather old. What she couldn't accept was that Wawan was not genuine. On the contrary, reports about him said that he was a person who was constantly divorcing and remarrying. That he was always trying it on with women. So even though she was constantly being hounded that she should get married, that did not mean that she would accept just anyone, she said to herself. It was these ideas of hers that people around her could not accept. Perhaps only her mother was not unduly anxious about the way she thought and always respected her opinions. This was perhaps the way of mothers who tried to understand their children's feelings.

Ceu Mimin, the woman who had a small kiosk next to the house, had a different opinion, which she let be known. She said, "Of course Nining will end up an old maid. She's too pious, the way she flaps around in her robes and head scarves. You'd think by the way she acts that men are the cause of sin. Getting to know men is sinful, shaking hands with a man is like touching filth."

Nining didn't respond to talk like that. But when she was praying, she pitched her head forward when she prostrated herself and wept. She resigned all her pain to the God who knew all. In her ears there still echoed the words of her spiritual guide in the prayer group to which she belonged, words which brought comfort and balm to her soul.

"For believers, everything that happens, happy events and sad ones, all turn out to have good consequences. If you find yourself in circumstances that cause you difficulties, you must be patient and bear them; and if you find yourself in circumstances that bring you happiness, you must be grateful for them. Don't despair, because we all have Allah to turn to. Follow the straight path, do everything as well as you can, and offer it up to the Almighty. And if God is bountiful, you will be guided."

"Oh God, may it be so, may it be so," she said with a choke in her voice in between her sobs. Her tears wetted her *mukena*, the light prayer cape which covered her. Sometimes after saying additional prayers, crying she would throw herself forward on her prayer mat. She clenched the mat tightly and screwed it her hands. "Oh God, how tired and exhausted I am," she said softly. But then immediately after, if she did this, she would hastily say *istighfar*, the word of repentance, and briskly wipe away her tears. Then she would open her small reading stand. She would read verses of the Quran aloud in a ringing voice until she heard the voice of the *azan* rising up from the mosque to the west of the house calling the faithful to prayer.

She continued to look hard at the calendar. Tomorrow she would be exactly thirty. "Oh, Mother, Nina, it's not that as the elder sister I want it like this. I don't want to stand in your way, Nina, if you want to get married and start your own family, but feel that you can't because you must wait for me to be married first. But this is how it is with me. What should I do, Mama, Nina? What should I do? God knows I have tried. How many times have I tried to find a suitable partner through religious meeting arrangements, but the results have never been successful. I'm told I have to be open and friendly. I should pray for this and that. I haven't omitted anything in the reading of the holy writings. It may be that Allah does not want me to get married yet, perhaps," she said to herself in some confusion.

Then she stood and observed her appearance in the mirror, looking at herself in the clothes she stood in. In the corners of her eyes the wrinkles were clearly visible. Her face, which never reeked of cosmetics, was wrapped around with a length of cloth which covered her hair down to her chest. And she wore a long gown covering her whole body. And then on top of that she wore a head cloth and a blouse matching it.

"I hope, please God, that it is not all this which is the cause of the problem. Please God no," she whispered, talking to herself.

Later that afternoon when she came back from her prayer group meeting, she felt calmer. The words of her spiritual guide had assuaged a little the pain she felt. She had recollected in passing some of the unsuccessful experiences she had had of meeting potential partners through religious channels. These memories took the form of recorded scenes of unhappy incidents replayed on a large screen. She had once in this way met a man who was a year's difference in age from herself. But it seemed they were not destined for each other, because after the man had received the relevant personal data about her, her spiritual guide informed her that the man had decided not to pursue the acquaintance. The reason he gave was that he was looking for someone younger than her.

Another time she was introduced to a man who was said to be ready to start a family. She had the data on the man she was to meet. So that she would not have regrets later, she looked at his Facebook page which she had access to because of the e-mail address she had been given in the personal data sheets. She immediately felt let down, her hopes cut away. Her body shook seeing the photographs of this man who had been matched with her. Photographs of him holding a woman tightly, photographs of him leaning against a woman, photographs of him in various poses, all with women, were there in profusion on his Facebook. She felt nauseated.

She didn't have to think long about it. Straightaway she phoned the spiritual guide and said that she was cancelling the appointment to meet the man.

The experience of several failed attempts at such arrangements had left her with a trauma. It led to a sense of panic every time mention was made of arranging another meeting. But her guide and her friends were forever trying to encourage her and keep up her spirits.

Without realizing it, she had reached the house on her motorbike. When she went up to the front door she had a sudden shock. She heard the muffled voice of a man and a woman giggling together. "Nina," she said to herself. She felt a hot flush in her chest. She opened the door and the flush grew hotter and burned through her. In the living room Nina, her sister, was snuggled up in the embrace of a man. Hearing the door open, the two of them were startled. Nina went pale, realizing that the person who had opened the door was her elder sister, who was always going on about the importance of wearing the headscarf and not exposing those parts of the body considered taboo by religion.

"Nining, you're home," she said, her voice all of a tremble.

Nining didn't pay any attention to her. She went straight to her room and covered her eyes, now brimming with tears. She sat there for a long time on the edge of the bed, then slowly she wiped the tears with the end of her head scarf. From her room she heard indistinctly the voices of Nina and her boyfriend muttering something. Then she heard the sound of the door shutting.

There was a knock at the door of her room. "Teh Ning, Teh Ning, can I come in?"

She didn't reply. She stayed as she was. Her lips were trembling; there were so many things she wanted to say, but they were all stuck in her throat. It would be painful if she gave free rein to her passion. A wave of emotion came over her. Her lips could only mumble the word *istighfar*.

Then the feeling of pain became mixed with a feeling that perhaps she was wrong. She felt that there was something slicing through her, taking her to a dark place. Everything seemed black. Black. She saw in her mind the faces of her father and mother, who felt sorry for her because she still had not found anyone who wanted to take care of her. Then her sister, who had someone, but was prevented from marrying him straightaway because of her. She remembered the conversation she had overheard that one evening between her mother and Nina.

"Nina, it's your sister who must marry first. It would be a great embarrassment if you should 'step over' your sister by marrying before her. You mustn't do it. You know how your sister would feel," Mother said.

"I won't, Mama. I know," Nina had replied.

"Try to understand her feelings, don't speak too much about Kang Arif in front of her."

Tap, tap. There was another knock on the door. "Teh, forgive me," Nina said with a choke in her voice.

She couldn't stop the tears welling from her eyes. A little later she heard her sister's steps moving away from the door. "You're good to me and I love you. It's I who have to ask your forgiveness for standing in the way of your happiness, Nina. It's perhaps because of my behavior that you are now hugging a man who is not yet your lawful husband. It's I your sister who must ask forgiveness, Nina," she said quietly to herself.

The calendar lay open and she stared at the dates again. Tomorrow would be her birthday. She would be thirty. Tomorrow would be her birthday. She resigned herself to the birthdays, which, as they came up, now caused so much distress and anxiety to those around her. Thinking it over with herself, she made a resolution: she would speak to her sister and to her parents. She would say straight out that Nina should let her love find its proper religiously lawful expression. She would tell her parents that in all sincerity she had no objection to being 'stepped over' and that she was ready and had the fortitude to face the gossip of the neighbors.

She ended the *maghrib* prayer with a long additional prayer. She spoke her heart to the Almighty, she gave vent to all her sorrow and her hopes. "*Robby la tadzarny fardan wa anta khoirul waritsiin,*" she said ending the prayer, the prayer that she had always said with a tremble in her lips, carrying her hopes, her pain, and her fears.

Héna Sumarni

Decided by a Stroke of Fate

"Grandfather, may you find happiness in eternity."

It was evening and a person stood looking up at the moon. Very still on the balcony of the second floor, she was gazing into the distance. A purple jumper clothed her well-formed figure. And a thin shawl around her neck was rippling gently, touched lightly by the evening breeze.

On that balcony of the second floor, her gaze settled on the tips of the tall *cemara* trees. The evening air was cold; it suited the mood of her thoughts. She was thinking of what had happened in the past and she turned her mind to her recollections of that time—a time that stood out in her memory, when her life had been decided by a stroke of fate.

"In my opinion, as your grandfather, I think it's best for you to go to university first. After you get your degree you can do whatever you want. I won't interfere. But if you don't continue your schooling now, Ina, I shall be embarrassed having to face your father's family."

Ina looked down. She mumbled to herself. "So that's it. Fine. I am being told to go to university. No asking me; just because he's embarrassed. I am being made to understand that I must listen to my grandfather. Grandfather doesn't care at all about Father being annoyed by his behavior. After all, Grandfather wasn't at all concerned when he took me away. And as for Mother, she only concerns herself with the day to day; nothing comes second to her work as a housewife."

"Look now, why don't you follow your young uncle's example? Mang Hudan doesn't question things; he follows my advice. The results are as you can see. And after all you're a woman, and its proper that you should be even more obedient than your uncle."

Ina felt even more dejected by this. She said silently, "Please, Grandfather, don't make me follow Mang Hudan's example in the rush of having to find the right course, making me want to go for something which is suitably 'womanly'."

"Tomorrow Mang Hudan will take you to the campus."

Grandfather went out of the room. What had just been decided was not open to further discussion. But in her heart of hearts she did not want to accept this, did not want to have things laid out for her as they had been for her uncle. When it was the choice of school, it was her grandfather who had decided; when it was a question of the choice of friends, again Grandfather had decided; a question of career and once more it was Grandfather who decided.

"Don't you feel worn out having to do what Grandfather says all the time, uncle?" Ina said when they were on the way to the campus next day.

"If his children and grandchildren don't listen to Grandfather, who will?"

"Rubbish. You're too soft and effeminate, just a *banci*," said Ina preceding him out of the campus parking lot. Her uncle was taken aback. He looked crossly at his young relative.

The days that followed went by quickly. Ina had begun her courses. She had lots of friends, both people in her own department and in other departments. And she had a lot of friends in other faculties, too. She was very easy-going, a loyal and warm person, so it wasn't difficult for her to make friends. But in her darker moments she was still not fully reconciled to what she had been forced to do. She couldn't banish what had happened. The happy expression which she always wore couldn't be kept up in the house. The sparkle disappeared from her eyes the moment she stepped over the threshold. And when she had gone into the house, she had no desire to talk or answer questions. Everything around her took on the appearance of big boulders, boulders the size of a buffalo. One by one they descended on her like punishments. One by one they left her feeling depressed. Her behavior seemed to be hemmed in by those boulders, which were her grandfather's dictates. When Aunt Tuti fled from the house, when Irma went off and never returned, when Uncle Ida found it much more to his liking to live abroad with Om Karlos, Grandfather's behavior changed dramatically. One by one his commands felt even more oppressive to those left behind. This was especially the case for Ina and her young uncle.

"Grandfather, I'm supposed to take part in a campus event. Nearby in Jayagiri. May I go?"

He folded up the newspaper he was reading and put it on the table. Then he reached for his cup of coffee and took a sip.

"Call your uncle. Say that Grandfather wants him."

Ina went into the house and soon came back followed by her uncle, Hudan.

"'Dan, what is this event in Jayagiri?" said Grandfather.

"Oh that. It's for freshmen. It's organized by the student union. It's intended to strengthen the bonds of students in the same department and bring them closer together."

"Are you going?"

"No. There's something else I have to attend. I need to go to Cireundeu with Sandi. But if Ina wants to take part, I can ask a friend to take care of her."

"All right. Just so long as I don't have to worry. Now that you mention Sandi, he hasn't called round here for some time. Has he been busy?'

"Yes, he has. Sandi is involved in a lot of things.'

"You have my permission to go to Jayagiri, Ina. But mind you, take care of yourself. Where are you meeting?"

"At the campus. Thank you, Grandfather, for permission."

"That's fine. Take care when you're there."

Ina was very pleased. She could imagine what fun it was going to be meeting her friends on campus. She loved joking around with them, laughing, looking out for one another; it was another world, a much wider one. At the moment, her world was only a small corner of a valley, a valley encircled by rocky cliffs which manifested themselves in her grandfather's commands, which to her mind were extraordinarily feudal and dictatorial.

She was so surprised that at first she hardly know how to react. It had just been a passing whim that she would have liked to take part in the event. Usually she would not have been allowed to. And so she would have felt rather indifferent to it all, since it was unlikely that she would be allowed to do anything she wanted. It was always up to her grandfather to decide whether something was worth attending. But now? Suddenly she was full of animation and eager to talk about what was planned. She couldn't believe her good fortune that her grandfather had agreed.

Arya Muldiawan, that was his name. The boy she had got to know on campus. She experienced a different kind of feeling every time she happened to bump into him, a feeling that she couldn't put a name to. In the stillness of his gaze, Ina looked to find the peace and calm that she had been looking for all this time. The depression she felt would perhaps lift if she could lean against his breast. She liked to fantasize: how beautiful her world would be if there could come a time when she could be constantly by his side: Arya.

"Ina, someone is asking for you," said Lia.

"Who?"

"I don't know. I haven't seen him before, but he looks as if he's a year or two above us."

Someone was coming towards her from the student office. Ina didn't know how to react. The person coming towards her was Arya. The boy she had just now been thinking about.

"Are you Ina?" he asked.

"That's right."

"Hudan's niece?"

'Yes."

"Are you coming to Jayagiri then?"

She nodded in answer. The expression on her face brightened. So here was a quick way to get to know him; a better way to get closer to him than if it was just the relationship of an older student to a younger one. What a surprise that he was a friend of her uncle's!

"When I come to pick you up at the house, I'd like to say hello to your grandfather. I visited a couple of times before, when I was in the first year," he said speaking as though he already felt close to her, like an elder brother.

"That's fine. We'll expect you," Ina said.

And it all worked out. After that one occasion, Arya came to the house frequently. One couldn't imagine how close a friend of Hudan's he had suddenly become. And as for Ina, she was overjoyed; she was at her happiest whenever she had to bring out a drink for the guest. She got to know what he liked, a cup of coffee; "coffee h.s.s.," she said, was the way Arya expressed it: coffee hot, sweet and strong. And to accompany it, a snack of boiled bananas made in her own way by Bi Iwen in the kitchen. Ina knew his dress style, too. "Casual." "Cool, very cool." Everything about him appeared to affect her deeply. Well, that was love for you.

They had been seeing each for several months. And he had now been a frequent visitor for some time, but Arya still hadn't expressly stated that he loved her. On the campus, by contrast, all her friends teased her. They all asked her when the big day was. They were all claiming the tax—the tax for celebrating the announcement. It was obligatory, they said to her. She would have to treat them, whether it was an outing to the noodle-soup restaurant or to the Cairo Lamb Roast place. Ina only smiled shyly when she was teased like this. When she replied that there was nothing between her and Arya, her friends didn't believe her.

Ina was a little surprised. She hoped it wasn't because Arya was afraid of her grandfather. Since he was a frequent visitor, Arya knew her grandfather's character very well. He knew the way in which her grandfather ruled the household with a rod of iron. That was it, perhaps; that was why he had not said anything about his love for her, Ina reasoned with herself.

"In the circumstances, there would be no embarrassment in the woman being the first to express her affection? Or have I been deceiving myself all this time? I hope it's not a case of a one-sided love affair?"

She got up from the settee and sat down at her desk.

"I feel like writing him a letter. Never mind that letter-writing isn't in fashion these days. I don't think that I need to have any religious scruples about it; there's nothing that says a woman shouldn't write first and express her feelings. In fact it's better than letting things drag on. After all, if there's no response to the letter, there will be no real embarrassment, because one's friends won't know about it. So I think I should write a letter."

She pursed her lips, half-anxious, half-smiling. Then she set about writing a letter, addressed to Arya, who she hoped had been in love with her all this time.

> *To Kang Arya, at his residence*
> *First of all please forgive me for having the presumption to send you this letter. I hope that you don't feel offended by it. Kang*

Arya, you know that it hasn't been a year yet since we have been acquainted with each other. I don't know how it began, but I immediately liked you. And naturally my feelings have become even stronger since you started visiting the house. My hopes have grown and flourished and they have now taken me over completely. I hope that these hidden feelings are not confined to me but are to be found within you too.
One who loves you constantly,
Marlina Adiwikarta

Before she put the letter in an envelope, she re-read it several times, looking to see whether there were any words which were not appropriate, or where the expression wasn't quite right. When she was sure, she put the letter on her dressing table. She intended to give it to her uncle to pass on. Later that afternoon Arya was bound to come to see her uncle. She sprawled out on her bed. Eyes wide open, she looked at the ceiling, and in her thoughts she anticipated Arya's arrival. Usually he went straight in to her uncle's room. They strummed around on guitars or played their favorite music, played electronic games, surfed the internet, and sometimes there was just silence if they went to sleep. They crept out of the room only if they heard Grandfather calling out to tell them it was time to eat or that it was time to go to the mosque to pray. And while she was daydreaming like this, she fell asleep.

She wasn't aware of it when Arya did arrive. It was Bi Iwen who had the privilege of receiving him.

"Your friend Arya is here," she said knocking on the door of Hudan's room.

"Ask him to come straight in, Bi. And ask Ina to make some coffee."

"Miss Ina's asleep. Let me do it." Arya entered the room and a little later Bi came in with a tray bringing the coffee.

Not long after that Ina woke up. She quickly looked at her watch. It was four in the afternoon. She jumped off the bed and reached for a comb. She tugged at her hair, combing the tresses that reached her waist. Then she went directly to the door of her room and opened it. In the lounge there was a jacket and a motorcycle helmet. They were of course Arya's. She drew the curtain and, yes, she saw Arya's Vixion motorbike standing in the drive. Ina went back into her room and took up the letter. Then she walked quietly to her uncle's room. There was silence. There was no sound of a guitar being plucked or music being played on the sound system. She smiled to herself.

"They must be asleep," she thought. "Just like two dozy snoozers. They study together for some assignment and then fall asleep and start snoring." She tried the door quietly. It hadn't been locked. She opened it. Then she shuddered as she had never shuddered before. She wanted to scream and scream but the scream didn't come. She covered her lips with the envelope she was carrying. What she saw was two bodies twined together in the lust of love-making. As she stood beside this scene of strange passion, her vision was clouded by darkness, and she wanted to weep. A howl seemed to be running through her whole person, but it found no expression. Instead what she said, in a voice which was almost a whisper, was, "Mang Hudan is a banci, Mang Hudan is a banci."

Déni A. Hendarsyah

The Boy in My Class

Sometimes I felt like slapping or kicking the boy, if I had been allowed to. You can imagine; from the time classes started, right through to the end of the day, all that boy in my class did was cause a disturbance. If you didn't watch him, he was forever interfering with the others who were getting on with their work. I had told him off endless times, but far from his behavior improving, it had got worse.

I was a new teacher in the school. It had only been a few months before that I had received my letter of appointment. Although I would be far from my parents and although I was a woman, I went out to the school. After I had presented my letter of appointment to the principal, I asked whether she could help me find a place I could rent. I was lucky because the headmistress said right away that I could stay at the official school house.

So I tried to make myself feel at home staying there. In the first two months, I was not entirely happy, but come the third month onward I had become used to it, although I was on my own and didn't have any company there—not because I was choosy, but because I was unmarried.

In the school I was the class teacher of the second year, and it was in that class that I came face to face with the pupil who was causing me so much grief. In terms of his appearance, he was a handsome boy, well turned out. He was clean and tidy even though he was a village boy. And his name, Budi—which as you know means of an honest and generous nature—matched his appearance. But I was at my wit's end in relation to his behavior. If I was good to him, this encouraged him to behave badly. If I threatened him, he would only mimic what I said and be quite indifferent. I didn't know what I could do to bring him under control. I thought to myself, just supposing I was married and had a child and that child behaved like the boy in my class, how awful it would be. The boy in the class was bad enough, and that was only five hours a day from seven to twelve. And on Sunday there was no school. But my thoughts were confined to my imagination, since at that point I wasn't even engaged.

I once asked the class teacher of the first year about him. She had taught the boy. What did she say? She told me this.

"Well, Ayi," she began, addressing me by the term for younger sister because, I suppose, I was younger than her, "In the first year Budi was very good, clever, no problem. And he was clean and tidy, unlike the other boys. And look at his reports; they're all good. And he was always first in the rankings in class in his first year."

"But why, Bu, has he become the way he is in the second year? Is it because of the way I'm teaching or is there something else?"

"I don't know, but it would be best, I think, if one tried to get close to him. Since in that way, one hopes, it may become clear what has led to him becoming like this. I am not making it up, in the first year he was well-behaved."

Hearing what she had to say, I was uncertain what to do. But now at least I had something to think about. There must have been some incident or something that had arisen in relation to the boy. In fact I had suspected this for some time. Because if I looked into his eyes, it was as though they were reflecting his feelings and something disturbing was going on there. This suspicion, coupled with the information which the first-year class teacher gave me, that he had been well-behaved in his first year, made it seem certain that something major had happened to Budi.

After talking to the first-year teacher and hearing her suggestion that I try to get close to Budi, I decided to follow her advice. Almost every day I tried to engage Budi in conversation at the end of school. I tried every way I could to reach him. Now whenever he was naughty in class, I didn't glare at him; I ignored his behavior. It was only after class that I held him back and asked him why he had disrupted the class by doing this and that. And if he happened not to have done his homework, I would question him and ask why he hadn't done it. And while he was explaining, I would look at him closely and pay attention to the way he spoke, to the explanation, in fact to everything. I even observed closely the expression in his eyes while he looked at me.

I had been trying to get to know Budi for about a month, and there was a very noticeable change in him after that. In class he was now not that badly behaved and didn't disturb his classmates any more. And he used to latch on to me. If I had finished my work, he would often approach me to talk. When I was teaching him something, I could see now how he became interested, although he still often didn't do his homework. But, well, his behavior certainly had changed from what it had been in the previous months. As I watched this change, I began to observe him even more closely. There wasn't any aspect of his behavior that I didn't pay attention to. I went further and tried to get to know him better, to get to know him as well as possible, so that everything would come out. In fact in my efforts to get to know him, I used to invite him to come to my house.

It was very clear that Budi was indeed changing. The more one paid attention to him, the better behaved he became; and he now came over to my house very frequently. This was of benefit to me, since I felt I had company in the house and I wasn't just alone.

But the change in Budi's behavior from being badly behaved to being good had been strange, because it had all happened in a relatively short time, in about a month and a half. I felt surprised and very happy about this. What had it been that had made Budi become badly behaved? I couldn't yet work it out, though I had been trying for a month and half to get close to him. I often had conversations with him, but not once had he talked about his family and how he got on with them. I had asked him several times but he never replied.

And then on one occasion I said to Budi that I wanted to visit his home. He seemed to ponder this.

"Why are you having to think about it, Budi? Am I not permitted to come to your house?"

"Yes, yes, you are, Miss. But I shall have to let my father know first, Miss."

"Of course, please do. Say that I should like to come to your house on Saturday. That's the day after tomorrow. So if you ask your father now whether I can come or not to your house, then tomorrow you can tell me what your father said."

"Yes, Miss."

The next day before classes began, Budi came up to me. From his expression he seemed very cheerful.

"Miss, Father said that he will expect you. So you'll come tomorrow?"

"Yes, yes, I will. So it's all right for me to come?"

"Yes, Miss. Father particularly said that he would expect you. We'll go there together."

I was pleased to hear this. I especially wanted to visit Budi's house because I wanted to know about his family. I had asked the other teachers in the school and I had even asked the headmistress, but no one knew anything. So that was a further reason for wanting to go to his home.

School ended at noon. I went briefly to my house and then I went off with Budi, happy to follow him to wherever his house was. The house turned out to be quite a long way from school. Furthermore, it seemed to take a long time, since one had to cut across rice fields. This explained why none of the teachers knew anything about Budi's family, since it was clear that the house was some way distant from the school.

We reached the house a little time after one o'clock.

"This is very impressive, this house of Budi's," I said to myself looking at the house. "No wonder Budi is different from the other children; he's from a well-off family." I gazed around as we went in through the front gate and walked towards the porch. But before I could say anything, the door was opened by someone inside. Out from the door came a good-looking man. I quickly said a greeting, "*Assalamualaikum.*"

"*Wa'alaikumsalam.* Welcome to the house. Please come in and sit down, Miss," said the good-looking man.

"Thank you," I replied without ceremony. Then I took off my shoes and looked at Budi.

Budi seemed to be expecting my glance, because he immediately said, "Miss, this is my father."

I just nodded hearing what he said, though in fact I was saying to myself, "He's very young, Budi's father. And good-looking. No wonder his son's handsome."

After taking off my shoes, I went into the house. I was rather taken aback when I entered. Just looking from the doorway I could already see that the furniture and trappings in the house were of high quality, whereas my own things were very modest.

"Please, Miss, sit down," said the owner of the house, inviting me to be at my ease. "I must thank you for taking the trouble to come to my modest dwelling," he went on.

"Oh not all, not at all," I replied in some confusion. Then, before sitting down, I shook hands and introduced myself. For a moment neither he nor I said anything.

"Excuse me just a moment. I want to get something from the back."

"Yes, please, go ahead."

He rose from his seat and went into the back of the house. He was soon back again, carrying a tray with two glasses of tea and some snacks.

"Oh, don't worry about me. Don't go to so much trouble."

"It's no trouble. Besides, I have to thank you again for being prepared to come to this house, such as it is. Please have some tea."

"Thank you, thank you. I seem to have inconvenienced you by my visit."

"Oh no, not at all. As it happens, I've just finished something I had to do. But may I ask straight away if there is any particular reason for your visit?"

"No, there isn't. I just wanted to make your acquaintance. It's just a friendly visit."

"Oh, I see. When Budi gets back from school he often talks about you. And he says he often goes round to your house, and that's the reason why he doesn't get back till late in the afternoon."

"Yes, that's right. Budi does often come round to the house. Do you mind? Perhaps it causes you concern."

"No, no. On the contrary, I must thank you, since Budi used to become rather moody staying here at home. So I'm grateful to you. Since he's taken to visiting you, when he comes back here he no longer gets into one of his moods."

"I see," I nodded. "May I ask? Is his mother out?"

But to my surprise he said nothing for a moment. The expression on his face changed to one of sadness. He looked down. For a few moments the atmosphere was not as it had been before. Then he got up again and spoke.

"The truth is that Budi's mother died when he was moving up into the second year."

"Oh goodness, I didn't mean to bring back painful memories."

"No, it's all right. Perhaps it was just fate. She died when she was giving birth to her second child. When it happened she bled a lot and there was nothing that could be done. And the child, who was premature, didn't survive either. It was that that led Budi to become depressed and moody. I felt it very much. And now there are just the two of us here in the house, no one else. I feel that I have neglected Budi. As far as his outward needs are concerned, he lacks nothing—but inside I don't know. I have heard that he's badly behaved in school. I was unable to do anything about it except work hard. I wanted so much to comfort him. But now he seems to me to be completely changed. And that is all since he started visiting you. In fact I had been wanting for some time to get to know you. I wanted to thank you because you've been so good, taking an interest in him."

I could only nod hearing what he said. Now everything was clear, even though I hadn't asked. I knew why Budi had become badly behaved. He wanted attention, it appeared. But why had no one at school been told that Budi's mother had passed away? I don't know, I was only new at the school.

After *ashar* I took my leave. I had spent a long time talking to Budi's father. Mostly we talked about Budi. Where Budi was at the time I don't know. In fact I enjoyed talking to his father, but it crossed my mind that it did not look quite proper to pay a visit to a widower like this, especially since there was no one else in the house.

But when I was taking my leave and going out of the gate, what he said then made me think.

"Just supposing, Miss, I was to come and visit you from time to time at your house. Would that be all right or not with you? I would like to get to know you better."

That's what he said. But to my surprise the light in his eye seemed to say something else. At the time I couldn't reply. I simply nodded.

Usép Romli H.M.

A Sackful of Earth

Who doesn't like the idea of an extensive plot of leveled land? One which lies on a plateau between the mountains, which faces north and so catches the sun which always shines bright and clear? Everyone likes the idea. And indeed there are people who are obsessed by it. They want to own it. If they have the money to buy it—or if the owner wants to sell— then it's just *clunk-clunk*, money down, and it's done. And then it would be cleared and prepared for the erection of a large villa, "Beautiful Tranquility." How pleasant it is to have such daydreams.

Barja, the *lurah*, the village head, had such thoughts. He wanted to own land like that. But not for himself. He would sell it on to that man called "Big Boss," whoever he was, a retired official or army officer, perhaps a successful business man. The thing was that the previous week he had come here from the town on purpose. He had gone around up and down the country roads around there, through the villages. He had been in an expensive four-wheel drive, a Rubicon. A well-built driver had sat behind the wheel. And he was accompanied by two men, a private secretary and a bodyguard. They both had flattened-down sleek hair.

They had come to the district of Pasir Pangematan and Situ Bungbulang and reached the village of Kelewih, which was under the authority of Barja. He was still young. In his forties.

"Do you know who owns the land? Would they be willing to sell it or not?" the Big Boss asked his secretary, who was following behind him. The person addressed quickly came to attention. He saluted and said, "I'm at your command, sir. I'll find out for you." He wanted to show due respect and express his readiness to fulfill the mission given to him.

While gazing at the lake, the Big Boss imagined what a villa would look like on that plot of land. It would stand out conspicuously on the plateau. It would be constructed in this and that fashion. He would commission the architect Jomantara, who had recently acquired a reputation for designing very expensive luxury buildings.

"Exactly right as a hideaway to keep Indah Jelita," Big Boss suddenly said to himself. His thoughts turned to the person he had married in a clandestine *kawin siri* religious ceremony four months previously. She had been starting out on a career as an actress. She had just had roles in two television series, and those were only servant roles. "I was lucky that I spotted her. If she had been allowed to become a well-known star then she would quickly have been snapped up by someone else. She has a lovely slim figure; it would be a pity not to enjoy it. A pointed chin, thin lips, an exotic face. She's tall; her skin is a glistening brown. Ah Indah, Indah. It was no sacrifice buying her a Lamborghini. And I shall give her a villa and some money in the bank...."

Big Boss sighed softly, carried away by his imaginings. He thoughts wandered. Why, why? If only he had met Indah fifteen or twenty years ago, then it would have been even more wonderful. When he was still full of the "joy and vision of life" he only had to see something and he became stiff with excitement. The principle underlying his life had been "life's struggle" or "living for the struggle." The passion and energy had just poured out of him.

It was different now. Now he had reached the stage of "struggling to live." It was very difficult to become involved with pretty women when business was always pressing.

"But back then I probably couldn't have afforded to 'buy'. I had a very humble position. I wasn't making anything from deals on the side. Never mind a Lamborghini or a Ferrari, even buying a second-hand minibus was only possible by taking a loan from the cooperative." Big Boss sighed regretfully. He experienced a sharp twinge of jealousy. When he was not there, who knows, Indah probably made out with someone else, with some young buck who was full of spirit and energy.

He ceased daydreaming. Two people had come to meet him—Barja accompanied by the village secretary.

"This is the village head I was referring to," his personal assistant explained.

Big Boss welcomed them and held out his hand to greet them. The village head and the secretary shook his hand in turns.

After briefly introducing themselves Big Boss asked them what the situation was in regard to the land and the lake in front of it. Barja quickly explained. He made everything seem simple and straightforward so that Big Boss would feel more eager to carry out his plan to buy. He imagined the commission he would get from the transaction. He would pick up a little something from both parties, from the seller and the purchaser. If the land was sold at Rp. 500,000 a *tumbak*, without a doubt that would be worth a few hundred million to him.

"That land has been left uncultivated for some time now, Big Boss," Barja said persuasively. "In total there's about two hectares. The land which extends down to the lake is four hundred *tumbak*. The owner doesn't seem to have any use for it, since he spends most of his time in town. If someone was to offer a good price for it, I am sure he would sell quickly."

"And how much is the going rate for land around here?" Big Boss said at the same time indicating to his assistant that he should take out his calculator.

"Ready." The assistant set his mobile phone on calculator mode.

"On average it's 700,000 per *tumbak*. The land which stretches down to the lake, however, would be two million." Barja made up a figure which matched his idea of a tidy profit for himself. In fact at the most the land around there was only 200,000. And as for the land extending down to the river, there was no certainty that the owner wanted to sell it. But Barja's thoughts had turned to Rosita, the PE teacher whom he tumbled whenever he could, who had a sexy figure, and an inviting smile. She had features like Chaterina Wilson, and for the last month she had been going on about wanting a Honda Jazz.

"I'm fed up with the motorbike. I can't stand the cold wind," was what Rosita had said while nestling up to his chest in a hotel room in Cipanas, before doing it twice in succession.

"Of course, darling." Barja closed his lips on hers. And then played tongues. Then withdrawing he said softly. "Of course you'll have a silver Honda Jazz…"

Hearing his whisper, she had stirred; she sighed, uttered a sharp cry of pleasure, kissed again, withdrew again. Whispered.

"Again? A third time, shall we?" She pushed out her lower lip.

Barja nodded. Saw the inviting look in her eye. Kissed the protruding lip.

And now the money for buying the Honda Jazz was there in front of him; he could see it.

Indeed he felt as though he already had it in his grasp, the money that would be forthcoming from this colonel. He imagined it all. Two hectares at 700,000 a *tumbak* would come to 980 million. For the owner of the land this would come to 280 million, leaving him with 700 million. And as for the village secretary and the various officials, the *camat*, the Koramil, police at the station, 200 million would be enough for them. He would divide it out among them.

The rest, 500 million would be all for him. He would use it to buy a Honda Jazz for Rosita. And the remainder he would use to have a good time, including trying to get his way with Neng Yenni, one of the tellers in the local *kecamatan* bank.

"Thank you, Almighty, for showing the way," Barja never ceased praying. He would be saved by this windfall, perhaps, since he had previously made up his mind that he would embezzle the money from the free distribution of rice.

But the money was not yet in his pocket. And indeed, not only was the transaction not yet concluded, he had not even yet approached the owners of the land and persuaded them to sell.

"But am I not the senior person in the village? Why shouldn't I be able to do it?" His heart thumped as Big Boss held out a thick envelope to him. For operational costs, he said.

On his return to the office, riding on the back of the village secretary's red number-plated official motorbike, he asked to stop off at Oboy's small roadside coffee shop, saying that he wanted to have a pee. He went to the toilet next to the kitchen and took out the envelope which the colonel had given him and counted the contents. There was three million. He took out three notes and quickly went out again. He said goodbye to the shop owner and got back on to the bike, which had kept its engine running.

And then on to the village office building. Lurah Barja went in to his office and called the village secretary.

"Take this 300,000 and use it. To help along the process of persuading the people of Pasir Pangematan to sell their land. Tell them that the price offered is 100,000 a *tumbak*. If they ask for more, don't go above 200,000." Lurah Barja held out the money to the village secretary, who had just sat down on the chair in front of the village head's desk.

The secretary didn't bother to say anything and quickly went out again. He called the *punduh* (village representative) under whose authority Pasir Pangematan lay. He gave him 100,000.

"Divide this up among the *hansip* village watch. So that they persuade the people of Pasir Pangematan to sell their land. It's important that they succeed. Once Big Boss has paid out, then we'll all get a bigger share."

The *punduh* nodded. He made a calculation. If he bought five packets of cigarettes, that would come to fifty thousand for the five young men of the watch. That would leave him with fifty thousand to add a bit more to his household expenditure that day.

"Of course the people of Pasir Pangematan will want to sell their land. Rather than let it remain idle, far better to sell it to someone who can make something of it. And then whatever is done with it, of course, the management of it will be handed to the people there. Casual labor will certainly be required," the village secretary quickly said. He hid his uneasiness at being caught fingering the two hundred thousand, before stuffing it into his shirt pocket.

A week later rumors were circulating in the village of Kelewih. They came from Pasir Pangematan. There were protests. People were asking about the village head's intentions. The news spread like wildfire. At that moment, a large number of people had assembled near the religious school. They could be heard loudly expressing their opinions:

"We're being treated like doormats by the village head. He's trampling on us to make some money for himself. It's not right; the Pasir Pangematan land is being valued for purchase at 50,00 a *tumbak*.

"Who's valuing it at that?" asked an astonished voice from the back.

"The *punduh* and Sanadi the *hansip*."

"Find the *punduh* and Sanadi and bring them here!" said a loud voice at the back.

"And bring the village head with them," an even louder voice added, increasing the general animosity.

"Drag them here, drag them here!" said the voices of some who were deliberately trying to provoke trouble. They shook their fists in the air.

It was the hottest part of the day. They had just said the noonday prayer. The pupils who were on their way to the religious school were thronging in front of the entrance to their classrooms.

"Burn! Burn!"

Some people were banging used paint cans by the school. There was a ringing noise as the metal flagpole was hit repeatedly. There were some people throwing their hats in the air. There were some who were jumping about with excitement. Feelings against the village head and *hansip* were running high.

"Come on, let's demonstrate in front of the village offices! A demo, a demo!" Some were egging the others on.

"There's no one at the offices," someone said in response to this. "The village head's at a meeting in the district office. And the village secretary and the others are God knows where."

"What's all this commotion?" said an authoritative voice. Those who were making the noise suddenly stopped. There was silence. Everyone looked towards the entrance of the religious school. Ajengan Holil, the head of the religious school, was looking at the crowd, examining their faces one by one.

"It's this, your honor, the matter of the Pasir Pangematan land," explained Pa Uja, a member of the village council.

"What's that?" asked Ajengan Holil.

Straightaway, the words tumbling out, Pa Uja explained. He said that there had been reports that the people felt they were being forced, compelled, by Sanadi to sell their land at 50,000 a *tumbak*. It wasn't just one or two people who felt they were being pressured to sell. There were around fourteen or fifteen people involved.

"But so far there has been no buying or selling?" asked Ajengan Holil.

"Not yet. There has just been mention of a price and the pressure," Pa Uja said.

After a moment's silence, Ajengan Holil said quietly, "Wait then, let's not rush into things. I'll go and see Barja. I'll tell him not to touch the land in Pasir Pangematan, or any other land in the countryside here around Kelewih. For the moment just disperse. But if my efforts come to nothing, then you can go ahead with your demonstrations."

Everyone agreed. People started drifting away until there was no one left in the courtyard of the school.

That evening, Ajengan Holil went to visit Barja, who received his guest warmly. Not because he was a religious teacher, but because he was of his father's generation. And because from the time when they were young, Ajengan Holil and Barja's father, Sobana, had been friends. Sobana had often said to his son that he should listen to Ajengan Holil and not contradict him in any way. Because Ajengan Holil was one of those people who were "exceptional." He possessed special qualities. He had spiritual powers which were the wonder of all, dating from the time that he was still studying at religious school.

Once a leopard had descended from Mount Handeuleum and had come into the neighborhood and preyed upon the goats and the chickens and other livestock, but it had been brought under control by Holil, who at that time had just returned from the religious school in Tasik. As it happened, the leopard had just been cornered, and the rifles of soldiers from a company who had been called out from their barracks for the purpose had been cocked ready to fire.

"Don't shoot," Holil abruptly said to them. "The leopard is protected under the law. It would be irresponsible to break the law. Let me tell it to go back."

Holil walked toward the jackfruit tree where the leopard was cowering. He picked up a handful of earth and grabbed it tight in his fist.

"Hey you, leopard. Go back to Mount Handeuleum at once. Don't ever come again. Go before this handful of earth is blown away in the wind." And he threw the handful of earth high into the air.

Whoosh, whoosh. The leopard as big as a young frisky goat jumped out towards a stand of *salak* trees. The leaves crackled underfoot as it leapt away through the shrubs straight back to the mountain.

That had been Sobana's story. It had happened in 1970. Barja had not yet been born. Another story of Sobana's about the amazing powers of Ajengan Holil concerned the general elections of 1977. Barja had a dim memory of the affair. At that time he was, after all, only five years old. The head of the *hansip* contingent at that time was being very intimidating towards people who had not put up in the windows of their houses posters showing a picture of the Banyan Tree, the symbol of the government party, Golkar. Those who put up pictures of the Kabah, the symbol of the Muslim party, or the Buffalo Head, the symbol of the Nationalist Party, were treated to a tongue-lashing. And indeed there were those whom he was inclined to slap. Including Holil, who at that time was still studying at the religious school in Tasik.

The *hansip* chief was looking for Holil, because it had been reported that he had been putting up pictures of the Kabah in various houses. He was searching all over for him and found him collecting coconuts from his plot of land.

"I was with him at the time," said Sobana to his son years later, when the boy had grown up and was in the midst of campaigning in the elections of the Reformation period post-1998.

All of a sudden the *hansip* chief had tried to hit Holil on his back with his stick. He wanted to grab hold of him and attack him when he wasn't expecting it. But the blow missed. In a trice the commander's arm was caught and held hard and Holil asked: "What are you doing?"

"It's your fault. Why the hell are you putting up pictures of the Kabah in the neighborhood?" the *hansip* chief cried out, grimacing at the pain of his arm being twisted.

"Am I not allowed to?" Holil replied curtly.

"N-n-no you're not," the man cried out in even more pain.

"Who says I'm not?" Holil snapped.

"My, my superiors…" the man whined. Holil concentrated, thus increasing the pain in the arm, making it unbearable.

"And who are these superiors of yours?" Holil snapped again.

"The… village head, the *babinsa* corporal, the police chief, the district head, the governor, the presi… dent ow, ow!" The *hansip* chief shrieked louder.

"You're a damned liar!" Holil interrupted. "This election has been called by the President. It is being contested by three parties with the symbols of the Kabah, the Banyan Tree and the Buffalo Head!"

"I don't… know about that, but my superiors have said that only the picture of the Banyan Tree can be displayed in the neighborhood. The other pictures are forbidden— Ow, ow!" The man yelled as Holil released him. He fell back, tottered and hit his head against a coconut tree. And then collapsed.

"Unless you apologize to me and lick a chicken's ass, you will be crippled for life."

The *hansip* chief stumbled away, trying to bear the pain and holding his crippled arm with his other hand. He immediately reported the matter to the village head and to the corporal of the local detachment. He showed them his crippled right arm. He said that he had been badly injured by Holil. Of course listening to him they were angry. Especially since it was all connected with the election, with the business of putting up a picture that was not the picture of the Banyan Tree.

A day or so later, Holil was summoned to the village office. The *babinsa* corporal walking beside him shouted at him. And indeed the man was on the point of hitting him with his stick. But he drew back when he heard Holil's threat, quietly uttered, but firm:

"If you want a fight, I'll cripple you like I did the *hansip*!"

Eventually the village head was ingratiating and begged Holil to treat the *hansip* chief, to make him better again. "Poor man, he can't use his mattock to work in his fields. Where will his wife and children turn if he is not able to provide for them?" the village head said in a wheedling voice.

"All right, I'll deal with him, but he must change his ways, not be so quick to use his hands. And he will have to ask forgiveness from all those he has slapped because they did not put up pictures of the Banyan Tree or put up pictures of the Kabah instead. Bring him here. I'll be able to treat him, I hope, and God permitting he'll be fit again."

The *hansip* chief was brought in to the village office. His face was pale, his eyes sunken. His right arm hung limp. For two days and two nights he had tossed and turned finding it difficult to sleep, difficult to eat.

"If you want to be fit again, you'll have to ask the forgiveness of all those people you've mistreated during this campaign period. Are you willing to do that?" Holil said to him sharply.

"Y-y-yes I am. Ow-ow," the man whined.

"And you, and you, Corporal," Holil addressed the village head and the *babinsa* corporal who were standing beside the *hansip* chief. "It's time now to catch a chicken. You must ask some of the *hansip* men to get it. Then all the time while I am massaging the *hansip* chief's arm, he will have to be licking the chicken's hole. And before that, that same hole will already have been licked five times each by you, and you, Corporal."

"What?" The village head and the corporal looked hard at him. They were dumbfounded that they should have to lick the chicken's asshole five times each.

"Wasn't the *hansip* chief so fierce on those who had put up pictures other than the Banyan Tree, because he was ordered to act like that by his superiors? By the village head and the corporal. Wasn't that the case, Hansip Chief?"

The *hansip* chief nodded weakly.

Straightaway the *hansip* men brought in a chicken tied up with string.

"Are you ready to start the cure that will restore the feeling to the *hansip* chief's arm as it was before?" Holil half-shouted at them. He said a *bismillah* and then mumbled another prayer. Then he turned to the village head and the corporal.

"Right. Now if the *hansip* chief's crippled arm is to be healed, you, and you, Corporal, have to lick the chicken's hole five times each. *Bismillah!*"

Being forced to do so, the village head and the detachment corporal took it in turns to lick the chicken's hole.

It was covered with shit. When they'd licked it, the two ran off to the gutter outside, tried to rinse their mouths out, and vomited repeatedly.

"Now it's your turn to lick the chicken's hole while your crippled arm is being massaged," said Holil, ordering the *hansip* men to put the chicken's ass to the *hansip* chief's lips. Several of those looking on shivered, while at the same time trying to suppress their smiles.

There were no unforeseen consequences. The *hansip* chief's arm was normal again. There was no sign of there having been any injury. It was just as it had been before. Before leaving, Holil spoke to them all, especially addressing his remarks to the village head and corporal.

"If you ever again intimidate anyone who doesn't put up a Banyan Tree picture or who doesn't vote for that party, you will all experience the same as happened to the *hansip* chief. And to treat the consequences will be more difficult. Because the next time you will have to lick a horse's hole!"

When Sobana asked why the treatment had to include the licking of the chicken's hole, Holil answered that he had only done it as a prank; there was no connection with the treatment. He had simply used an opportunity. When else would he have a chance to order the *hansip* chief and the village head and the *babinsa* to lick a chicken's hole?

All this was why Barja had a lot of respect for Ajengan Holil. So when the latter came to the house, he asked him immediately what he could do for him. Ajengan Holil asked him how matters really stood with the Pasir Pangematan land. Barja could not avoid the question, any more than he could lie about it. Whether he wanted to or not he had to be open about what the situation was and he spared no detail. He even mentioned the price of 200,000 a *tumbak* which he was going to sell to Big Boss for 700,000.

"Why did *hansip* Sanadi only offer 50,000 a *tumbak*," Ajengan Holil reproached him.

"That damn Sanadi; he's still a kid. He wanted too big a share for himself," Barja said tightening his mouth. He had no compunction about saying that someone else wanted too big a share, although he himself was trying to get even more.

"Well, let's leave that for the moment. Now let's go to Pasir Pangematan," Ajengan Holil interrupted.

"Now?" said the village head surprised.

"Yes, now. We have to act quickly. Do you want to wait until the people who are gathering to protest burn down the village office?" Ajengan Holil looked at him sharply.

They went out accompanied by one of the *hansip* men and the village secretary who had been picked up en route. They were told to bring a mattock, a shovel, and a sack.

Arriving at the place, Ajengan told the *hansip* man to dig up some earth, then to shovel it into the sack. When it was full to the top, Ajengan Holil told Lurah Barja to lift up the sack.

"Now use all your strength. Lift it on to your shoulders, my friend!"

Heaving and pulling, heaving again, Barja tried to lift the sack full of earth. But he couldn't. Never mind lifting it to his shoulders, he couldn't even lift it to his waist. Eventually he gave up and collapsed. He sat down in a heap, panting for breath, puffed out.

"You see you don't even have the strength to carry one sack. What will it be like then in eternity when you have to carry the earth of the whole of Pasir Pangematan?" Ajengan Holil admonished Barja. The village secretary and the *hansip* man looked on open-mouthed.

"Yes that's true, what you say, everything... everything..." the village secretary replied hoarsely.

"So tomorrow early, announce that the Pasir Pangematan land is not going to be sold after all!"

Ajengan Holil strode off looking neither to right or left, plunging through the gathering darkness of the evening.

"Whether we want to or not, sir, we'll have to obey," said the *hansip* man. "If we don't want to be burdened for eternity with the earth of Pasir Pangematan. Heaven forbid."

Barja resigned himself to it. He would have to return the three million expenses to Big Boss. He would have to bury the dream of buying a Honda Jazz for Rosita as well as that of trying to get round Neng Yenni, the teller at the *kecamatan* bank. There was absolutely nothing he could do, he was thinking, when his mobile phone went off. It was a call from Big Boss asking how the land business was coming along.

"Be quick about it. Fix it," Big Boss said to him in an abrupt tone. Barja trembled. Just as Big Boss was trembling; he had been nagged about the villa by Indah Jelita who had just arrived to ask about it. He had a week; she was going to join a club of Lamborghini owners who were intending to tour sites in Java and Bali.

Yus R. Ismail

The Leaf

"Teashur, Teashur, why is the color of leafs green?" asked Ujang who still lisped a little. The kindergarten teacher thought for moment and was silent. Yes, that's a good question, why green, she said to herself. But her actual reply was:

"It has to be green, dear."

"Who has decided it must be green?"

"Well, it's just been like that ever since."

"Ever since what?

"Leaves want to be green. Come along now; everyone has gone to play outside. They're making a snake-line. Look at your friends there; they've all left the classroom."

Ujang nodded, then walked off in search of his friends who were playing about in the schoolyard. But the teacher didn't go with him. Because she had begun to wonder, why are leaves green? She grew disturbed thinking about it. So she went off to the headmistress's room. The headmistress was in the middle of writing something, and she thought and said nothing. Then the teacher went off. She was now back to her normal self and wasn't disturbed anymore, because the cause of her feeling ill at ease had now been passed on to the headmistress.

It was the headmistress now who became ill at ease. She didn't carry on writing, because turning in her mind was the question, why is the color of leaves green? One day the headmistress went off to see the head of the local Education Department. And after she had seen him she went home. And going home she was back to her normal self; she went to the market first and bought some *petay* beans with some smoked fish, her husband's favorite. Oh, and she remembered, too, to buy a toy car for her son, who had cried because his toy car had been run over by his father's motorbike and was now in bits.

The head of the Education Department, who had been organizing the payment for some books from a publisher, could not shake off a feeling of uneasiness. When the headmistress of the school had been there, he had just said to her: "Yes, that's a very good matter for us to think about. We'll put it on the agenda for our next meeting." But when she had gone home, the head of the Education Department had shaken his head. He had just taken in the headmistress's question, "Why is the color of leaves green?" And now his mind was full of the question. Yes, why was the color of leaves green? He kept puzzling over it. So when there was a telephone call from the publisher he just said, yes, yes, and did not mention the figure he was expecting.

The head of the Education Department had still not come up with an answer. He went round to the garden at the back of the office and approached a bougainvillea flower in blossom.

"Hey, leaf, why is your color green then?" said the head of the Education Department.

The leaf, which was waving at the bee who was sucking nectar from the flower, was very surprised. And the bougainvillea flower was put out, because this was the first time that anyone had asked this.

"Come on, out with it. Why is your color green?" said the head of the Department, appearing to be angry.

"I don't know, sir. I've always been green from way back in the past."

"That may be the case, but who asked you to be green? You must know…"

"I swear, sir, I don't."

As this was happening, the breeze approached. The breeze had come along from who knows where. And just like the breeze when it comes along, it then played with the leaves. It tickled the leaves. Leaves of course are ticklish, and their twists and turns spread to the branches, which also began bobbing up and down.

The head of the Department nodded looking at them. No mistake, this was who was responsible, said the head of the Department to himself.

"Hey, breeze, you're the one then who's responsible."

The breeze was unhappy at this. He stopped playing with the leaves.

"What do you mean by responsible?"

"Come on, why is the color of leaves green? What have you done to them?"

"I swear I have done nothing to them. I've only been playing with them. And that's because the leaves are ticklish, so they like a bit of fun."

"That fun of yours is excessive. You're at it every day, aren't you? Admit it."

"But don't you know that the leaves are my friends? You can't accuse me just like that," said the breeze rather annoyed and not liking, perhaps, suddenly to be accused like that.

"Well, if it's not you, who is it then?"

"I have no idea. Look, why don't you ask the sun?" The breeze whooshed off to the west. Perhaps he was venting his anger there, because the guava fruit which was growing in profusion in the tree fell to the ground, blown down by the wind.

The head of the Department nodded his head, up and down like a horse. Yes, that was it. It looked as if it was the sun was the cause of it, he said to himself. But how could he talk to the sun? Perhaps he should shout from here, but it was too far. So the head of the Department went straight home, changed his clothes, and put on his mountain climbing gear. Then he went and climbed the Himalayas. And when he had reached the peak, yes, the sun was there, close.

"Hey, sun, why is the color of leaves green?" said the head of the Department.

The sun was put out that someone strange was asking him a question. Because as far as he knew, it was only stone cutters who persistently asked him anything.

"Hey, person, why are you asking that? Aren't I a sky creature and aren't the leaves earth creatures? Why ask me?'

"Because, and you know this, leaves like to bask in the sun and then their leaves are green."

"I don't know a thing about that. That's earth business. And are there lots of creatures that like to bask in the sun. Tortoises like basking, roof-tiles like basking, the sea also likes to bask, and cats like to bask. And Miss Imas, whom you like to wink at, she likes to bask in the sun, too."

And now it was the head of the Department's turn to feel unhappy. That was because the sun knew his secret, his winking at Miss Imas. The head of the Department went home. It was easy going home from the peak of the mountain; all you had to do was slide, like going down the slide in the children's playground at the kindergarten.

And now the problems whirling around in his head had been added to. Because now it was not only the matter of the leaves being green but also the matter of Miss Imas, who was surprised now, because for two days the head of the Department had not winked at her. Has the head of the Department some eye trouble? Miss Imas asked herself.

Because there was no one who owned up, the head of the Department reported the matter to the Regional Head of the Education Department. And the Regional Head reported it to the Provincial Head. The Provincial Head then reported it to the Minister of Education. The Minister also started to get a headache thinking, why is the color of leaves green. As it happened, the Minister was at that time about to go on a comparative study tour to Ethiopia with a team of people from Parliament. The comparative study was to do with school buildings which often collapsed. Because in Ethiopia there were no school buildings, they never collapsed. In Ethiopia school takes place in tents.

So the comparative study tour of the Minster and the members of parliament was called off, because an emergency meeting had to be held. The issue of why the color of leaves was green had to be settled first, the Minister said. The meeting went on for a day and then into the evening. The security guards who were on duty started to snore in their sleep. And the demonstrators who were out in the yard of the parliament building became bored and went off to eat some noodles and have some *cendol* as something sweet.

The meeting almost looked as though it would come to no conclusion. Because no one could be found who could come up with an answer to why the color of leaves was green. But members of Parliament are smart, aren't they? There was someone who came up with an answer, namely: who was it that had begun the question which was causing everyone's head to spin: why was the color of leaves green? The Minister called the Provincial Head of the Department, the Provincial Head called the Regional Head and the Regional Head called the Local District Head and the Local District Head called the Head of the School and the Head of the School called the teacher. The teacher trembled when she pointed to Ujang. Then the police officer with a moustache like a caterpillar immediately arrested Ujang. He was handcuffed and put into a car.

He screamed and sobbed on and on. Poor boy. No one came to help him. His father and mother were very upset when someone telephoned to tell them the news. They went off to the school, and from there to the police station. But Ujang had already been put in a cell. Poor fellow; there was no television in his cell, no refrigerator, no decent mattress, no possibility of going off to Bali to have some fun, not being able to get a manicure in Singapore or being able to watch Wimbledon, or being able to watch Barcelona play Real Madrid.

After Ujang had been put in prison, all the fathers and mothers sealed their children's lips with tape. So they couldn't say anything, so they couldn't ask anything. "You'll learn by just taking in the lesson. Work hard at memorizing it. It's easy to learn now. Isn't mathematics being taught in Indonesian now? You don't need to know the regional language, nor English nor Mandarin. And aren't the national exams just a matter of knowing things by heart?" said the mothers and fathers to their children. Only after the children had graduated from university was the tape removed. And then they got jobs. There were those who became civil servants, those who became police, those who became doctors, those who became businessmen, those who became tax officers, those who became the heads of parties, those who became members of parliament, those who became district heads, and many who became servants in foreign countries because they could speak a little English while at the same time they were despised by the foreigners because they knew nothing about their own culture, and there were those who became....

Dadan Wahyudin

Traffic Jams

"**A** traffic jam, dear," said Odih, throwing himself into a rickety bamboo chair on the veranda of his house. He was tired out. He deliberately came home at *lohor* to rest. He could say his *lohor* prayers and also eat at home, saving some money.

"Where was it this time, Kang?" His wife Imas was anxious. She seemed startled as she gathered up the sticks and dead wood for the fire. This was the wood she had managed to gather from the hillside that morning.

"Oh, it was the usual jams around Lebaran which seem to go on and on. It's been almost a week now. They're difficult to avoid," said Odih wiping off the sweat with the small towel that always hung round his neck. The sun was burning down and it was hot and uncomfortable.

"Really. Where are they all going to…?" Imas said, but didn't continue. She stirred the coffee and then handed it to her husband.

"There's an exceptional lot of traffic about," Odih said taking her up quickly while he stretched his legs. He was stiff from constantly applying the brakes, changing gear and pushing down the accelerator pedal.

"One thing I'll say. No one shows any road manners. Lots of drivers cut in from the left. They think it's their right that others should make way for them, especially if they're big trucks.

Fortunately, one can usually brake to let them in. But the result is bad traffic jams. Add to that people going back to their villages for Lebaran, hundreds of motorbikes swarming like flying ants," Odih added. Then he took a gulp of his coffee.

"Did you get many fares?" Imas half-smiled at her husband. She really meant was, is there any money from the takings for her that day. Usually before he took his rest, Odih filled up the tank of his *angkot* minibus with gasoline and brought home his takings. The daily deposit money for the hire of the *angkot* he paid out of his takings in the afternoon.

"There's about five thousand," said Odih handing over some one thousand rupiah notes. Then he got up from the chair and went to the pigeon-roost at the side of the house. Odih had three pairs of pigeons. He opened the plastic bagful of kernels of sweet corn he had bought specially at the bus terminal. He scattered them from his hand. *Kuk geruk, kuk geruk kuk.* Si Badud, the biggest pigeon, was overjoyed to be fed corn, his favorite. As well as pigeons, Odih also had chickens and ducks. It all helped. If things were tight and the money from fares had not come up to expectations, they could always eat the eggs of the chickens and ducks to stave off the children's hunger. And the chickens and ducks could always be turned into cash if there was an urgent need for money.

"Badud, Badud." Odih clicked his fingers at the pigeon. Badud cooed even louder. He participated in the fun of it all. *Kuk geruk, kuk.* Odih's smile broadened. The pigeons, the hens, the ducks— they were his pets. The medicine that soothed him. If he was to be constantly thinking of how difficult it was to earn a living, there would be no end to it. It would give him a perpetual headache. It would make him thoroughly ill. As soon as the cost of gasoline went up, the price of all daily necessities went up, too. And that meant that the cost of spare parts went up also, and this became an excuse for raising the cost of the daily hire of the *angkot*. On the

211

other hand, the number of *angkot* passengers was declining. The number of vehicles on the road, including motorbikes, was rapidly increasing. Traffic jams all along the route of Odih's *angkot* had now become a daily occurrence.

The daily route taken by Odih's *angkot,* which belonged to Haji Bana, was from Cileunyi to Sumedang. This route wasn't just for the Lebaran period. There were frequent accidents on the road when trailer trucks had tipped over or broken down. They hadn't been able to make the steep climbs or they had gone too far over to the side of the road and their wheels had caught in a ditch. Sometimes their axles snapped because the loads they were carrying were too heavy. There were also those who had taken risks in forcing a way through and had met oncoming trucks carrying coal or sand. If you weren't prepared to take on the challenges of driving in these conditions, you yourself became a cause of the traffic jam.

But the holdups lasted only an hour or so. The people whose responsibility it was soon shifted the trucks which had tipped over or had broken down. But if there was a holdup, even if it only lasted an hour, it led to stress. There was nothing to be done except be patient. If the drivers of buses and *angkot* did not have the patience, the passengers were off-loaded on to other vehicles at Cikuda. Then the *angkot* would turn around and go back. There were also those who pressed for the vehicle to go faster, but this was always accompanied by the grumbling of the driver. All throughout the journey he would mumble and complain, saying that the price of gasoline had gone up, that he had gone over his time, that daily necessities were now all very expensive. It was all designed to persuade the passengers that they should make more allowance, in other words that they should add something to the normal fare.

But Odih was not like that, even though he was in the same position and had the same problems in relation to time and gas.

He felt a sense of responsibility as the driver of an *angkot* in those circumstances. Passengers should not be inconvenienced. As far as he could, he had to take passengers to their destination in as much comfort as possible. Even if he had pressing commitments, the passenger should not suffer. He would immediately talk the matter over with a fellow driver. And then it would just remain for the passengers to clamber out of one *angkot* into another without having to pay any more.

Having a job as an *angkot* driver had not been what Odih had planned for himself. As a young man he had wanted to go into the army. But he had not been able to follow it through, since his family were simple tillers of the soil: there wasn't the money to pursue the matter. He had only completed junior high school. Fate had determined that his life would be spent on the road. From that time onwards, he had often travelled in his uncle's *angkot*. And from that experience he had learned how to drive it. And so that had become his profession.

Earning one's livelihood on the road meant working in an environment where tempers flared and people quickly became worked up. It was exactly as the *ustad* said: if you looked closely at people's behavior, it was like seeing people at a football match or a crowd on the streets. People swore and shouted and their emotions quickly came to the surface in whatever words they found to convey them. And it was quite usual to swear coarsely naming filthy animals when a person was angry. On the road, a person who in his daily life seemed a quiet sort, would glare if he was overtaken, and glower and look daggers. Then he would press down on the accelerator and chase the car that had overtaken him. On the road there were a lot of people who let emotions take over from their reason. One amusing thing that one sometimes saw was when an old clapped-out pickup truck, intended only for collecting pieces of junk, was slightly bumped, perhaps by a motorbike. The driver would get out and, arms akimbo, would walk around and wipe his rusty bumper. He would put on an angry expression, even before he had had a chance to look clearly to see whether there had been any real damage.

The *angkot* business was not what it had been in the past. Then the owners of the *angkot*, the patrons, were well-known, prosperous rich men. They had dozens of *angkot* in their fleet. They had employed lots of people. But now the situation was pitiful. Many *angkot* now lay idle, their spare parts cannibalized. Haji Bana, Odih's patron, from having dozens of *angkot* now only had two, one of which was the one Odih used.

And it wasn't only the patrons; the drivers were no different in terms of worsening conditions. After the hire of the vehicle and the cost of the gasoline had been paid, there was sometimes nothing left. And that was often because in these difficult times there were numerous "devils" who had to be paid off with offerings. Besides the daily cost of the official road duty tax, drivers often had to report in to those who were in charge in their area of operation. There were many unofficial tolls, money for waiting for passengers in a particular spot or at a place by the side of the road—all sorts of unexpected things, all requiring the payment of offerings. If one tried to call out to possible fares at the side of the road, there were always *calo*, middle-men, there, who also had to be given a little something, even though all they did was to wipe the side-mirror of the *angkot*. On the other hand, there were occasions when an *angkot* set out with a full complement of passengers, having spent some time waiting at a terminal. And then somewhere along the road, the *angkot* would get a puncture. The passengers would scramble out, not sparing a look behind them and leaving the driver to it. They wouldn't pay. There was nothing to be done. That was just the lot of drivers. In the blazing heat of the day, with the traffic whizzing by, the driver had to jack up the car. He had to work as fast as possible changing the spare tire. Cars with punctures in the middle of the road would lead to holdups.

Sometimes Odih thought about traffic jams when he was taking a break at a terminal. Clearly some people benefited from them. He wondered to himself: supposing there were no traffic jams, all those street peddlers walking from car to car offering bean curd and fruit and fried snacks—who waited at the side of the road, who were used to making a living that way—those peddlers would just be idly walking around. But they, too, had wives and children. How would they be able to make a living? The men who used performing monkeys at the road side and traffic light junctions to entertain the drivers and passengers—how would they earn a living? The Almighty was fair to all. Although holdups led to short tempers and outbreaks of emotion, some of God's creatures drew some benefit from the traffic jam.

Holdups could be regarded as a rebuke to everyone. The roads needed to be improved; they were narrow, full of potholes, and consequently when it was pitch-dark at night they were a potential cause of holdups. And then there was the behavior of people who had no conception of road manners, who felt that the road belonged to them, who cut into the path of others, who ignored traffic lights, who went very fast or caused others to have accidents. And there was the matter of government policy, which put no restrictions on people owning vehicles. And that caused holdups everywhere.

Odih had once talked over the problem of holdups with his fellow drivers.

"When there are holdups, drivers should be able to ask for extra money from passengers. There should be a proper calculation of this when fares are being negotiated. That should happen, because after all drivers depend on time to make sufficient journeys along their routes." Robin was quite firm about this when he was discussing the matter with Odih during a break at the terminal in Cileunyi.

"But the regulation for fare increases is always determined by the government, even in relation to individual routes," Odih replied.

"But when you're on the road, it's a different matter isn't it, 'Dih? It could be that there's a holdup with your woman, too. Ha ha." said Sitohang, a driver from Sumatra, butting in to the conversation and laughing. He was laughing at Odih's innocence.

"No, you couldn't do that. Not all passengers have that bit extra. Many of them just have the fare. That's why they choose to go by *angkot*, because they can't afford to take a taxi or buy their own car."

Although there are traffic jams every day, I hope my feelings don't get jammed, too. God keep my feelings charitable. I hope that I shall always be open to helping others, Odih said to himself while he stared, surprised, watching one of the terminal *calo* banging the back of a city bus slowly moving off out of the terminal. It looked as though the conductor had not yet paid the *calo* his money.

Érwin Wahyudi

My Wife

I had been working at this company for just a year, after having been made redundant from my previous job. I had had a stroke of good luck when I met old Rendi, a friend from university days.

When I had asked him a few times whether he knew of any jobs going, it chanced that his father's main office was looking to open a new branch in this town.

I was overjoyed when I received the news that I had passed the recruitment test. Not only was the place of work near my house, I had been accepted to start straight away as a manager, because it appeared they had seen that I had had previous experience as a supervisor. I was given a company car. And my staff gave me no problems. Everything was very comfortable.

But human nature being what it is, a person is never happy with what he's got. Changed circumstances affect him. Given one, he wants two. Given two, he wants three. And so it goes on and on; one is never satisfied. That was especially the case with my wife. First of all she was taken under the wing of the other women who lived in the housing estate, as well as by the mothers in our eldest child's school.

Her lifestyle became consumerist. Beginning with clothes and bags, shoes, cosmetics, all of them had to be well-known brands if one didn't want to be left behind by one's friends. There were all sorts of *arisan*, savings clubs, to join, for jewelry, pearls, kitchen gadgets, whose cost was sky-high.

As for *arisan* in which money was at issue, I don't know how many she joined. Of course one had to look one's prettiest each time there was an *arisan* taking place; and the venues had to keep on changing. At first it was small traditional eating places or restaurants in town, then they moved on from there and it was places outside town.

And one time she herself suggested to the other women that they hold their *arisan* in Bali. And when she came back from Bali she brought all sorts of things. But there was no real need for them, things like paintings, accessories, carvings and other items.

She once asked beforehand when it was the children's holiday, "Please say you agree; Bu Cakra has invited me to go with her to Singapore." And she snuggled up to me, speaking in a wheedling tone. When I asked her where was the money coming from, she only frowned. She replied by talking about something else.

"What a pity you're so busy. Just say it's OK. I want a bit of fun; I get bored in the house, and the children are now on holiday." I didn't want to drag it out; it would only be wasting time. I gave in; I had to say I agreed to it. I had to dip into office funds to pay for it all.

Every time she returned from an outing where she had been enjoying herself, the debt on the credit card would swell. Her behavior grew more extravagant; all her wants had to be met.

As time went on, things became worse. All our electrical white goods had to be replaced with new ones; the house had almost constantly to be renovated and designs changed. When I asked her about it, her reply was simply, "Everything's out of date, these are yesterday's brands and designs, dear."

And it was true, the furniture in the house was now of a sturdier design and the house was brighter and looked fresher. The jewelry she wore was more conspicuous. Her clothes were brightly colored and stood out. The children were given everything they wanted. Only, unfortunately, bit by bit I became more reckless: I was more daring taking money out of the office till for purposes for which it was not intended. I made fictitious reports and added mark-ups and used other deceits to cover my wife's expenses, which knew no bounds.

I was not the only one behaving like that. Leni, the office secretary—whose lifestyle was little different from my wife's—also became carried away by it all. She used the same methods, and in fact it was often she who showed me the way.

This day I had a splitting headache, and in addition it was very hot and stuffy in the room. The hot dry season was at its height and to make matters worse the air-conditioning was being serviced. In addition, I had not been feeling well since the morning. My heart was beating irregularly. I looked up at the wall clock. The small hand pointed to the figure two.

Kring! The office telephone rang.

"Hallo, Len. Everything OK?" I said, as I massaged my head with my free hand.

"Sir, I have just received information from the head office. They say that an audit team is coming to visit us tomorrow," said Leni and she sounded anxious.

"All right then. Thank you." *Bang.* I almost slammed down the receiver.

"Damn it." I dug my nails into my scalp. My head was spinning even more now. I suddenly felt weak, and my limbs were on the point of collapse knowing that an audit team was about to arrive next day.

I was dazed. I breathed deeply trying to relax myself. I thought about what I was going to face the next day. I gripped the table. I breathed deeply again and my gaze traveled around the room. Then it lighted on the photo of my family hanging on the wall.

"Oh God. The shame of it all," I said to myself. Suddenly I took hold of the office ledger and threw it across the room. It hit a vase of flowers on top of the low guest table. I sat down again.

It was the end of the day in the office, and I met Leni in the clocking-off area.

"What about tomorrow, Pa?" She was worried. She looked pale.

"Stay calm, Len. Just give me time to think about it at home," I said, trying to reassure her, though my mind was in just as much turmoil as hers.

I opened the door of the car and got in and slowly drove back home. Along the way my thoughts couldn't settle; they turned to this and that; but most of all I kept thinking of how I could find a way out of what would happen tomorrow. But in my dilemma, far from being able to find a way out, my thoughts became even more confused. The perspiration continued to trickle down my brow.

And then halt; I brought the car to a stop in the drive.

"Hallo, darling..." My wife greeted me from the porch. I didn't look at her; I felt disgusted. "Hey, why the sour face all of a sudden? Are you angry with me?" My wife rattled away just as she always did.

I took off my jacket and loosened my tie. Then I flopped down on the sofa.

"What's the matter, darling?" she asked again. I didn't reply. Instead I lit a cigarette, taking one from the packet lying on the table. Strolling away, she went inside, and a little later she appeared again bringing a glass of coffee.

"Have some coffee now. You'll feel better for it," she said. I took the glass and quickly drank the contents. It was true I brightened up after drinking the coffee. The air was hazy; smoke from the cigarette drifted round the room.

"Is there something I've done wrong?" Her tone was quiet and submissive.

"This is all your fault. And I am the one that has to bear the consequences."

Her mouth tightened.

"What's the matter?" She didn't hide her surprise.

"An audit team is coming to visit the office tomorrow."

The expression on her face changed. There was an intake of breath. But after a short time she spoke.

"Just keep your head, darling. There's a solution for every problem, isn't there?" Her voice was hesitant. I didn't interrupt. I just sat there smoking.

The room was silent for a time. I looked at her out of the corner of my eye. She was thinking again. I finished two cigarettes but still nothing. When I was putting out the stub of my cigarette in the ashtray, she suddenly exclaimed with glee.

"Darling, I have a brilliant idea," she said.

"What sort of idea?" I leaned forward to hear, then she whispered it to me.

"You're mad. It's impossible. Find another way."

I frowned angrily rejecting her suggestion.

"There's no other way, dear. "

She kissed my right cheek while she stroked my head. Thinking again about it, I decided that, actually, it was a good plan, especially when we were pressed for time like this. I should give my wife praise. Her ideas are sometimes very original compared to what other people come up with. I thought about it again, taking my time, and then decided that, like it or not, I would follow through with her suggestion, even though my conscience was not happy about it.

Feeling a bit uneasy, I took out my mobile phone and rang Leni. I told her my wife's idea. At first she, too, was unhappy about it, as though she couldn't believe what she was being asked to do. Then after I had worked hard to persuade her and told her that there was no other way, she finally agreed.

"Be careful; don't forget you have to fix it with the watchman who is on duty."

"Understood, boss."

Almost the whole night I was unable to sleep, thinking about what was going to be done next morning and whether the plan would succeed. But looking across at my wife, I saw that she was not restless at all; she was fast asleep. I shook my head in disbelief at her composure.

It was the very early hours of the morning. I sat up in bed. Quickly I got everything ready in preparation. I walked off to the garage. I started the car and let the engine warm up.

Soon after, my wife came up to me, still drowsy with sleep; she put her arm around my shoulders.

"Take care, darling," she said, speaking gently as though to show me how concerned she was.

The car left the house and slowly went on its way pushing through the cold night air of that transitional time of the year between the wet and the dry seasons.

The *azan* had not yet made the dawn call to prayer by the time the car reached the dark cul-de-sac just in front of the unused garden plot behind the office. It was very quiet. I saw Leni's car already sitting there. I got out and approached it. The window of the car came down slowly. Leni put her head out and gave a sign.

"Is everything OK, Pa?" she asked me.

"All in order. Quick now; it'll soon be daylight," I said. The door of the car opened. She got out and then went to the trunk of the car at the back. She opened it and there, visible, were two white cans each containing twenty liters of gasoline.

They hung down from my arms as I carried them off. Then, looking right and left, I examined everything around. I went into the garden and she followed. And because I was full of my purpose, the fear left me, even though there was a lot of rustling of leaves as we pushed our way through the garden, which was also quite dark.

"Here's the key, Pa," said Leni when we arrived at the back door of the office. There was a slight click as the key turned. We went in. I shivered slightly as I entered the storeroom, which had been empty for some time. I switched on the flashlight. Treading carefully, we made our way to the front.

Then we reached the office where I worked every day. We both took a hand in splashing the contents of the cans around the room, especially in the area where the books and the accounts were kept.

It wasn't long before the cans were empty. Leni handed me the lighter. I took it. I pressed to get the flame, and then I lit a scrap of newspaper and quickly put it to a pile of paper. *Shuup!* The flames began to spread. For a moment we looked at each other open-mouthed.

We began to feel the heat.

"Quickly, let's get out," I commanded, not wanting to dawdle any longer. We sped off, running as fast as we could back the way we had come.

Before getting back into the car again, I had a quick look around, scouring the area. There was no one in the cul-de-sac. Just before I left the place, I heard from the mosque to the west of the office buildings the voice of the *azan* calling the faithful to the dawn prayer.

Glossary

ajengan	A term of respect, used in west Java in particular, for a religious teacher especially for one who is the head of a *pesantren*.
akang	Often abbreviated to *kang*, meaning elder brother but often used by a wife to her husband.
angkot	A form of cheap public transport. *Angkot* are minibuses carrying about twelve passengers at a squeeze. They ply specific routes in the main cities of Indonesia, and the color of the *angkot* helps the passenger at the side of the road to know where the *angkot* is heading.
Arjuna	The third of the five Pandawa brothers in the *Mahabharata*. He is known for his bravery and his chivalry, as well as for his good looks and his fondness for women.
aki	Literally grandfather, but frequently used for any elderly man who might be of one's grandfather's generation.
arisan	A rotating credit association. These are very common in Indonesia and are found at all levels of society where they function both as savings clubs and as social institutions for neighbors and friends to get together.
asar	The late afternoon prayer in Islam. It is announced between three and four o'clock depending on the time of year and the exact geographical location of a mosque in Indonesia.
Astrajingga	A character from the *wayang* world.
ayi	A term of address for younger sibling in Sundanese society. This can become Ai, Yi or Rai depending on the custom within an individual family.

azan	The person responsible for issuing the call to prayer from the mosque five times a day. Any male who is capable of doing so and is at the mosque at the appropriate time can be the *azan*.
babinsa	Badan Pembina Desa, the body for the security of the village, a group representing elements of the security forces who operate at the village level. Like KORAMIL, it was one of those bodies that was especially important during the New Order period under Soeharto for ensuring rigid conformity with the instructions of the political and military authorities emanating from Jakarta.
bakung	A kind of white narcissus flower.
banci	A common but derogatory term used for a male cross-dresser and has a connotation of effeminate behavior.
barjanzi	A sung recitation in praise of the Prophet Muhammad and describing his life, performed especially during the month of Maulud honoring his birth.
bata	A measure of land of about 14.2 square meters.
berenuk	A kind of tree, *Crescentia Cujete*, of the *Bignoniaceae* family.
bibi	Aunt, used as a common form of address for a woman of one's mother's generation.
bismillah	A short invocation of God commonly said at the outset of any enterprise, the beginning of a journey or the start of a meal.
BP7	Acronym for "Badan Panitia Penasehat Presiden tentang Pedoman Penghayatan dan Pengamalan Pancasila," The Body of the Committee of Presidential Advisers concerned with the Handbook for the Interiorization and Implementation of Pancasila (see below).
bu	A shortened form of *ibu* meaning mother. It is very commonly used throughout Indonesia to address women one doesn't know, in shops, on the street, in an office and in most other day-to-day encounters.
bupati	The elected head of a district, a *kabupaten*. Indonesia comprises thirty-three provinces, and each province comprises several *kabupaten*, each of which has a *dewan*, an elected council or assembly to which a *bupati* is accountable.

calo	A ticket tout or a middleman who can arrange deals and business transactions for a negotiated fee.
camat	The appointed head of a *kecamatan*, a government sub-district below the level of a *kabupaten*. See *bupati* above.
cendol	A very popular sweet dessert-snack made of coconut milk and pearls of rice flour.
Cepot	One of the clown figures in the Sundanese *wayang golek* repertoire. He is recognizable from the red color of his face and a protruding front tooth and is an especially popular figure among the Sundanese. His scrapes evoke much laughter but at the same time lead spectators to reflect on their day to day lives.
ceu	Short for *ceuceu*, the term of address for elder sister, sometimes used as a general term of address for senior women with whom one has some acquaintance.
dalang	The puppet master in performances of shadow plays and *wayang golek* theatre.
dangdut	A catchy popular style of singing which people often dance to.
Dayak	A native inhabitant of Kalimantan (Borneo). In other areas of Indonesia, Dayak people have a reputation for great fierceness.
DPR	Dewan Perwakilan Rakyat, Assembly of the People's Representative, Parliament
dukun	A generic term for a traditional specialist; many *dukun* are considered to have special magical powers in relation to healing, finding lost objects, casting spells and other similar arts.
fitrah	A religious tax; a designated sum paid at the end of the fasting month and given to the poor of the community.
gudeg	A soup-stew dish associated very strongly with Central Java, the main ingredient of which is jackfruit.
hansip	The civil guard found in villages throughout Indonesia whose main function is to assist the authorities to ensure law and order. The institution which survived for several decades was abolished in 2014.
iket	The band of cloth worn round the head by men, it is considered to be part of a traditional Sundanese costume. This "reinvented" tradition has recently become popular, and civil servants and school pupils in Bandung are now encouraged to wear the *iket* with accompanying black trousers and black blouson every Wednesday.

isya	The evening prayer, the last prayer of the day, announced shortly after seven.
istighfar	A religious exclamation requesting God's assistance.
ITB	Institut Teknologi Bandung, the oldest institution of higher education in Indonesia, set up in the Dutch colonial period in the 1920s. It is a very prestigious institution and one of four leading universities in the country. As its name suggests, it is a technology-science-based university, but there is also a long-established Faculty of Fine Arts as well as a highly regarded School of Business and Management which was opened in 2004.
jabon	A kind of tree, *Sarcocephalus cordatus Miq.* A member of the *Rubiaceae* family. Its fruit is used for medicinal purposes, and other parts of the tree provide dyes.
jang	Short for *ujang*, usually used familiarly as a term of address for a man younger than the speaker.
Japanese period	The period between 1942 and 1945 during which the Japanese occupied Indonesia in the Pacific War.
kebaya	A light-weight embroidered traditional blouse worn by women; the *kebaya pendek*, or short *kebaya*, coming down to the waist is considered part of the national costume for women, worn on official occasions as well as to formal ceremonies; the *kebaya panjangor*, long *kebaya*, coming down to the knees is especially worn in Sumatra.
kecapi	A kind of zither with copper strings often played as an accompaniment to the recitation of traditional stories and songs.
kang	Short for *akang* meaning elder brother. It is often used as a polite form of address to a young man whom one doesn't know. With the addition of a personal name, e.g., Kang Acep, it is the usual way to refer to a third person (male) in a conversation. It is the male equivalent of *teh* or *teteh* when addressing men in the public domain, shops and offices.
kawin siri	An institution of temporary marriage much frowned upon in orthodox Muslim circles in Indonesia. It permits men and women to contract a temporary marriage, not recognized under national law, but acceptable to the parties concerned because it bestows a quasi-religious legitimacy to casual relationships.
KORAMIL	Komando Rayon Militer, a regional military base.

KOTRAR	Komando Tertinggi Retooling Aparatur Revolusi. One of the numerous bodies set up in the late Sukarno period, this was intended to overhaul the structure of the bureaucracy.
KPK	Komisi Pemberantas Korupsi, the Commission to Stamp out Corruption. This government body set up in 2002 has taken very serious strides in dealing with endemic corruption in Indonesia. Over the years there have been a number of spectacular cases at the national and local level which have given it a prominent status in the eyes of the population at large.
kuwu	Another title for a village head.
Lebaran	The celebration at the end of the fasting month when many people *mudik*, that is, go back to their villages to visit relatives.
lohor	The midday prayer announced between 11:45 AM and 1 PM according to the time of year.
lotek	A kind of vegetable salad served with a spicy sauce, a common snack.
lurah	The minor official who heads a *kelurahan*, the district level below that of *kecamatan*. See *camat* above.
madrasah	Religious school at which priority is given to religious instruction, though in modern *madrasah* the national school curriculum is also followed.
maghrib	The dusk prayer which falls between about 5:45 PM and 6:15 PM.
mang	Literally uncle, but often used as term of address for a senior man. Recently it has fallen into disfavor, because as a form of address it has a slight connotation of the speaker taking a condescending attitude to the addressee. In the context of most if not all of the stories translated here that connotation is absent.
melati	The jasmine flower.
MPR	Majelis Permusyawaratan Rakyat, the Assembly for the People's Deliberations. For many years this was the upper house of Parliament, which largely had only a ceremonial role though it met at least every five years officially to elect the President. It no longer performs this function, and has been superseded by other constitutional assemblies since 1999.

mudik	Literally this means to go north or upstream. It is now taken to mean the exodus of people back to their family villages from the cities during the Lebaran holiday at the end of Ramadan.
mukena	The special cloth women use for covering their heads and shoulders when they perform the five ritual prayers.
nangka	Jackfruit, which has rather a bulbous shape.
neng	A polite form of address for young (unmarried) women. It can be used on its own or followed by a name. *Angkot* drivers trying to drum up fares will try to attract the attention of schoolgirls at the side of the road by calling out, "Neng, Neng." The story translated here as "Miss Maya" is in the original Sundanese "Neng Maya."
New Order	See Orde Baru.
nyi	A term of polite address for a married woman, usually followed by a name or by the title held by her husband.
Old Order	See the information under Orde Baru
oncom	A sort of cake made out of soybean, a very common snack in west Java.
Orde Baru (Orba)	Literally the New Order, this refers to the period of the Soeharto regime from 1966 to 1998. Called New to distinguish it from the Old Order, Orde Lama (Orla), designating the Sukarno period, between 1950 and 1965.
P4	Pedoman Penghayatan dan Pengamalan Pancasila. Guide for the Interiorization and Implementation of Pancasila, a handbook produced during the New Order period in the late 1970s, for the promulgation of the New Order interpretation of the Pancasila (q.v.) the five principles of the State.
pa	The usual form of address for a senior man one respects. Note that in west Java, unlike common practice elsewhere in Indonesian, the word is not spelled Pak. I am told that this is because in Sundanese the final /k/ is pronounced hard unlike in Indonesian where it is end-stopped, hence to emulate the Indonesian pronunciation and to avoid the confusion which the spelling Pak may cause, Sundanese prefer the spelling Pa.

pahlawan	Hero, a heavily laden word in Indonesia to indicate those who have fought for the country against foreign aggressors or who have contributed in some way to the struggle for national self-esteem. There is a specific list of accredited *pahlawan negara*, national heroes, to which names are added each year after an assessment is made of the candidates whose names have been put forward by regional committees. In many big cities, especially in Java, there is a special cemetery, Taman Makam Pahlawan, for the dead who played some kind of role as heroes. Hari Pahlawan, Heroes Day, is celebrated on November 10th every year.
Pancasila	The national creed; five principles of the Indonesian state to which all citizens should subscribe. They are: (1) Belief in the existence of one God (monotheism); (2) Humanity that is just and civilized, (3) The Unity of Indonesia, (4) Democracy for the people pursued through representative deliberation, (5) Social justice for all Indonesians.
pesantren	The term used in Java for a religious boarding school; it usually refers to a traditional religious school, but there are "modern" *pesantren*.
PETA	Pembela Tanah Air, the national defense force set up by the Japanese during the occupation and intended by them to act as a pro-Japanese anti-western military force. During the period of the Revolution, many of those trained in PETA camps became leaders of guerilla forces against the Dutch, some of which were incorporated into the national army.
petay	A kind of bean, a frequently used vegetable in Sundanese dishes, with a distinctive and, to Western tastes, unpleasant odor.
POLSEK	The sectoral police station, of varying size, found in all *kecamatan*.
PKI	Partai Komunis Indonesia, the Communist Party of Indonesia. It was outlawed and destroyed in 1965/1966 during a period of great violence in Indonesia when hundreds of thousands of PKI members and supporters were brutally murdered.
punduh	The title of a junior village head.
rebab	A two-stringed fiddle.

rupiah	The Indonesian currency. At time of first writing (October 2014) the rate of the rupiah to dollars was about Rp. 13,500, having varied between 9,000 and 14,000 in the past ten years. In some of the stories which take place in earlier times, the rate was considerably different.
sarjana muda	This is a first higher education degree in the Indonesian university system taking three years to complete. It is intended as preliminary rather than a terminal degree. The latter is achieved after two further years of study and is known as a *sarjana* degree. At least this was the situation in place at the time referred to in the story *The '66 Album* until changes in the education system in the 1980s led to the introduction of a new *sarjana* degree lasting four years, which is now regarded as a terminal degree. This new system obtains throughout Indonesia now.
saung	A sheltered place of rest, usually for those working in rice fields, but also to be found in the middle of ornamental ponds, reached by bridges. The structure is a square platform on stilts open on all four sides and covered by a simple straw roof. People sit on mats on the platform drinking coffee and tea and smoking.
SD	*Sekolah Dasar*, Primary School. Pupils are admitted at the age of six or seven, and primary education lasts six years. *Sekolah Dasar* were formerly known as *Sekolah Rakyat*, People's School.
sedap malam	A kind of flower which gives off a very pleasant fragrance in the evenings.
SEKDES	The village secretary, an official post subordinate to the village head (Kades) or *lurah*.
sengon	The local name for the *albizzia chinensis*, a fast growing soft wood used for cheap furniture, and the manufacture of chopsticks and matchsticks.
SMA	*Sekolah Menengah Atas*, Senior secondary school. For pupils coming up from SMP (q.v.) at the age of sixteen. SMA are three-year schools. They are relatively elite since most families cannot afford to send their children to school beyond SMP.
SMP	*Sekolah Menengah Pertama*: Junior secondary school of three years' duration.
subuh	The dawn prayer which is announced between 4:00 AM and 4:30 AM.

surabi	A kind of thick pancake often served with syrup or coconut milk.
tadarus	The ritual reading of the Quran together during the fasting month of Ramadan.
tahu	Bean curd, a favorite fried snack throughout Java.
tarawangsa	A traditional two or three-stringed fiddle played with a horsehair bow and often played in combination with a *kecapi* (q.v) and a *suling* (flute) to accompany recitations and songs.
taraweh	The additional prayers said in the evening after *isya* during the fasting month of Ramadan.
tarekat	Communities of believers within Islam who follow particular mystical religious practices and trace their origins back to a founder figure who established these practices as a way of becoming closer to an experience of the divine.
teh	Short for *teteh*, elder sister, almost identical to *ceuceu*. It is frequently used as a term of address for shop assistants or young women who hold official positions
tuan	Sir or master, a title especially used in the Dutch period for Dutch and other expatriates. It is only occasionally heard now.
tukang ojeg	A person who drives a motorbike as a taxi. In the last thirty years *tukang ojeg (ojek* in Indonesian*)* have rapidly expanded in number and are to be found the length and breadth of Indonesia. They are found not only in urban areas, where they are popular for their capacity to avoid being held up by traffic jams, but also in rural areas where roads are often impassable by four-wheeled transport. There are *tukang ojeg* stands where groups of drivers wait together for fares. There are a few female *tukang ojeg*. Many women who are prepared to ride pillion and use the services of a *tukang ojeg* do so by sitting side-saddle on the bike.
tumbak	A measure of land, roughly 14.2 square meters; as a measure of length it is approximately 3.77 meters.
umroh	A religious pilgrimage to Mecca which takes place outside the period of the hajj pilgrimage. With the increasing ease of air transport and the growth of a prosperous upper middle class in Indonesia, *umroh* pilgrimages have become extremely popular in the last thirty years.

ustad	A commonly bestowed title on a religious teacher known for his preaching and his knowledge of religious texts.
waringin	Banyan tree.
wayang	The traditional puppet theatre of Java with stories drawn in particular from the Ramayana and Mahabharata. In west Java, where the puppets are three dimensional, the theatre is known as *wayang golek*. In central and eastern Java where the puppets are two-dimensional and their silhouettes are shown on a screen, the performance is known as *wayang kulit*. In both cases the puppeteer, who controls all the figures, is known as the *dalang*.
zakat	A religious wealth tax.
zikir	A repeated religious chanting of the Arabic statement of belief that Allah is the one and only God, often performed communally in the mosque.

Acknowledgments

Thanks are owed first of all to the writers of the short stories for allowing their stories to be translated and included in this selection. In this context, too, I thank *Tribun Jabar* where the stories first appeared for permission to reproduce the stories here. Also thanks to the editor of *Galura* for the story "All Quiet in the Small Hours of the Night in Cijeléreun."

I should like to thank collectively several Sundanese and English friends. My Sundanese friends, including some of the authors of the stories, have cleared up the meaning of some of the Sundanese phrases and sentences which I found difficult to understand. They of course bear no responsibility for any mistakes in the translation, of which I am sure there remain some. English friends to whom I described the difficulties of finding good English translations and equivalents helped me with useful suggestions.

I should like particularly to thank Rachmat Taufiq Hidayat of the publishing house Kiblat. It was he who suggested I consider translating some stories. If he had not encouraged me and then given me his support I would not have embarked on the translations

I thank too Taylor and Francis the publishers of *Indonesia and the Malay World* where two of the translated stories appeared for the first time for permitting the reprinting of the translations.

R.R. Hardjadibrata's *Sundanese-English Dictionary*, (2003, Jakarta: Pustaka Jaya) has been of considerable help to me. This dictionary is based on F.S. Eringa's comprehensive *Soendanees-*

Nederlands Woordenboek(1984, Dordrecht: KITLV) but had I had to use only the latter the translations would have taken much longer.

And of course thanks to the family for all sorts of support given freely and liberally in Canterbury and Bandung.

Further Reading in English

Jedamski, Doris. "Balai Pustaka: A Colonial Wolf in Sheep's Clothing," in *Archipel* 44, pp. 23-46, 1992. A brief account extracted from her German language thesis, this article describes the role of Balai Pustaka in the promotion of a modern Indonesian literature.

Jedamski, Doris. "Popular Literature and Postcolonial Subjectivities: Robinson Crusoe, the Count of Monte Cristo and Sherlock Holmes in Colonial Indonesia," in Keith Foulcher and Tony Day (eds.) *Clearing a Space: Postcolonial Readings of Modern Indonesian Literature*, (Leiden: KITLV Press, pp. 19-47, 2002) describes some of the popular European literature translations of which were the first examples of a new prose fiction in Malay-Indonesian

Moriyama, Mikihiro. *Sundanese Print Culture and Modernity in Nineteenth Century West Java* (Singapore: Singapore University Press, 2005). The last chapter in this book describes the development of Sundanese modern prose writing in the first three decades of the twentieth century.

Moriyama, Mikihiro. "Regional Languages and Decentralisation in Post-New Order Indonesia: The Case of Sundanese," in Keith Foulcher, Mikihiro Moriyama, and Manneke Budiman (eds.) *Words in Motion: Languages and Discourse in Post-New Order Indonesia*. (Tokyo: Research Institute for Languages and Cultures of Asia and Africa Tokyo University of Foreign Studies, pp.82-100, 2012.) This is a very useful account of the situation in west Java today and of the way in which successive government language policies have affected the preservation and development of Sundanese. It concludes that there are grounds for optimism.

Sanoesi, Mohd. *Siti Rayati*, translated into English and with an introduction by Wendy Mukherjee(Bandung: Kiblat, 2006). First original Sundanese edition, 1928. As far as I know this is the only Sundanese novel which has been translated into English. The excellent introduction gives a lot of useful historical background as well as informative biographical details about the author of the novel.

Watson, C.W. "Bangsat. A Sundanese Short Story," in *Indonesia and the Malay World*, Vol. 40, No. 118, November, pp. 315-331, 2012. This is the first appearance of the translation of the story reprinted in the collection here. It contains an introduction and copious notes on linguistic, cultural and historical matters relating to Sundanese.

Watson, CW. "The Wonder of it All: Yus. R. Ismail's Sundanese Story, 'Imah Kontrakan'(The Rented House)," in *Indonesia and the Malay World*, Vol. 42, No. 124, November, pp. 358-379, 2014. The first publication of the story which appears in the collection. It also contains an introduction and copious footnotes.

Biographical Information

THE AUTHORS

AAN MERDÉKA PERMANA (born Bandung, 1950) is a journalist and has worked as an editor for *Manglé, Sipatahunan,* and *Galura.* A productive writer, his Sundanese short stories and poems have appeared in *Manglé, Hanuang,* and *Galura,* and his Indonesian-language stories have appeared in *Pikiran Rakyat* and *Sinar Harapan.* He has written a number of historical novels in Sundanese, and his children's book, *Sasakala Bojongemas* (*The Legend of Bojongemas*) won the annual Samsoedi Award from the Rancagé Foundation in 2011.

ABSURDITAS MALKA (born 1982) is a farmer in Karawang. His Sundanese stories have appeared in *Manglé* and *Tribun Jabar,* and his writings in Indonesian have been published in *Kompas, Pikiran Rakyat, Radar Surabaya,* and *Tribun Jabar.* His book *The Road to Freedom* was published by Dar! Mizan in 2004. In 2014 he was selected as an emerging writer in the Ubud Writers & Readers Festival.

DADAN WAHYUDIN (born Pagaden, Subang, 1972) is currently working in the Indonesian Language and Literature Postgraduate program of Suryakanca University in Cianjur. His first and second degrees were from Nusantara University in Bandung. His stories and articles have been published in *Kompas, Galamedia,* and *Manglé.* Several of his stories have also been published in *Tribun Jabar.*

Déni A. Fajar (born Bandung, 1968) is a graduate from the department of Sundanese literature of Padjadjaran University where he was active in the Sundanese student theater group. He writes fiction in Indonesian and Sundanese, and his collection of poetry *Lagupadungdung* (*Drum Music*) won the prestigious Rancagé prize in 2013. His short stories have appeared in *Manglé, Galura,* and *Pikiran Rakyat.* He currently works as a reporter at *Tribun Jabar* where he frequently writes about sports.

Déni A. Hendarsyah (born Cimahi, 1972) graduated from the Indonesian Literature and Language Department of the Indonesian's Teachers' College of Bandung (IKIP-Bandung, now the Education University of Indonesia) in 1996, then went on to obtain a higher degree from the same institution in 2014. Having worked as a teacher since 2000 at a state junior secondary school in Cimahi, he has also written for numerous newspapers and weeklies and has published several books, including a collection of poetry, books of literary criticism, and school textbooks.

Erwin Wahyudi (born Tasikmalaya, 1980) has published work in several newspapers and weeklies, including *Priangan, Manglé,* and *Tribun Jabar.* As a writer, he is especially fond of short short-stories of 100–250 words, and has had work published in two anthologies of mini-fiction, *Serat Sapamidangan* (*Written at Leisure*) and *Lembur Cahaya* (*The Sunshine Village*).

Fitria Puji Lestari (born Sumedang, 1992), a graduate of the Regional Languages Department of the Education University of Indonesia (UPI), works full-time at home. She has written several short stories which have been published in *Manglé* and *Seni Budaya.* Nine of her stories have appeared in *Tribun Jabar.*

Héna Sumarni (born Subang, 1972) graduated from the Department of Regional Languages of the Indonesian's Teachers'

College in Bandung (IKIP-Bandung, now the Education University of Indonesia) in 1998 and then went on to do a postgraduate degree there in 2014, specializing in Sundanese language and literature. Her stories have appeared in *Manglé* and *Tribun Jabar*, and she has authored numerous short-short stories or mini-fiction, a very popular literary genre among Sundanese writers today. At present she is a teacher of Sundanese at a state junior secondary school in Cimahi.

LUGIENA DÉ (born Bandung, 1983), the pen name of Dea Lugina, is a graduate of the Regional Languages Department of Indonesian University of Education (UPI) and an instructor of Sundanese. This award-winning author writes in both Sundanese and Indonesian, and his stories have been published in *Manglé, Cupumanik, Galura,* and *Tribun Jabar*. His plays *Rucah* (*Riotous Living*) and *Dayeuh Simpé* (*The Quiet Village*) were selected in 2014 and 2016, respectively, for inclusion in the biannual Sundanese Drama Festival. His short story collection *Jeruk* (*The Orange*) was published in 2016 and was short-listed for a Rancagé award in 2017.

MAMAT SASMITA (born Tasikmalaya, 1951) worked as a satellite transmissions engineer for PT TELKOM, the state-owned telecommunications company, for most of his adult life, during which time he was stationed at several locations in Indonesia, including Pontianak, Jambi, and Fakfak. He retired from PT Telkom in 2007 and now manages Rumah Baca Buku Sunda, a lending library of Sundanese books, which he established in 2004. From 2009 to 2012, he edited the Sundanese journal *Cupumanik*, and he has published work in both Sundanese and Indonesian in *Pikiran Rakyat, Tribun Jabar, Manglé* and *Mata Baca*.

MULYANA SURYA ATMAJA (born Karawang, 1970), who goes by the pen name Musa, graduated from the Indonesian Teachers College of Bandung (IKIP-Bandung now UPI) and worked as a secondary school teacher before doing a further degree and then working as a teacher in Saudi Arabia. After a varied career which included time in the Middle East and the United States where he took part in a program for Leadership and Assistance for Science Education Reform, he went on to do a PhD at Pakuan University which he completed in 2015. He is now active in the Karawang branch of the Indonesian National Teachers Association (PGRI). His writings have appeared in *Suara Daerah* and *Galura*.

NINA RAHAYU NADÉA (born Garut, 1975) works in the regional office of the Department of Education in the municipality of Bandung. She writes in Sundanese and Indonesian, and her articles and stories have appeared in numerous journals and newspapers including *Pikiran Rakyat, Majalah Kartini, Majalah Baca Banda Aceh, Suara Karya, Kompas, Manglé,* and *Galura*. She collaborates with the Miyaz agency in producing school textbooks on the social sciences.

USÉP ROMLI (born Garut, 1949), a prolific writer and highly respected journalist, writes regularly for *Pikiran Rakyat, Manglé,* and *Galura*. His journalism includes accounts of travels in several Muslim countries in the Middle East and North Africa as well as Bosnia. He also writes on political and religious issues. He has written over thirty books in Indonesian and Sundanese, and in 2010 his short story collection *Sanggeus Umur Tunggang Gunung* (*Having Reached the Sunset Age*) won the Rancagé prize.

YUS R. ISMAIL (born Sumedang, 1970) is a prolific writer and has published short stories in Indonesian in a number of national and regional newspapers and weeklies, including *Kompas* and *Koran Tempo*. His Sundanese stories appear regularly in *Galura, Manglé,* and *Tribun Jabar*. He has written novels and short stories and published a collection of poetry. Recent works include *Humor Klasik Kabayan* (2017) and an e-book titled *Mahacinta* (2017). After working as a journalist for some time, he decided to become a full-time writer of fiction.

THE TRANSLATOR

C.W. (BILL) WATSON retired in 2008 from the University of Kent in the UK where he taught in the School of Anthropology. Since then he has been teaching in the School of Business and Management at the Bandung Institute of Technology (ITB). Over the years he has written several articles relating to the history, anthropology, and literature of modern Indonesia. His books include *Of Self and Injustice* (2006), *Multiculturalism* (2000) and *Kinship, Property and Inheritance in Kerinci, Central Sumatra* (1992). He has been reading modern Sundanese literature, after a fashion, since 2010.